A GAMBLE EITHER WAY

The Bishop Smoky Mountain Thrillers
Book 4

LAUREN STREET

STERLING & STONE

Chapter One

WINSTON BURKETT WAS ALWAYS careful to wear light-colored clothing when he went out for a run at night, had flashing lights on his shoes and strips of reflector tape on his jacket and pants. If his wife Margaret had her way, she would have wrapped him up in reflector tape from head to toe, even though very few of the five-to-seven miles he ran every day were anywhere near the streets and traffic. The mountain roads in Yarmouth County, Tennessee, were far too narrow for anything as fancy as a bike lane, so Winston did most of his running in Burnt Oak Park. He lived less than a mile from the park, so he dressed at home and counted the trip to and from the park as part of his run.

It was a frigid January night, his breath coming out in big puffy clouds in front of him. He didn't check the temperature because if he had, Maggie might have noticed, might have decided it was too cold for him to run. All that freezing air couldn't be good for your lungs. Maybe the cold nipping at his exposed ears and fingers — he'd forgot his hat and gloves— was the reason he was thinking about fried shrimp. Oh, how he'd love to have some fried shrimp. The kind Maggie learned to make when they'd lived in Louisiana, where fresh shrimp was plentiful. She used a special recipe her neighbor had given her for the batter. Had sworn a sacred oath never to reveal the ingredients even if she was tortured. It made his mouth water just to think about them. Maybe he could get her to make some for dinner on Sunday, but where would he get fresh shrimp?

The flap, flap, flap of his shoes on the sidewalk in front of his house became a different tune when he stepped out onto the asphalt of the street, passing below a streetlight that set him aglow like a firefly. He ran facing the oncoming traffic so he couldn't get clipped from behind by a car he didn't see coming.

But even facing the traffic like that, he still never stood a chance.

When a car doing sixty miles an hour topped a hill aimed right at him, he had two or maybe three heartbeats until he was *gone*.

Winston probably had time to wonder why the car coming toward him so fast suddenly flipped off its headlights. Time to wonder why it swerved over onto the side of the road so there was nowhere to go.

Maybe he even had time to figure it out, saw the face of the driver and understood that death sat in the front seat of that car and his time had come.

The car hit him square, like the hood ornament was a sniper's sight. The impact threw Winston's body up into the air so high it didn't crash down until the car had passed beneath it and was a hundred feet down the road.

He lay on his broken back on the cold asphalt, his arms and legs stretched out at impossible angles from his body, blood bubbling out his mouth between his broken teeth. He was drowning on his own blood, but was miraculously conscious, aware. He couldn't move his head, but he could still see the red taillights of the car that hit him as it slowly began to back toward him.

He watched it come, watched the left rear tire get bigger and bigger until it filled all his vision. Perhaps he felt it, but only for an instant, when the tire rolled over his head and his skull made a mushy popping sound.

When the man in the passenger seat of the car heard that sound, it sent a jolt like an electric shock through his whole body. He watched the road in front of the car expectantly, waiting for the body to be visible there, and when he saw it, he made a sound that had no description, a grunting moan like an orgasm without the sweet release afterward.

He gestured toward the bloody, headless corpse and said one word.

"Again!"

The driver pulled forward over the body again, angling the wheels so they crossed over the torso this time. When the man in the passenger seat heard the crunching, crackling sounds from beneath the car as it bumped up and over the corpse, he let out a tiny bleat of laughter. If he'd been driving, he would have driven back and forth across the body until it was as flattened as a road-kill frog.

But that part was over now. The fun part.

The driver stopped the car a few feet in front of the mangled corpse, and the passenger helped him pick it up and dump it into the trunk. Then the car sped away into the cold darkness. They got rid of the body — wouldn't have to worry about dental records since it didn't have a head. And they chopped his hands off so there'd be no fingerprints to match just in case someone found the body before it decomposed, which they wouldn't. Construction on the house it was buried under would be complete as soon as the weather got warm.

The car they'd used went to a chop shop and was reduced to resale parts before the sun came up the next day. The only thing that remained of Winston Burkett was the memory of his final moments on this earth, carried with something like reverence in a special place in the mind of one of his murderers. He would not forget Winston Burkett, would re-live the sounds of Winston's head and bones crunching again and again and again. Those gory sounds fundamentally changed who he was on a molecular level. Everything from that point forward was a brand-new world.

Chapter Two

RILEIGH BISHOP WAS HIT with a sinking feeling in her belly as she turned onto Main Street in the Forge. There was nowhere to park on this street, and she could see cars lining all the cross streets she passed. Yup, tonight was definitely going to be difficult. But that was the point, wasn't it? And it wasn't likely to be as difficult for her as it was going to be for High Mount Development Company. It was clear already that their night was *not* going to end well. A big turnout at a Yarmouth County Zoning Board meeting was never a sign of smooth waters ahead — people only showed up at a public hearing when they were pissed about something. And if the level of pissed-ness could be judged by the number of cars on the street, High Mount was about to get their asses kicked.

If you wanted to construct anything in Yarmouth County, Tennessee, beyond turning your one-hole outhouse into a two-holer, you had to slog through three successive public hearings in front of the zoning board. During those hearings, anybody who thought they had a dog in the fight was welcome to take the microphone and weigh in.

Rileigh found a place to park on a side street and leapt out of the car as soon as she pulled in, then stood leaning against the door panting in relief. She could hear the ticking of the cooling engine and wished she could put her hands on it to warm her fingers. She'd cranked the heater as high as it would go in the old Honda Accord, but it was no match for the frigid air blowing into the car with all the windows open. Rileigh should have them rolled up, of course. But she ... *couldn't.*

Opening the car door, she reached in and turned the key back on so she could to raise the windows before turning the car off and locking it up again. Then she stood beside it, waves of dread washing over her like she was a shell on a beach.

She didn't have to do this.

Yes, she did.

No, she didn't. She could leave, get back into the car and drive away. No harm, no foul.

The very depth of her yearning to do just that was all the proof she needed that she couldn't.

Summoning the resolve that had prodded her to get out of her pitifully-shrunken "comfort zone" and face the world tonight, she pulled her coat tighter around her and hurried up the street to Main, where she joined the ranks of a few other stragglers moving toward the courthouse.

Yarmouth County Courthouse was a big old four-story red brick building that looked like every other county courthouse in Tennessee. The first, second, and third floors were used for public functions. As was the basement, where the county sheriff's office housed its whole operation. The fourth floor was attic and storage.

The front of the courthouse also looked like every

other front-of-a-courthouse in the state, its steps leading up to a wide flat porch with stately columns stretching up to the porch roof, concrete railings, and extra-large double doors. Inside those doors was an entryway with stairs leading up and stairs leading down.

You could go downstairs to the sheriff's office or upstairs to the first floor for district court and the county clerk's office; to the second floor to the PVA office, the water district office and the sanitation department; or to the third floor for circuit court. Public hearings were always conducted in the circuit courtroom, which was enormous, taking up almost all the third floor, with a judge's bench three steps higher than the rest of the court, a witness chair attached to one side and a table for the court stenographer on the other. The tables for the prosecution and the defense faced the judge's bench, and the jury sat in seats along the far wall. The whole front area was cordoned off from the rest of the room by an ornate wooden railing. The area from the railing to the big double doors in the back was filled with "spectator" seating.

The courthouse was packed with people filling the stair wells and the wide-open area between the offices where the state seal was emblazoned on the granite.

Rileigh absolutely could *not* shove her way through that crowd into the courtroom, but she knew a better way to get there, having spent a lot of time in the courthouse as a teenager, working in the Property Valuation Administrator's office. Not to mention her own clandestine after-hours activities. She went up the side stairs and through hallways until she came to an unmarked room at the back of the building. It was the jury room, where a defendant's twelve peers sat to deliberate his fate after a trial. She stepped inside, turned on the lights, and crossed the room to the door on the other side, which led to a small alcove behind the jury box in the big circuit courtroom. She stepped into the alcove, relieved to be out of the teeming crowd outside … and surprised to find she wasn't the only person who'd had this idea.

The man jumped when she approached, as surprised to see her as she was to see him. Charlie Hayden. If she'd had to come up with a person she'd like to avoid spending time with in a tiny alcove, she couldn't have done any better than Charlie Hayden.

"'Lo Rileigh," he said. "You didn't want to watch the proceedings with the teeming masses out there either, huh?"

Charlie didn't look good. He hadn't looked good in a long time, barely able to hold together the debonair exterior he presented to the world. The owner of Blarney Stone Realty Company was a man on a slippery slope to nowhere good. Rileigh had talked to him last summer about his "loan-shark" operation that had made a fifty-percent interest loan to a murdered teenager. He'd had his shit together then, his business raking in so much money he could afford to keep throwing it into the ravenous maw of his gambling addiction.

But his life had hit the skids in the fall, at the same time Rileigh's had — for the same reason, but with different results. Rileigh's mother had told her all about it. Which begged the question how much of what Mama had said was true and how much dementia-fabrication. It was often hard to tell, but what was totally undisputed was Mama's pipeline of information. That woman knew about every husband who was sleeping around on his wife before he got his pants zipped back up. Her knowledge of the local gossip was legendary.

"Finding that body while he was out for a run has done pushed Charlie Hayden over the edge," Mama had said as

Rileigh helped her make popcorn balls for the church's Halloween Trick or Treat event. "Least that's what I hear."

She was referring to the body of one of Aunt Daisy's roommates at the psychiatric ward, a woman brutally murdered by the same serial killer who'd come after Rileigh. Stumbling upon a dead woman murdered by a rat chewing through her body … yeah, that'd be traumatic alright. "Charlie got where he couldn't sleep, started taking pills, stronger and stronger," Mama had said. "He's hooked big time now. Not just sleeping pills anymore."

Around Thanksgiving, Mama had reported that Charlie's third, maybe fourth wife had left him. Now he was gambling so much even he couldn't make enough to cover his losses. He'd disappeared over the Christmas holidays — not just Vegas, private invitation-only games *somewhere*. Tonight, Mama would have said he looked like death on a cracker.

The pupils of his eyes were dilated, looking like twin pools where some small creature drowned. His face was thin and drawn, and a nervous tic had settled in his left eye and kept it twitching.

"What are you doing here?" Rileigh asked.

He made a gesture at the scene beyond the alcove, merely said, "Crowd."

They were both here to escape the crowd — Rileigh because she just *couldn't*, and Charlie because he didn't want their scrutiny. Maybe their shared motivation should have made her feel a bond with him, but she didn't.

She stepped up beside him, smelling the combination of his expensive cologne and something else. Sweat. Fear sweat. She didn't like being this close, but it was a small alcove, left in shadow by the big overhead lights in the courtroom, and he got here first.

She immediately spotted Mitch up front, conferring

with the deputies whose job it would be to keep order in the court. For tonight's hearing, the seven members of the zoning board had been seated in the jury box. A small podium had been set up facing the jury box, so people could step up one by one and tell the board members what they thought about the Gum Tree Hollow Development plan. The circuit judge was in attendance, seated on the bench: this was his courtroom and he was in charge. He would ensure an orderly meeting, quickly banishing the unruly to be hauled out by Mitch and his deputies.

Rileigh had a good view of the proceedings, could see the faces of all the citizens who stepped forward to have their say. She scanned the crowd behind them, picked out Ian McGinnis, her best friend Georgia's brother. Georgia would be home with her five kids and her drug-dealing husband, who wasn't the sort to attend a zoning board meeting. Though he'd never admitted it, Rileigh believed Ian was the head of the mysterious "Save Gum Tree Hollow Association," a group whose members refused to be identified, but who were responsible for signs protesting the development tacked to telephone poles and trees all over the county — and uglier ones spray-painted on bridge abutments and the sides of buildings, threatening ones that showed stick figures hanging from trees or beheaded.

At precisely seven o'clock, Judge Michael Hall banged his gavel for order and the hubbub of conversation in the big room silenced.

Judge Hall was an intimidating man, even when he wasn't sitting three feet above everybody else in a black robe. He was probably 6'6", had thick black hair, and a lone black unibrow over penetrating blue eyes. A dirty look from those eyes had been known to cause internal bleeding. His voice was the thing, though. Mike Hall could beat you up with his voice. It was deep and gravelly, reminding

Rileigh of chains being dragged across the metal deck of a ship. The voice alone was enough to intimidate, but coupled with his size and his scowl, he was a man few crossed and lived to tell the tale.

"I want to make this clear from the start," Judge Hall's rumbling voice filled up the room. "This is my courtroom, and you will be respectful here or the sheriff will drag you out. I know this is an issue where emotions are running high, but you had best check those emotions at the door, because they won't be tolerated in my courtroom. Is that clear?" He looked around the room, his gaze penetrating. No one made a sound.

"Here's the way this is going to go. Everybody in this room has a right to speak and make your views known to the zoning board. We're here to provide that right, not abridge it. But we can't have everybody making thirty-minute speeches or we'll be here until dawn. So I brought this."

He held high an egg timer in the shape of a baby chick. It was so incongruous in his big hand, reaching out of the sleeve of his black robe, that a titter of giggling rippled across the room.

"I'm going to set this for six minutes every time someone takes the microphone. That's how long you'll have to say whatever you have to say. When this timer goes off, you're done."

He looked around again. "Any questions?"

With the perfect unison of a Greek chorus, everyone in the room shook their heads.

"Good enough."

The judge banged his gavel again and gestured with his chin toward the head of the zoning board.

"Showtime," he said.

Chapter Three

THE CHAIRPERSON of the Yarmouth County Zoning Board was a woman in her mid-40s. She didn't seem like the type to be a chairperson. She was a little too sexy to be a soccer mom with her long blonde hair curled in seductive waves, Fuck-me red lipstick, and clothes that look like they'd been painted on. This evening, however, she presented no cleavage to distract. Her blouse was not low-cut, and she didn't have the top two buttons of the not low-cut blouse undone. Ruby Cunningham looked proper and professional.

"I want to thank everybody for coming out tonight to let us know your feelings about the proposed development project in Gum Tree Hollow," she said in a soft voice, almost a whisper. "We need your input to make an informed decision on the land use applications that the construction company has applied for, and the variance in zoning regulations we will have to put into effect in order for them to proceed. Before we begin taking comments from the audience, we'll hear from Hunter Dobson, the owner of High Mount Real Estate, about the development proposition he has presented to the board."

She turned her head toward a man who reminded Rileigh a little of Charlie Hayden, except Charlie was all hat and no cattle, and from the looks of this man, he had a full herd. He was not overdressed as Charlie tended to be. His hair was modest, wasn't cut in some funky hairstyle to match some equally funky trend. He merely looked well-groomed and responsible, which she supposed was probably the image he was trying to project. He stepped up in front of the zoning board, then turned his back on them and directed his remarks to the courtroom full of people.

"My vision is that five years from now Gum Tree Hollow will be the most environmentally-friendly land development in the Smoky Mountains."

There was a disbelieving grumble from the crowd.

Gum Tree Hollow was pristine, had so far escaped the fate of the other mountain hollows where beautiful woodlands had gradually been transformed into forests of golden arches and Taco Bell signs and treeless streets named Oak and Maple and Hickory.

There had never been any development in Gum Tree Hollow. And there were those who proclaimed there never would be, that bulldozers would have to chew tread marks into their dead bodies to get there. Not entirely an idle threat. Equipment belonging to High Mount Development Company at other construction sites had been vandalized: sugar in the gas tank of a dump truck, severed hydraulic lines on a crane. The Save Gum Tree Hollow Association took the blame for the crimes, though it was clear the existence of the association emboldened other lowlifes who knew the organization would be the scapegoats for whatever they did.

"These mountains are beautiful and we intend to keep

them that way," Dobson said. "We won't cut down the forests. We will build around them."

She'd heard other developers make that empty promise. But it was flat-out too expensive to operate heavy equipment and leave the trees where they were. It was cheaper to cut them all down. Land development was just that, developing the land, and the trees on top of it were an inconvenience for the construction crews.

When a hum of disbelief arose from the crowd, he held up his hands.

"It's a lofty goal, but I pledge to you tonight that we will attain it. We will leave Gum Tree Hollow as untouched as is humanly possible. We will build in it structures that match the hollow's ethos, and we will incorporate the character of the mountains, the atmosphere, using stone and natural building materials native to the mountains. We will preserve the character — the *soul* of Gum Tree Hollow."

He continued, speaking over grumbles.

"This is not a development for tourists. There will be no souvenir stores, no ticky-tacky rubber tomahawks for sale, no taffy/fudge/ice cream/funnel cake shops lining the streets. This will be a planned *community* where people will move in and raise their families."

He had brought a map of the proposed development and put it on an easel so everyone could see. Rileigh hadn't realized how extensive the development would be, and most of the people in the crowd who had come to protest a small development hadn't realized it either. It looked like the kind of community people moved to Florida for, cookie cutter housing only a golf cart ride away from big shopping centers. But golf carts wouldn't cut it here, not in the wintertime.

With every word he spoke, it became more and more

clear how culturally removed Hunter Dobson was from the people he was speaking to.

When Dobson was finished with his presentation, Ruby Cunningham held up a clipboard where people who wanted to speak had signed up earlier.

"We will take speakers in the order that their names appear on this list," she said, casting a glance toward the judge. "As Judge Hall said, each speaker will only have six minutes to present their case. This meeting will adjourn at 10 p.m. sharp."

She looked down at the sheet and called out the first name on it. "Mr. Clarence Underwood."

If you could hear a smile from a group of people, Rileigh heard one now. Uncle Clarence had come to have his say.

Clarence Underwood could have been anywhere between seventy-five and a hundred and ten years old. There wasn't an inch of his face that didn't have a wrinkle on it. He wore a slouchy hat pulled down low over his eyes. But when he stepped up to the little podium in front of the zoning board, he took it off, nodding to the ladies on the board, revealing a massive mane of white hair that he had obviously cut himself. Perhaps not with scissors, either. Maybe with a knife. His beard stretched from his mouth all the way over the top of his belt buckle. But he wore a clean plaid shirt under his clean overalls. He'd spiffied himself up for the occasion.

After greeting the zoning board, he turned toward the table that would have been the prosecutor's bench if this had been a trial, and spoke to Hunter Dobson and the three men and one woman he had brought with him.

Clarence pointed toward the diagram of the proposed project.

"You done a lot of work to put that together," he said,

"so you musta spent a considerable amount of time in Yarmouth County. I don't mean no offense, but it's plain as the nose on your face that you still don't know jack shit about this place or the people who live here."

There was a murmur of approval.

"All them trees you's talking about working around and not cutting down, do you know the names of any of 'em?" He paused for long enough that it dawned on the people he was addressing it wasn't a rhetorical question.

Hunter Dobson cleared his throat. "We understand that there are hardwood forests in that hollow."

"Yep. Could you maybe name a hardwood tree?"

Clarence waited, but there was no response.

"*Any* hardwood tree."

Silence.

"Gum Tree Hollow's got hickory trees and basswood trees and yellow birch. You ever seen a Douglas fir? You know the difference between a black cherry tree and a black walnut tree?" He paused, caught himself. "I ain't got but six minutes or I'd tell you about all the trees that's in the woods in Gum Tree Hollow that you don't know the names of."

He drew a breath.

"But I will tell you that ninety-nine percent of all the old growth trees on the whole east coast of the United States has been chopped down. Did you know that Gum Tree Hollow's got some of the oldest and tallest trees in the country? The Great Smoky Mountains National Park is right next door to where you plan on bulldozing dirt, and it has more than a hundred native species of trees. Other national parks got maybe 15, but the Smokies has got over 100, with more than a dozen different species of oak tree. 'Cause it's a park, somebody studied up on it, catalogued all the trees there, but them forests don't stop at the boundary of the park. The oldest tree there's a black gum tree that's five hundred sixty-eight years old. I ain't no history authority, but I looked it up."

He grinned, showing a mouth full of empty spaces with a few blackened teeth like the stumps in a forest after a fire, and held up an iPhone.

"I asked Siri, and she told me that five hundred sixty-eight years ago, the Gutenberg Bible was just coming hot off the first printing press. Chew on that. I didn't have to ask Siri to know there wasn't no United States of America. That tree was growing in that forest when Christopher Columbus was in diapers."

He zeroed in then and spoke only to Hunter Dobson.

"Son, are you siting there telling me you're going to drive your bulldozers *around* trees that old? Do think I'm so stupid I believe that? Ain't no way in hell you could do it even if you intended to, and ain't a person in this room believes you intend to. You're gonna bulldoze Gum Tree Hollow and build from the dirt up. You ain't got no respect for trees you don't even know the names of, for meadows you ain't never walked through and creeks you ain't never waded in. You don't give a rat's ass about any of it except how much money it can make you."

The swell of approval had to be quelled by Judge Hall's gavel.

"And what you're planning to build on all that bare dirt, you said it'd be … 'a place families can move in and raise their children.'"

He leaned closer, then hooked his thumb over his shoulder at the crowd seated behind him.

"You look around in this room and tell me if you see a single human being who could afford the houses you want to build."

A voice cried, "Amen!"

"Is there anybody in this room you think's got money for the trinkets and doodads, fancy clothes and the like you gonna sell in the stores you're gonna build? This development ain't about *us*. It's about you. It's about *you* making a place for people just like you in *our* mountains. And they're our mountains, not yours."

A spontaneous cheer rose up from the crowd so unexpectedly that Judge Hall had to hammer his gavel to calm it down.

Uncle Clarence looked at Dobson quizzically. "You really think we're buying your line of bullshit, don't you?" He shook his head in disbelief. "If it was raining soup, you'd go running outside with a fork."

There was a roar of laughter and applause that the judge gaveled into silence. He looked at the little egg timer in the shape of a chick and said, "You have one minute left, sir."

"Hell, I done said everything I have to say. And all the people who come after me is going to say the same things." He turned from the judge to Dobson. "We don't want you here. You rich people think you can waltz into Yarmouth County with your flowery language and empty promises and bamboozle the poor, dumb people who live here. We may be poor, but we ain't dumb, and we got one thing you can't buy — these mountains. And we will thank you to keep your greedy hands off 'em."

Clarence turned back to the zoning board and nodded to Ruby Cunningham.

"Thank you, Ms. Cunningham." He looked at the other members of the board, made eye contact with each one individually. "And you Mr. Cassidy … Mrs. Hanover … Mr. Alvarez … Mr. Onassis … Mrs. O'Reilly … Mr. Tackett. Don't you listen to that man's sweet-talking lies. Don't you take his bribes, and make no mistake about it —

he's paying for that cruise on the lake to buy your votes. You know how this county feels about that development. We expect you to deny the application for the Gum Tree Hollow Development because that's the will of the people."

There was a roar of approval so loud that the judge didn't even try to quell it, he had to let it die down before his banging gavel could be heard.

Ruby Cunningham read off the next name on the list, and Clarence Cunningham was right — all the speakers who followed him said the same thing he had, droning on and on.

Rileigh stood for more than an hour listening to the speakers. Her feet hurt and her shoulders ached. She'd have left, but she was waiting to hear what Ian McGinnis had to say. She reached up and massaged her neck with her fingers. Then she felt other hands on her shoulders, kneading the knotted muscles.

Charlie Hayden was standing behind her, whispered into her ear.

"Need a back rub?"

She whirled on him in rage, slapped him with such force he slammed into the closed jury room door behind him and banged his head.

"Keep your hands off me, you pathetic creep," she hissed.

He looked genuinely surprised. Did he actually think she *wanted* him to touch her?

But in a heartbeat, his surprise morphed into a look of black rage darker than her own.

"You bitch! You—"

"Mr. Ian McGinnis," Ruby Cunningham announced, and Rileigh turned back toward the courtroom and ignored the rest of his obscene response.

Ian wasted no time getting to the point.

"Members of the zoning board, *this* is what Yarmouth County thinks about the High Mount Development Company's Gum Tree Hollow plan," he said, his voice loud. Rileigh could hear a commotion in the crowd and stepped to the edge of the alcove to see what was going on.

At least half of the people in the crowd had leapt to their feet, unfurling signs they had sneaked into the courtroom.

"Hands off Gum Tree Hollow!"

"Save our Hollow!"

"No compromise! No development!"

"Mess with our mountains, we'll mess with *you!*"

The group burst into a chant then, and after they'd repeated it a couple of times, the rest of the crowd joined in. In seconds, every person in the gallery was on their feet chanting and stomping in unison.

"High Mount!" Stomp, stomp. "*Hell* no!" Stomp, stomp. "High Mount." Stomp, stomp. "*Hell* no!" Stomp, stomp.

The roar was deafening.

Judge Hall banged his gavel to no avail, so he nodded to Mitch. Rileigh could read his lips.

"Clear the courtroom!"

When Mitch and his deputies tried to usher the crowd out of the room, scuffling broke out, then fists began to fly and it became a brawl on its way to a full-bore riot.

Rileigh watched in dismay as Mitch and his deputies waded into the fray, she remained well out of their way in the alcove. If she couldn't cope with the crush of a crowd, a riot was … she had to get out of here. The zoning board wasn't interested in hanging around for the show either, and came rushing out of the jury box through the alcove where she stood, carrying her along with them like a leaf in a stream, finally depositing her on the courthouse steps. Rileigh could hear the commotion growing louder on the third floor. She turned away and headed back to her car.

As she walked through the cold night air, she remembered what Ian had said to her when she'd stumbled upon a meeting of the Save Gum Tree Hollow Association at the Wheaton Estate last summer, though she hadn't known at the time there was such a group, and still didn't know who the members were. She'd demanded an explanation but Ian had refused to give one. She'd pointed out that secret societies were responsible for all manner of evil in the world and he'd bristled.

"Make no mistake," he'd told her. "We are *not* the Ku Klux Klan in this. We're the Underground Railroad. We're *the rescuers.* Our goal is to *save* the mountains — for our children and their children and all the future generations who have a right to live in these mountains as God made them, free of the pollution of greedy developers who rape and pillage and gorge their gluttonous gullets on the spoils of our destruction."

Ian could be poetic when he put his mind to it.

He'd told her, "We haven't broken any laws. *Yet.*"

The rest of what he'd said then rang in her head now, as chilling as the icy wind caressing her neck:

"One of these days, Rileigh girl, you're going to have to pick a side."

Chapter Four

RILEIGH TURNED off the road and up the driveway to her mother's house, accelerated just enough so she would make it over the hump of rock at the top, then hit the brake so she wouldn't go crashing through the front yard fence. The challenge of her driveway was enough to pry her thoughts away from the near-riot she'd just witnessed at the courthouse. It had been chilling, and she was still chilled, but no longer because of the altercation at the zoning board meeting. The valiant little heater in her car had fought bravely against the attack of cold wind through open windows and had gone down in noble defeat a few miles outside the Forge, spewing cold air after that. Truth was, the heater only worked sometimes and not others, and most of tonight had been a "not others" time. She had to get the heater repaired. It was January, a lot of winter left before spring. But … money.

To have money, one had to have a job. She had only worked off and on since mid-October, and she'd have been homeless under a bridge if it weren't for her mother's generosity. But Mama wouldn't allow the words *thank you* to get all the way out of Rileigh's mouth before leaping into her mama bear suit and proclaiming that the house belonged to the Bishop family, was Rileigh's as much as it was hers ... "and that's the beginning and the end of it."

Rileigh's fingers were stiff from clutching the freezing steering wheel. She knew she was being absurd, reacting to weather in the 20s as if she were in Antarctica at minus 60 degrees Celsius. But most of her life had been spent in warm Tennessee and in places much hotter than that, and much less scenic. It was hot enough to fry an egg on the hood of a Jeep in parts of Afghanistan.

Distracted by driving with frozen fingers, she didn't notice until she turned off the engine that her mother was sitting outside on the porch swing.

Rileigh leapt out of the car, calling as she went, "Mama, what are you doing out here in this cold? You're going to freeze to death."

She could see that her mother was wrapped up warm. She had a coat on and boots, and had wrapped the Afghan off the living room couch around her shoulders. It was the last thing that Aunt Daisy had knitted before she forgot how. She kept knitting after that, of course, lumpy balls of tangled yarn that Mama unraveled so Daisy could do it again.

Leaping to her feet, Mama barreled down the porch steps, and threw herself at Rileigh.

"Oh, sugar, I'm so glad you're home. I've been waiting so long."

"Mama, I've only been gone a couple of hours."

"Don't be silly, dear you've been gone for a week, but you're home now! And I've just been waiting and waiting, so excited I can't hardly sit still."

"How about we go inside and you be so excited you

23

can't sit still in a warm house instead of out here in the cold?"

"It's the most wonderful news!" Mama said as Rileigh directed her up the steps and across the porch.

"You can tell me all about it as soon as—"

"Oh, sugar, Jillian's coming home!"

No matter how many times it happened, and it happened frequently, Rileigh felt like she had been kicked in the stomach by a mule. Mama had not mentioned Jillian half a dozen times when Rileigh was growing up, but as she got older and wandered further into the LaLaLand of dementia, her filters began to fade away. In the past few years, Mama's mind strayed more and more often to her oldest daughter, Rileigh's big sister who had disappeared on the night before her wedding and had not been seen since. Mama never gave up on Jillian. Mama believed, *chose* to believe, that Jillian was still out there somewhere and would come home.

All Rileigh could do was grit her teeth when Mama started talking about Jillie, even though it was staggeringly hard to hear.

"Hurry up. Come on. Wait till you see. Just wait. Wait till you see!"

Lily dragged Rileigh into the kitchen and pointed triumphantly at what lay on the kitchen table. If Rileigh had been kicked in the stomach by her mother's announcement that Jillian was coming home, the sight of the postcard lying picture side up on the table felt like a wrecking ball had slammed into her chest.

She stared at the postcard. Her vision narrowed until it seemed like the postcard was all she could see. She walked toward it slowly, reluctantly, ambivalent emotions tearing at her like two vicious dogs as they always did, her desire to put her hands on the postcard to somehow maybe be close to Jillian, and her revulsion at the sight of it, because it brought up all the agony around her sister's disappearance and fed the flame of her mother's delusion. Jillian had vanished 19 years ago, when Rileigh was six years old. Rileigh had gone into her big sister's bedroom that night to leave a picture and a note in her suitcase, begging Jillian not to forget her. What she'd walked into was a murder scene, blood everywhere and a severed human tongue lying on a fresh white pillowcase on display there for all to see. Terrified, Rileigh had run away. She'd come back hours later, tried to tell the adults what she'd seen, and they'd checked Jillian's room. It looked perfectly normal. No mess, no blood, no tongue, nothing to support Rileigh's story except the fact that there was also no Jillian, and there had been no Jillian since then.

Postcards had started arriving about a year after Jillian disappeared, just a postcard from some faraway place: New York, Chicago, San Francisco. And after a while, foreign cities: Paris, London, Rome. There was never any handwriting on the postcards, no message, nothing but a handdrawn smiley face. Jillian had loved smiley faces.

She walked slowly to the table as her mother hopped around her like a cricket, as excited as a little kid who needs to go to the bathroom, babbling something that Rileigh could not hear because of the roaring in her ears. She stepped up to the table but didn't touch the postcard laying on it, just looked down at it. It was a cityscape at night, bright lights outlining buildings that weren't familiar enough for her to recognize where the picture had been taken. But she didn't have to. The location was printed right there on the front in big bold letters: *Atlanta, a city not too busy to care.*

With trembling fingers, she reached out and picked up

the card and turned it over to find what she knew she would. No message, just a hand-drawn smiley face.

She stared at it, trying to calm herself, and eventually her mother's words began to penetrate the cocoon of isolation she had woven around herself.

"And look there. Look where it's from. Just look. It's Atlanta."

Rileigh looked at the postmark. It wasn't just a picture of Atlanta. The card had been mailed from Atlanta, which wasn't more than a couple of hours' drive from Black Bear Forge, Tennessee. It was the closest postcard they'd ever gotten. The last one had been from Venezuela.

"You see what that means, don't you? She's right here. She's coming home. Oh, Rileigh, Jillian's coming home."

Mama threw her arms around her, hugging her tight, and Rileigh stood as stiff as the bedpost on her bed. She didn't need this right now. God knew she didn't need this right now, not with everything else that was going on in her life.

"Mama, sit down and calm down. Let me make you some tea."

"Why ain't you excited about it?"

"I'm not excited about it because it doesn't mean anything." Rileigh tried to hold her tongue, and usually she was successful, having given up years ago trying to pry this precious delusion out of her mother's clutching fingers. But the words slipped out this time. "None of the postcards mean anything, Mama. Jillian's not sending them. Somebody is messing with us."

She took her mother's shoulders in her hands and looked down into her face. "Mama, Jillian's not coming home — not now, not ever."

To her utter surprise, her mother reached up and slapped her in the face. Even with the little force her mother was able to put behind the blow, it stung. She thought of Charlie Hayden. He deserved an apology for her overreaction.

"Don't you say your sister's not coming home. She's getting closer and closer every time. Didn't you say them phone calls you was getting was from Texas? Well, Texas is closer than Venezuela. And Atlanta's closer than Texas. She's coming home."

Rileigh suddenly felt very tired, bone weary, and she let go of her mother's shoulders, folded her into a gentle hug, then kissed her on the forehead. "I'm going to bed, Mama. It's been a long day."

Rileigh had gotten all the way out of the kitchen before she heard her mother's voice trailing after her.

"Did you fill that prescription for them pills the doctor give you so you could sleep?"

Rileigh froze. Yes, she had gotten the prescription filled, but she was not going to take them. Her mother had browbeat her into going to the doctor. But she had better sense than to take the pills he'd prescribed, "something mild" to help her sleep. Riiiiight. Charlie Hayden was a walking, talking advertisement for *why not*. That man had been higher than the Goodyear blimp when he'd put his hands on her tonight to "massage her shoulders." And it had all started with taking something to help him sleep. She didn't want to end up like Charlie — addicted to pills to help her sleep, and then to other pills to wake her up. Besides, she'd heard all kinds of bizarre stories about what happened to people when they took Ambien. Stephanie Papadopoulos, the screechy-voiced girl who was a receptionist at the Good Guys Investigation Agency in Gatlinburg, had been telling her "Ambien story" one day when Rileigh was in the office.

"I was sitting up in my bed with my computer in my

lap, just surfing the Internet after I took my regular Ambien pill. And as God is my witness, two weeks later the doorbell rang and a UPS delivery man was on my porch with all these boxes. He said they were for me, that I'd ordered what was in them. just refused delivery and they all went back. But damn, it's hard to believe I ordered six different wedding dresses."

No wedding dresses for Rileigh, thank you very much. She'd prefer to lay buggy-eyed in her bed staring at the ceiling until dawn.

Trouble was, she didn't lay there buggy-eyed. She went to sleep. Then she dreamed.

TOO TIGHT, jammed in a box. Can't move.

She opens her eyes and sees the wood of the lid only inches from her face. The sides of the box are tight against her shoulders. No room. No air.

She tries to reach up — her hands are tied. Her feet are tied.

She gasps. No air!

Smothering.

A sound above her, a clunking sound on the lid of the box. Thump. Clunk-clunk. Dirt sifts down into her eyes through the cracks between the boards. She sucks in a breath that's full of dust. Tries to scream but her tongue is coated with dirt, her throat dry.

And there's no air to scream.

She loses it, thrashes around, bangs her head on the wood above and below her, kicks and screams with no air and no sound as the dust filters down through the cracks where there'd been a little light. It's gone now. The dirt has covered the cracks, shovelfuls falling in rhythm on the wood.

Dirt on the top of the coffin.

Buried alive.

28

Rileigh sat up in a tangle of sweat-soaked sheets, a scream on her lips, her breathing coming in harsh gasps, her heart hammering like a jackhammer in her chest.

No, no, no!

It wasn't real, only a nightmare. At home in her room in her own bed. She wasn't in a crudely made coffin, with dirt falling —

She leapt out of the bed and dashed to the window, pulled frantically until it came open, stuck her head out into the frigid air and dragged in great lungfuls so cold it was painful. Gasped again and again until the cold woke her fully, sobered her, turned her damp nightgown frigid. Then she closed the window firmly and got back into the warm bed. Beginning to shake, she pulled the sheet and blankets up around her neck and lay in the dark, trying to get full control of her breathing. Trying to calm down.

She took deep, cleansing breaths and let the air out slowly, ticking off in her mind the simple life tasks she couldn't do anymore. Going into the chicken house to collect the eggs. Into her closet to pick out her clothes, into the pantry for a can of soup, into the bathroom to pee.

She ground her teeth. She *could* do those things. She did do them, forced herself to. But it was hard. Dear God in heaven, it was so hard. Staring at the ceiling in the dark, she felt warm tears slide down the sides of her face.

Chapter Five

RILEIGH WAS AT WORK, the only work she did these days. She liked calling it "working remotely." Hell, half the people in the country worked remotely now, dressed in a coat and tie from the waist up and in their underwear from the waist down, doing Zoom meetings with people all over the world.

Unfortunately, most of her job at the Good GI's Investigation Agency in Gatlinburg wasn't the kind of work you could do sitting at home on a computer. It was hands-on: stakeouts, watching philandering husbands and unfaithful wives and rent-jumpers, delivering summonses, investigating the possibility of fraud in insurance claims. You couldn't do any of that sitting in your underwear in your basement. But she did what she could do from home. The tedious, mind-numbing tasks like background checks and documenting the previous owners of a property for a title search. Boring but safe. She didn't have to leave the house to do it, didn't have to get in a car or an elevator or a public bathroom space.

Her telephone rang and when she saw that it was Mitch, she smiled and punched the green button.

"Hello there, Sheriff. How are you this fine morning?" Mitch called almost every day to check up on her. It annoyed her to death and thrilled her soul all at the same time. "Calling to make sure I'm still breathing in and out on a regular basis?"

"Well, if you put it that way …"

"Because I should be the one asking if *you're* all right."

"How so?"

"Apparently you didn't get your lights punched out last night."

"How do you know about that?"

"I was there, saw it all."

"I didn't see you."

"I didn't want to be right out in the middle of things, and as it turned out, that was a pretty good decision. If I'd sat down front for the proceedings, I might have been hauled off to jail."

"So you saw the protest."

"Protest? That's a weasel word, if ever I heard one. It was a scuffle, then a fight, then a brawl, and probably, after I left, a riot."

"Never made it to riot, but it was a pretty good brawl. I'd figured it was going to get ugly, but after a while, I decided maybe everybody was going to keep their cool. And they would have if it hadn't been for Ian McGinnis."

"It wasn't totally his fault. Apparently, it was a planned demonstration by that whole group."

"Uh-huh. The group that Ian McGinnis is in charge of."

"How do you know that?"

"You don't think he is?"

Actually, she was just about certain that he was, so she

tried to change the subject. "What did you think of that Dobson guy's presentation? Until I saw the map, I had no idea how big the Gum Tree Project is supposed to be."

"Well, that's kinda, sorta what I'm calling about. Not the Gum Tree Project, but the man who's selling it. Hunter Dobson. You know he's invited the immediate world to go on a cruise on the Queen of the Smokies on Friday?"

"Yeah, I heard about the bribe."

"He says it's just to smooth the community's ruffled feathers, but it does smell like a bribe to me, too. So, you want to go with me?"

"What?"

"How many things can 'do you want to go with me' mean? I'm inviting you to go on the cruise on the Queen of the Smokies Friday … as my date."

Rileigh was astonished. "I can't believe Dobson invited you. I can't believe you're actually going."

"Have to — gun to my head. Preston Rutherford, the honorable Yarmouth County mayor and chief asshole in general says I have to."

"Seriously?"

"Serious as a heart attack. I figured if I had to do it, maybe I could twist your arm into accompanying me. The old lemon/lemonade thing. Actually, a New Year's Eve party might be a good time."

"Friday is January 5."

"It's the thought that counts. He's ringing in 2024 with a masquerade ball. It's got a storybook theme. I was thinking of going as Tinkerbell. What do you think?"

"You're more the Big Bad Wolf type."

"That's a great idea. We could go as Little Red Riding Hood and the Big Bad Wolf. What do you say?"

Say no, cried the voice of fear inside her. *Tell him you can't. Make up some excuse. You have a cold. You feel a migraine coming on. You have to do your laundry. Tell him your left leg just fell off … something! … just say no.*

"Yes, sure, why not?" she said, and hoped her voice sounded steady. She absolutely, 100% did *not* want to do it, which was why she needed to do it. Just like she needed to go to that hearing last night. She had to force her way through her fear or it would eat up her whole life. She swallowed hard and said, "Little Red Riding Hood, I think I could pull a costume together for that. But the Big Bad Wolf…"

"Can you say, *rent a costume in Knoxville?*"

"All right, I'll go to the masquerade party with you. But not as a date." The date part was a bridge too far. "I'll go because I want to keep an eye on Mama. Mildred Hanover's been at loose ends since Herb died, and she didn't want to go alone, so she asked Mama to be her guest. Mama's all excited about it. She wants to go as Pippi Longstocking or a fairy godmother. I'm pulling for the fairy godmother. I think braids sticking out the sides of your head would get old pretty quick."

Rileigh sighed.

"Mildred's just like the rest of Mama's friends — in denial. All Mama's lapses in memory, the imaginary people, the random irrational statements are just 'Lily being charming.' None of them is willing to admit she has dementia. Mildred doesn't understand that Mama might decide she wants to go for a swim in the lake or something equally loony. I was going to ask Georgia to watch after her, but I guess it's a job I ought to do myself."

"Georgia's going?"

"Yep. She and Ian are going as Wesley and the Princess Bride. At least that's what she told me yesterday."

"Ian."

She didn't like the way Mitch said that.

"What about Ian?"

"You mean the guy who tried to start a riot last night?"

"Ian *didn't* start a riot."

"Right. It was all … just an accident."

Before she could argue with him, he grabbed the conversational ball and dribbled off in a different direction.

"According to the mayor, Dobson has spread his net wide, and I don't know how many fish he'll catch. But I'm betting the place is going to be …" he paused. "*Crowded.*" He paused for another beat and continued. "The ship is set to sail at six o'clock."

"Not sail, paddle. And it's not a ship, it's a boat."

The Queen of the Smokies was a paddle-wheel river boat, it just wasn't in a river. It cruised the waters of Big Puddle Lake, the biggest of half a dozen beautiful lakes in east Tennessee.

"There will be dinner, and gambling, of course. Dobson's picking up the tab for all of it. See you Friday night," Mitch what she supposed was meant to sound like a wolf's growl. It came out more like a clogged garbage disposal.

She sat holding the telephone long after she had punched the little red button to disconnect. What had she gotten herself into? Then she shook off the dread, squared her shoulders and called out to her mother, "Hey, Mama, I'm going to that masquerade party on Friday night, too. Mitch and I are going to be Little Red Riding Hood and Big Bad Wolf. Think you could help me come up with a costume?"

Her mother breezed into the room with a smile.

"Little Red Riding Hood you say? Hmmmm." She paused, thought, then her face brightened. "Why them old drapes we took down last summer — they're a little faded,

34

but still red enough. I could whip you up a red cloak out of that fabric. Wouldn't take me long at all."

Her mother was grinning. "You go get me my sewing things. I ain't climbing that ladder up to the attic."

The attic. Small and dark and confining. Rileigh shuddered.

Chapter Six

HER MOTHER FELL into making costumes for the two of them with an enthusiasm that didn't surprise Rileigh. Once her mother sunk her teeth into something, she was as tenacious as a terrier with a bone. She buzzed into Gatlinburg the next day and came back with packages from half a dozen different stores — fabric and thread and bows and patterns, and a brand-new pair of scissors because Rileigh had used her "good sewing scissors" to cut paper, which was as big a no-no now as it had been when Rileigh was in elementary school.

Mama had sewn almost everything Raleigh wore when she was a little girl. But when Mama went to work full-time, she set the sewing machine aside, and Rileigh had store-bought clothes like everybody else. Mama had kept the hobby alive in fits and spurts, though, and now she was a woman on a mission.

Rileigh downloaded images of a fairy godmother and Little Red Riding Hood off the internet for inspiration. Little Red Riding Hood, who was often depicted not as a little girl but as a sexy young woman in a dress so low-cut she definitely was *not* on her way to her grandmother's house, or so Rileigh's mother said. She had a red cape stretched all the way down to the floor with a hood that draped over her shoulders. Beneath the cape, she wore a simple red peasant dress with a floor-length skirt.

"I got red satin at Michael's to line the cape with, and we can use some of that to make the bodice of the dress. The material from our old drapes will do for the cloak. It's heavy enough to hold its shape."

The costume for the fairy godmother was similar to the one for Little Red Riding Hood, just in different colors: a blue hooded cape lined in pink, and a gigantic pink bow at her throat above a white blouse and a billowing blue skirt.

Mama had purchased some kind of dark blue material for the fairy godmother cape and the two long skirts. She already had a blouse whose big billowing sleeves she planned to line with pink satin. The magic wand was harder than Rileigh had expected, but they finally settled on covering a fly swatter's handle in silver duct tape and replacing the swatter with a shiny silver star from the Christmas decorations box.

Mama's enthusiasm was contagious, and pretty soon Rileigh was as excited about making the garments as her mother was, but she was no seamstress —Mama had never had time to teach her. So she became Mama's enthusiastic assistant, pinning the pattern to the fabric as her mother directed, cutting the fabric with the new pair of scissors, and holding the big pockets on both the capes while Mama basted them in place.

"We need pockets," Mama had said. "I don't think Fairy Godmothers carried purses."

Rileigh served as the mannequin, too, standing on a step stool while her mother knelt on one knee, her mouth full of pins, directing Rileigh to turn around slowly so she could pin up the hems on the long skirts.

"I swear, girl, you're skinnier than you were a month ago," Mama said when she held up the finished Red Riding Hood peasant dress. "Nobody loses weight over the Christmas holidays. This dress would fit a ten-year-old."

Rileigh divided the world into two kinds of people — those who eat when they're upset and those who can't eat when they're upset. Her best friend Georgia fell into Category A. Rileigh was pure Category B, all the way.

When Mitch showed up to collect the two of them on Friday evening, Rileigh felt like a little kid on her way to a birthday party. The excitement and enthusiasm of making the costumes had shoved her dread of the party into the background. After all, it would be fun to prance around in a costume, playing make believe.

She opened the door at Mitch's knock, and standing on the other side of the screen door was a big furry black wolf so lifelike it was frightening. She took an involuntary step back.

Mitch reached up and grabbed a handful of fur on the top of his head to lift the full-head mask off, but he was still a black wolf from the chin down.

"I'll huff and I'll puff and I'll blow your house down," Mitch said in a low grumbling voice.

"Wrong fairy tale. That's the three little pigs and the Big Bad Wolf."

"Oh, it's the same Big Bad Wolf. He went to grandma's house after he finished off the three little pigs."

"If I'm remembering my fairy tales correctly, the Big Bad Wolf fell down the chimney of the third little pig's house and landed in a pot of boiling water," said Mama, coming out from behind Rileigh, waving her magic wand in the air in front of her.

Mitch cringed away from the wand. "Be careful with that thing, it might go off and you'll turn me into a mouse."

"Well, I was planning on turning your cruiser into a carriage, but—"

"We couldn't find any spells in the magic book for police cruisers," Rileigh said. "Just pumpkins, and where are you going to find a pumpkin in January?"

Mitch bowed low and said, "My humble conveyance, such as it is, awaits you."

In his car, Rileigh insisted her mother sit in the front seat because there was more legroom there and her mother had an arthritic hip that gave her trouble when she sat too long in one place. Or at least that's what Rileigh *said* was her reasoning. In truth, she wanted to have the whole back seat to herself. Less claustrophobic that way.

As soon as Mitch got into the car and closed the door, Rileigh's breath caught in her throat. Too tight. It was almost as if she could see the sides of the car moving slowly toward her, the roof sinking down, the floorboard moving upward.

No, no, not going to happen. Not going to hyperventilate. Not here, not now.

She gritted her teeth and balled her hands into fists so tight her fingernails cut into the palms of her hand. Thankfully, Mama and Mitch kept up a lighthearted, bantering conversation in the front seat that didn't require much participation from Rileigh. But as soon as they pulled up at the dock on Big Puddle Lake, she was out of the car in a flash, dragging in big lungfuls of cold air to calm herself.

Mitch walked around his cruiser and eyed her. She had seen him watching her in the rearview mirror, and was pretty sure he knew she was uncomfortable. That's why he had kept Mama talking and giggling in the front seat, to give Rileigh some space. She was surprised at how tender that seemed to her at the moment, how kind and thoughtful. She smiled at him.

Hooking her arm through his, she asked, "Is this your maiden voyage on the Queen of the Smokies?"

"Yes, it's my first time, so be gentle."

Rileigh elbowed him in the ribs.

"Are you a cherry, too?" Mitch asked.

"No, I've … well, actually, maybe I am. All I've seen on the boat is the children's play area."

Rileigh mimicked Georgia's Tennessee accent. "Aw come on, Riles … we'll lay out on the sundeck drinking mai-tais while the kids play in the playroom. Bring a book so you don't get bored." Rileigh paused. "Riiiight."

GEORGIA IS WADDLING. Literally. Though Rileigh doesn't have intimate knowledge of such things, she is afraid her best friend will go into labor right there on the dock before they ever even get on the paddleboat. Rileigh is carrying one-year old Mason in one arm and has a diaper bag the size, shape, and weight of a streamer trunk over her other shoulder. Georgia is herding Liam, Eli, and Conner down the dock toward the boat.

They give their tickets to the steward, who directs them to the children's play area on the bottom deck. Conner is a late bloomer, still in the throws of his terrible twos at age three-and-a-half. He refuses to hold either of his older brothers' hands, declaring "Con-con do it!" He wanders off down the wrong passageways, and pitches a fit when he's dragged back the right way.

When they step into the play area, Conner looks like he has died and gone to heaven.

It is impressive. Rileigh has never seen anything like it, a McDonald's play area on steroids. A bright-colored sign invites chil-

dren (under age 12) to play in Gerbil Village. It features slides and steps and monkey bars. There are bells to ring, horns to honk and other gadgets that each have a distinctive sound. The cacophony of different noises, mixed with the squealing/crying of children and the strident voices of attendant parents sounds like a battlefield without the blood. Rileigh is instantly shell-shocked.

The biggest piece of play equipment takes up two-thirds of the deck area — a gigantic maze of tunnels that look just like the plastic tunnels for gerbils Rileigh has seen in pet stores. Stretching in a snarl from the floor to the ceiling, the interconnected child-sized tunnels snake up and down, tangle with each other like a lump of hollow spaghetti dumped in the center of the room. Each section of connecting tunnel is a different color — red, blue, yellow, orange, purple, green, with a clear section about every ten feet or so. On the deck outside, there's a water park of sorts called Gerbil Pond — a kiddie pool where an enormous green frog squirts water out its mouth and ears, and there are jets in the floor that squirt whoever steps on them. There's an entrance to the gerbil tunnels from out there.

Unfortunately, the tunnels have been roped off with a sign that says, "Temporarily closed for cleaning." But the round doors closing off the tunnels aren't latched. They're standing open, and of course, Conner barrels toward the openings.

"No, Conner, you can't—" cries Georgia.

"Conner, don't—" cries Rileigh.

The child ignores them both, slips beneath the rope and disappears into the right of two openings in the tunnel system. Apparently, all the tunnels eventually wind back to one of those openings or to the opening outside. Before Rileigh can stop her, Georgia dispatches eight-year-old Liam and six-year-old Eli to "go find your brother."

Now there are three kids crawling through the otherwise empty maze of tunnels.

It takes two excruciating hours to extract all the children.

Eli finally finds Conner. The children have a brawl inside the tunnels and both crawl away in different directions, crying. Rileigh *suspects Liam is intentionally trying to stay lost because he's having fun.*

Though the tunnels can be opened at various places from the outside — a three-foot section of the top of the tunnel is hinged and latched on the outside — Conner scoots away and escapes all the adults' efforts to snatch him out one of those openings.

Though Rileigh volunteers to go into the tunnels after the children — it would be a tight squeeze, but she'd fit — the deck crew of the boat won't allow it. Right about the time a crewman extracts the final child kicking and screaming from the roped-off, closed-down play equipment, Georgia has her first contraction. Mayella is born a frantic few hours later, in the emergency room of the hospital. Never made it upstairs.

RILEIGH CONSIDERED FOR A MOMENT, then told Mitch, "Yeah, this is my first time on the Queen of the Smokies. Nothing you do in the company of four, soon-to-be-five little kids counts as a real adult experience."

Chapter Seven

MITCH, Rileigh, and her mother started down the incline toward the dock that stretched out into the lake where the mammoth Queen of the Smokies was moored on one side. The dock had always put Rileigh in mind of train stations in England where passengers waited on a center island and trains sped by in opposite directions on both sides. There was nothing moored on the other side of the dock from the boat, but the Queen of the Smokies took up the entire dock, her tail end sticking out far behind it.

"I'm surprised every time I see it," said Mama. "It's like it gets bigger and bigger and bigger."

"It doesn't need to get any bigger," said Rileigh. "It's enormous now."

The boat was an impressive sight cruising slowly around on the huge Big Puddle Lake with the Smoky Mountains as a backdrop. With its bright red paddle, the boat looked like it just sailed out of the Victorian era, trailing behind it calliope music that brought to Rileigh's mind the dusty smell of a cheap carnival and the taste of cotton candy slowly melting in her mouth.

The Queen of the Smokies was a shameless rip-off of the American Queen, just not as big and pretentious. Both were recreations of a Mississippi riverboat.

As the largest paddlewheel steamboat ever built, the American Queen boasted two hundred twenty-two staterooms, four hundred guests, and a crew of a hundred sixty-five. The Queen of the Smokies was condensed version of the original, with one hundred seventy-five staterooms, three hundred guests and a crew of ninety-five. The guest list for tonight's party cruise would likely top out at a hundred-fifty. How many of those invited would actually show up — anybody's guess.

While the American Queen had six decks, the Queen of the Smokies had only five. The whole of the bottom deck was called the hold, which would have been below water level on a sea-going ship not built for the shallow waters of a lake. In the hold resided the mechanics of the boat: engine, communication room, storage, cargo, and some guest cabins. At least half the hold was devoted to Gerbil Village.

Above the hold was Deck Two, where the crews' quarters and kitchen were located, along with the main kitchen for the guest restaurants on upper decks. The gift shop, was there, too, plus the theatre and a chart room with delightfully nerdy navigational materials.

Deck Three was the main deck, the showpiece, featuring a large and lavish dining room, a nightclub lounge with dancing and a stage for live performances. And, of course, the casino. On the stern of the main deck was a giant calliope.

A large buffet-style restaurant was open 24/7 on Deck Four, where most of the guest cabins were located. There was also a library, a video game room, hair salon and coffee shop. Deck Five was the roof of the boat, devoted to deck chairs and sunbathing, along with the pilot house.

All the decks were surrounded by verandas with ornate railings, and the high ceilings were decorated with lacy filigree. The open areas on the stern and bow of Decks Two and Four were for outdoor activities.

At more than four hundred feet long, the boat was a massive craft that looked like a cruise ship when it was moored at the dock. And it was a steamboat, all right, but unlike its bigger cousin, the Queen of the Smokies's only power was that paddle wheel. If there was an emergency on the Queen of the Smokies, the crew would just have to put oars in the water and row.

Tonight's outing was special indeed, since the boat spent all winter in dry dock. Rileigh couldn't imagine what it had cost Hunter Dobson to get it up and running in the dead of winter for just one cruise. Evidence that Dobson was a man determined to get his land development approved by the zoning board and would spend whatever it cost to grease the skids.

Several cars pulled into the parking lot at the same time as Mitch's cruiser, disgorging a small crowd of people on their way down to the dock. Rileigh held back as if she were admiring the sleek lines of the paddle wheeler and let the other people go down to the dock ahead of them. Truth was, she didn't want to have to stand in a crowd waiting to be checked off the invitation list by the uniformed man at the base of the ramp leading from the dock to the boat.

As they watched, storybook figures filed past them, smiling greetings. Pinocchio, and Tom Thumb, and at least two of the three little pigs. Surely there was a third coming along later.

"Now see," Rileigh's mother cried, pointing to a

woman coming down the dock toward the ramp. "That's the costume I should have made." Rileigh looked at pigtails sticking straight out from Mona Carrington's head.

"Mama, every time you turned around, you'd be whacking somebody in the face with those pigtails."

"And besides, Pippi Longstocking doesn't have a magic wand," Mitch said, "If somebody cuts in front of you in the punch bowl line, turn them into a frog."

Mama smiled and nodded. Surely she didn't think she could really do a thing like that … but then she thought she was dating Rhett Butler, so who knew what Mama believed was possible?

Ruby Cunningham, who chaired the zoning board, had come as Mother Goose, complete with yarn and knitting needles. Her husband was dressed as a pig. He wasn't the missing one of the trio, because his costume didn't match. When Rileigh saw Hansel Cassidy, another member of the zoning board, as Christopher Robin to his wife's Winnie the Pooh, she figured that Ruby's husband must be Piglet. She heard Stephanie Papadopoulos, the curvaceous receptionist at the Good GI's investigation Agency in Gatlinburg, long before she saw her. The girl's squeaky voice carried in the cold night air. Maybe she was supposed to be the Velveteen Rabbit. She was wearing a rabbit suit all right, but it looked more like something a playboy bunny would wear than a much-loved stuffed animal.

Mildred Hanover, the woman who had invited Mama to be her guest at the party, came hurrying down the dock, all in a dither.

"Oh, I'm so sorry I'm late, Lily," she said. She was dressed as Mary Poppins—who obviously had gained a hundred pounds as she aged. But surely that's who Millie was supposed to be, with that carpet bag and black umbrella.

"Oh, don't you worry a thing about it, Millie. We just got here ourselves."

With the crowd ahead of them now, Rileigh, her mother, the sheriff, and Mildred made their way down the plank deck toward the uniformed man checking invitations. It was possible he was supposed to be one of the Nutcracker soldiers, but more likely the was just wearing the uniform he wore as a member of the ship's crew.

As Mitch pulled out his invitation, Rileigh heard someone call her name. She turned to see Ian and Georgia hurrying down the slope to the dock.

"Wait up," Georgia cried.

Ian made a pretty good Wesley from the Princess Bride, in a rakish outfit with a rapier at his waist, a little stick-on mustache and his hair pulled back in a ponytail. But Georgia looked odd, and from this distance, Rileigh couldn't figure out why. She was supposed to be the Princess Bride, and she had a wig of long, blonde hair trailing down her back. But her dress was … what in the world? Then she got close enough for Rileigh to see, and Rileigh burst out laughing. When her mother turned to look, she started laughing, too. Mitch couldn't figure out what they had found so funny.

"Private joke?" he asked.

"More or less," Rileigh said, grinning. Georgia came huffing and puffing toward them, holding up the skirt of her dress so she wouldn't trip over it. A dress that was made out of duct tape. *Red duct tape.*

It looked like she had woven strips of duct tape into a single piece to use for the long skirt. From the waist up she was wrapped in tape, but she had somehow managed to make the poofy sleeves below the shoulders, and when

Georgia saw Rileigh looking at them, she said merely, "Wrapped the tape around a cantaloupe."

"But how did you get the cantaloupe out of —?"

Georgia waved the question aside.

"It's been my experience in life that you can do *anything* if you have a good enough reason," she raised an eyebrow and winked.

"Is anybody going to tell me what this is about?" Mitch asked.

"It's a really long story," Rileigh said.

"And a really funny story," her mother added.

Georgia shooed them on ahead of her up the ramp as she said, "A sad but true tale of love and friendship and larceny."

Rileigh saw Mitch cast a glance at Ian, who hadn't said more than hello since he and Georgia arrived. Finally, Mitch said, "Good to see you, Ian."

Ian merely nodded and said nothing.

Georgia looked from Ian to Mitch and back to Ian, then leaned over and whispered in Rileigh's ear, "It was already cold out here, now it's freezing."

Chapter Eight

IT FELT wonderful to get inside the boat out of the cold. Rileigh hadn't wanted to wear a coat because it would cover up the Little Red Riding Hood costume that she and her mother had worked so hard on. As she looked around, she could tell that most people felt the same way. They were coatless and shivering just like she was.

It was a strange indeed to be on a riverboat listening to a calliope cranking out its hinky-tinky music in the dead of winter. That was a summertime thing. This boat would normally cruise from one dock on the lake to the next and the next and the next, picking up and disgorging passengers. Tonight there would be no other passengers waiting in the cold on the other docks around the lake. The boat would just pull majestically out into the middle of the lake and drop anchor there. The passengers could look out the windows at the twinkling shore lights — from inside, where it was warm. Probably the only person onboard who'd be interested in braving the cold on the observation decks was Mitch, who was dressed in a furry Big Bad Wolf costume and was already sweating.

And the shore light vista was a little iffy tonight as well. On their way to the dock, they had listened to the news on the radio. There was a cold front moving through, and storms in the mountains were the screwiest storms in the world. It could be snowing in one hollow and raining in the hollow on the other side of the mountain. But they weren't predicting snow in the forecast she heard. The forecasters were warning about the possibility of an ice storm.

Standing just outside the grand salon of the boat, the boat captain greeted boarding passengers as they passed by. Georgia had run off to the ladies' room as soon as she got on the boat because some of her tape was coming loose. Wesley had just evaporated into the crowd. Mama and her friend Mildred couldn't wait to try their luck at the slot machines. Mitch's warning that "they're not called one-armed *bandits* for nothing" fell on deaf ears. Thankfully, her mother didn't have a whole lot of money on her to lose.

When Mitch and Rileigh approached the captain, he was speaking to someone who had his back to them. It was a heated discussion and Rileigh was a little embarrassed, feeling like she was intruding. It wasn't an argument, though, because only one of them was pissed off — and it wasn't the captain.

"Today's my birthday, for crying out loud," said the man with his back turned to Rileigh and Mitch. "I had to walk out on my own birthday party."

The captain apologized, told the man he was sorry it had worked out this way.

"No need for *you* to be sorry," the man said. "The person who should be sorry is Winston Burkett. Where the hell is he? My wife baked a cake, invited half a dozen friends over, made a great big taco salad,and I'm missing it all to cover for his sorry ass. I—"

By that time, Mitch and Rileigh had reached the other two. When the man with his back to them saw the captain looking past him, he turned and fell silent.

"Welcome aboard," said the man dressed as Jack Sparrow. "My name is Elijah Rowe and I'm the captain of the Queen of the Smokies."

Elijah was tall and good-looking, his skin a deep ebony. If he hadn't played football or some other grown-men-hitting-each-other kind of sport, he should have. He filled out his Jack Sparrow costume way better than Johnny Depp ever had.

The man he was speaking to was even bigger. With his broad shoulders, muscular build, and thick chest, he'd have been perfect as a lumberjack, but he was dressed in some kind of outfit Rileigh couldn't quite place: a floppy red hat, baggy vest, shirt, and pants, and a half mask that consisted of a big red bulbous nose and a long beard stretching down from it to his waist. If she had to guess, she would say that he was supposed to be one of the seven dwarves. Rileigh was quickly figuring out that partying with people dressed up in costumes messed with reality. It was hard to take anybody seriously when they were dressed like Jack Sparrow or a giant dwarf.

The definitely-not-a-*dwarf* man pulled his mask down past his chin, revealing his whole face, and reached out to shake Mitch's hand.

"My name is Donovan McCreary, and I'm the—" he glanced at the captain, then returned his gaze to Mitch. "I'm the head of security on this cruise tonight. You'll be able to pick out the rest of my team; there are seven of us and we're all dressed as dwarves." He pointed to the monogram that Rileigh hadn't noticed on his floppy red hat. It identified him as Grumpy.

Elijah said to McCreary, "The Big Bad Wolf here is the county sheriff, when he's not covered in fur."

Rileigh leaned forward, "I'm Rileigh Bishop," she said, shook hands all around, then cocked her thumb at Mitch, "And you need to know that he's not wearing a costume. He looks like this every time there's a full moon."

The others chuckled.

"I hope you enjoy yourselves tonight," Captain Rowe said. "We'll be serving hors d'oeuvres and drinks from six until seven. You're welcome to wander around and explore the boat."

The whole boat was open for business, he said, all five decks, though it wasn't likely anybody would avail themselves of the lounge chairs on the top deck for sunbathing. Only the staterooms not in use were closed off. Rileigh glanced around as the captain spoke to them, impressed by the turnout. She had thought, given the near-riot at the zoning board meeting, that people might boycott what many were calling the Bribe Tour paid for by Hunter Dobson. And there was this storm looming, maybe an ice storm, which could be really nasty in the mountains. The roads were bad enough even when they weren't covered with a sheen of ice.

But plenty of people had shown up, which was the good news for Hunter Dobson and the bad news for Rileigh Bishop. It would be hard to avoid getting jammed into tight places in a crowd this size. But one of the decks had a walking track all the way around it. She could always retreat to that. And all of the decks had walkways in front of the interior rooms where summertime visitors could sit in Adirondack chairs and look at the scenery. The stern deck had a viewing area where you could watch the paddle wheel splashing in the water as it moved the boat forward — a singularly cold activity tonight.

Captain Rowe said that at the end of the hour of drinks and hors d'oeuvres, the boat would be at anchor in the middle of the lake. At that point, there would be a brief welcome by Hunter Dobson, then dinner would be served in the dining room.

"At the stern end of the dining room, there's a raised stage for a band when we have live music. It's cordoned off now with drapes, and apparently Mr. Dobson intends to read us all a fairy tale," Captain Rowe added. He's dressed as that little green eyeball dude, Mike Wazowski. He paused. "He promised it would be brief. We'll have the boat back here at the dock promptly at ten o'clock."

The captain turned aside to greet more passengers boarding the boat, so Rileigh and Mitch wandered off into the grand salon. Rileigh steered them away from groups of people. Thankfully, the rooms in this boat were huge, with tall ceilings and giant chandeliers hanging down. She'd be able to find someplace less crowded when she felt the need, and that in itself relaxed her. She was trying very hard to keep Mitch from noticing that under her cheery exterior, anxiety was pulsing like a sore tooth.

Rileigh saw Mitch break into a big smile, and she turned to follow his gaze. Walking toward them was a man dressed all in black — carrying his head in his hands. The Ichabod Crane costume had been wonderfully well-crafted. The whole top of the outfit had been made larger, the shoulders raised up so that the head of the person wearing the costume fit beneath them. On either side of the top brass button on the front of the black jacket you could barely see two small holes where eyes were peering out of them.

"The Headless Horseman. Right on, pal." Mitch gave the man a fist bump, then turned to Rileigh. "You remember our friend here, don't you?"

"Actually, Ichabod and I were never really close."

"Good one," came a muffled voice from within the chest of the headless man in front of her. "Hold this," he handed her his head. Then he unbuttoned his shirt and out popped the face of Gus Hazleton, the county coroner. Rileigh didn't know the man well at all, but she had heard all about him from Mitch. He was a medical doctor, a pathologist, and had several other degrees as well. He ran the most sophisticated coroner's office in East Tennessee and perhaps in the whole state.

That wasn't because he had been funded by Yarmouth County, which paid a pittance to its coroner. Gus had outfitted the coroner's office and the lab out of his own pocket. And Gus's pockets were deep. He was an extremely lucky man … he had won the lottery. No joke. According to Mitch, the man had bought a single lottery ticket at a convenience store because he had to make a purchase or they wouldn't let him use the bathroom in the building, and he had netted millions of dollars. A dedicated pathologist and an "odd duck" was how Mitch had described him. It had been Gus who had called from a chartered fishing boat somewhere in the Gulf of Mexico last fall to tell Mitch that he'd remembered a serial killer named Alex Cullen had killed his victims by chopping off their heads, and then sent the heads to the next of kin— which had led Mitch to track down Brandon Hollister and save Rileigh from a very early grave.

"The Big Bad Wolf?" Gus said. "You told me you were coming to the party as Tinkerbell. That's the only reason I came — to see you in a tutu."

"Wish I'd stuck with my original idea." Mitch reached up a furry arm and wiped sweat off his forehead. "This was a serious fashion blunder."

"Want to go stand out on the deck?" Rileigh asked Mitch. She looked around at the growing crowd. "I wouldn't mind getting out of here myself."

"Join us?" Mitch asked Gus.

"I want food. My mama used to say she was so hungry, her stomach thought her throat was cut." He made a slicing gesture below the spot where his head should have been. "That's me."

He took his head back from Rileigh and melted into the crowd.

She and Mitch made their way through the dining room and the casino, toward the doors on the other side of the boat. Rileigh couldn't help gawking, remembering a line from the brochure advertising the boat tours. "We like to think this boat looks just like it did when Mark Twain was aboard."

They had definitely succeeded, though Twain had been dead for more than a century before this boat was built. Rileigh loved the glistening mahogany woodwork, beautiful flowered rugs on glassy smooth and shining hardwood floors. The Tiffany glass lamps glittering on huge antique furniture surrounded by overstuffed chairs and settees. Giant chandeliers dangled from the high ceiling, glistening, casting sparkling light all around the room.

Mitchell looked around, like he was searching for something or someone.

"Looking for celebrities? I don't imagine there are any, well except for Elvis, and he's been showing up in all kinda places ever since he died."

"I'm looking for … no, I guess they're not here tonight. The dispatcher at the office said the coolest thing about a cruise on the Queen of the Smokies was the mimes. Apparently, they set out lifelike mannequins dressed in period costumes, all over the boat. But some of them aren't mannequins, they're mimes, and they suddenly come to life and start talking to scare the bejeebers out of people."

When they passed through the casino, they found Mama and Millie camped at one of the slot machines. Mama was feeding chips into it one after another and cranking the arm, watching the spinning shapes as they came to rest in the viewer window on the front of the machine.

Clunk. A cherry.

Clunk. An apple.

Clunk. A sunflower.

Clunk. A wild card, which would have matched for a win if the other four had matched each other.

"Mama, try not to lose your shirt in the first five minutes."

Mama blew her off with a wave of her hand. "Oh, I won't lose my shirt. I'm a fairy godmother. If this sucker doesn't give me a win pretty soon, I'm gonna take my magic wand and–"

"Beat the shit out of it?" Mitch offered.

"Put a spell on it," Mama corrected. "If this puppy can do mice, surely there's a setting on it somewhere for slot machines."

A man dressed as the Mad Hatter passed through the casino without stopping. Rileigh poked Mitch. "Is that Charlie Hayden?"

"I think so."

"He and I crossed paths the night of the zoning board meeting." She paused. "I owe him an apology."

"What for?"

"I slapped him."

"Did he deserve it?"

"If he had deserved it, I wouldn't be apologizing."

"You gonna tell me the story?"

"Nope." She took him by the arm and headed toward the outside doors. "Let's get you outside before you develop heat stroke."

Chapter Nine

THE THOUGHT WENT off in his head like a nuclear explosion, blasted out in all directions, flattened every part of his psyche, reduced to dust the rest of who he was. *He was going to kill a man.* What rose up from the explosion within was not a mushroom cloud, though, it was ... fireworks.

A spray of fireworks formed before his eyes. Tiny burning specks fell down on him and he could feel them burn through his clothing, that stupid outfit he wore. He could feel the pain of tiny flames all up and down his arms and his back and his neck, could smell the acrid stench of his hair when the sparks landed in it. And he wondered how it could be. Was it real, the fireworks? The burns all up and down his body testified to the reality and he relished the pain as proof, would have gloried in the fire if his clothing had burst into flames.

Tonight. In only a few minutes, he would kill.

Oh, he understood that the fireworks were not real, not out there beyond who he was, out there in the world. Fireworks needed a black backdrop. And that's why his mind had conjured up the image of fireworks *inside,* where he was a cheering audience of one.

The explosion, the fireworks — those were because this was his first time, because he was a virgin. He would be busting his cherry in only a few minutes, tasting blood for the first time. He tasted blood in his mouth then, and realized he had clamped his teeth down on his tongue so hard to hold onto his anticipation, that he'd bitten into it. The taste was salty. He'd never noticed before that blood tasted salty. It might not be this way at all the next time. And there *would* be a next time.

His heart ramped up into a gallop, thundering through his chest, pounding the urgency through his veins. His hands didn't shake, though. The hands that held the claw hammer were as still and calm as a brain surgeon's. He almost giggled at that. A brain surgeon? Yes. That's what he was. He was a brain surgeon about to open up the skull of his first patient.

But his absolute glee was not a universal response, shared by all the delegates to the grand convention of Who He Was. There still existed somewhere inside him the High Court of Morality, or Virtue, or just … Sanity.

And that part of him rebelled in every possible way, trying to stop him by all means necessary. "Don't do this," Morality/Virtue/Sanity screamed, "for God's sake, don't do this. You're not a killer!" And if he were to make an appearance in that court to plead his case, he could have provided all manner of logical explanations for what he was about to do. He had a reason, after all. This wasn't just a random act of killing.

Except yes, it was.

If he hadn't had any reason at all to kill anybody tonight, he still would have done it. He had come too far to turn back now, had drunk too deeply from that cup. He was in a boat, his face set, his vision clear, rowing hard out to into the turbulent water and he would not allow the single line still hooked to the dock stop him. He slipped the rope off the cleat and watched it drop with a plunk and a splash into the water. Then he turned back to his oars and began rowing rhythmically out to sea, farther and farther from the dock of reason until he couldn't even see it in the darkness anymore.

Murder. He would murder now. He'd seen it, witnessed it, reveled in it. Now it was his turn.

Gripping the ten-pound claw hammer in steady hands, he moved as quiet as a shadow through the darkness behind the drawn curtains. He could hear the rumble of conversation on the other side, the crowd out there waiting. He stopped, remained motionless, melted into the dark at the back of the stage. Waiting.

He didn't have to wait long. He spotted the glow from a penlight on the other side of the stage as Hunter Dobson used it to find his way to the chair that sat facing out toward the curtains and the crowd beyond. If Dobson lifted that penlight just the slightest bit, turned it to the side for some reason, he would have seen his doom standing there with bright eyes and an itchy claw hammer.

Dobson settled himself in the chair. It was a huge, over-stuffed armchair, the kind you sink down into. He picked up a big children's story book off the small table beside it and opened it on his lap.

Showtime.

The killer imagined himself a shadow, snaking silently through the darkness as he approached Dobson to stand directly behind the chair. He lifted the hammer high in the air, and the thrill that went through him when he brought it down on the top of the Dobson's head was almost sexual in the pleasure and relief. The claw end of the hammer made a crunching sound as it dug deep into the top of his skull. And he wanted to cry out in jubilation, wanted maybe to roar like a lion. Or scream like that mountain lion he'd heard once when he was a kid. That cry, oh to make that cry.

Dobson didn't lurch or jump, just went rigid, making some kind of groaning gurgle before he slumped back into the chair. The curtain would slide open any second now. What if they opened the curtains and found him standing there with his hands on the hammer buried in Dobson's head? He had to finish the job and leave.

But he *couldn't*, not yet. He *had* to feel that sensation one more time. He tried to pull the hammer out of the skull, but he had buried it two inches deep, the whole claw head of it, and it was stuck, wouldn't come free.

Just one more time.

Tugging, yanking, he wrenched the hammer out of the bone and lifted it high, slamming it down into the top of the Dobson's head a second time with a satisfying crunching sound.

When he did, a lightning bolt of pure pleasure surged in his groin and he almost groaned out loud.

Seconds. He only had a handful left.

With a lightning motion, he pulled a knife out of the scabbard inside his sleeve, leaned over the body from behind to avoid the gushing blood, and stabbed it into Dobson's right side. He sliced the knife all the way across the man's belly above his naval, wiped it on Dobson's shirt as he withdrew it and stuck it back up his sleeve. Then he pulled the piece of cardboard from his pocket and set it in Dobson's lap atop his guts. As he turned toward the shadows, the killer believed he could hear the sliding, greasy sound of Hunter Dobson's intestines spilling across the pages of the children's book.

The curtain began to move.

The killer stepped into the darkness at the back of the stage as the curtains opened wider. Then he vanished, moving in the darkness behind the stage. He was already gone before the lights came on and the screaming started.

Chapter Ten

RILEIGH TRIED to get her breathing under control but wasn't having a whole lot of success. She had to get out of here fast or she was likely to make a fool of herself. This was the captain's fault. He had spotted Rileigh and Mitch as they came back in off the promenade deck and ushered them inside, depositing them right in front of the stage where Hunter Dobson was supposed to appear when the curtains opened, sitting in a chair to read them a children's story. It wasn't so bad in the beginning, but as it got closer and closer to the time when Hunter was to make his welcome speech, more and more people closed in around them.

Closer and closer.

She felt a woman nudge her from behind, and a man bumped into her on the right side.

She started breathing faster. Sweat popped out on her forehead and upper lip. Mitch took her hand and squeezed. Then he let go and stepped behind her, placing his hands on her shoulders and pushing her a few feet closer to the stage. Then he took a broad stance behind her, feet spread wide apart, somehow managing to keep people from crowding in any closer. It wasn't perfect. Perfect would be out of here completely, but it was a lot better than getting squashed by the crowd.

Rileigh looked back over her shoulder and smiled. Mitch had put his Big Bad Wolf mask back on, so she couldn't tell if he smiled back.

"Whatever you paid for that mask, you got your money's worth," she said, keeping her voice steady and light. "It even has nose hairs."

When they'd been standing outside earlier, Rileigh had asked Mitch what he was wearing under the Big Bad Wolf suit. He'd shrugged and said, "My uniform."

"Seriously?" She began to laugh.

"Why is that so funny?"

"Why didn't you just wear that and say you'd dressed up as the county sheriff?" she asked.

"Because that's not a storybook character. Also, the Big Bad Wolf and Little Red Riding Hood sounded like a good idea at the time."

"And now?"

"I no longer feel sorry for wildlife outside in the snow."

The lights in the room began to dim, and the hum of conversation died down as the room got darker.

All Rileigh could think was, "Come on, people, get this show on the road so we can go eat." She had a table picked out over by the windows, with no other tables around it.

Then the room went completely dark. Rileigh went rigid. Mitch took her hand, but it was like holding hands with a stuffed animal. She gritted her teeth, then slowly forced herself to relax. It was just the closed in feeling and the darkness. She felt her heart kick into a gallop.

In the darkness, she heard the sound of the curtains being drawn back from the stage. It wouldn't be but a few more seconds. As soon as the curtains were drawn back, the lights would come back on.

Hold on.

Though she couldn't see anything at all, as soon as the curtains began to spread apart, she *smelled* something. She recognized it immediately. She wanted to believe that she was imagining it. No, it was real. Once you'd smelled it, the copper stench, you never forgot it. Blood, a whole lot of blood.

Mitch whispered something into her hair, but she couldn't hear him because there was a sudden humming sound in her head.

Then the lights began to come up. The rest of the room remained completely dark, but there were two spotlights focused on the front of the stage. At first they were so dim, you really couldn't tell what was up there.

She could only make out the shape of a man and a chair. As the lights grew brighter, she could see more and more clearly. It was a man, obviously Hunter Dobson, who was dressed as Mike Wazowski from Monsters Inc. From his neck to his waist, he was a green ball, with one enormous eyeball in the center, a grinning mouth beneath, and green arms and legs. He was sitting in a big, overstuffed chair with a storybook open on his lap — but the smell, the stench had been real.

There was a grumble around her, disbelief. Mitch stiffened. The lights grew brighter and brighter.

Up on the stage, blood pooled beneath Dobson's chair, and his internal organs had gushed out on top of the book in his lap through a slit where somebody had cut him open, the gash stretching across his belly just below the eyeball costume, from one side to the other. And on the top of his head, a claw hammer was buried in his skull.

"Holy shit," she heard Mitch mumble.

Then hysteria hit, exploded like a bomb in the crowd behind her, shrieking and screaming, the sound of a crowd of people thundering away like a single frightened beast, knocking over furniture, bumping into each other, elbowing each other out of the way. Total pandemonium.

Rileigh didn't move, stood frozen right where she was as the crowd around her fell away. Mitch walked slowly toward the stage, toward the dead body sitting in a chair preparing to read a story. Then Rileigh noticed that the man the captain had introduced to her — what was his name again? The head of security. Something McCreary. His Grumpy the Dwarf mask was pulled down off his face, the attached beard hanging down his chest, and he now stood at Mitch's elbow.

"Holy shit," McCreary said.

Both men leaned toward the other thing lying on the storybook in Dobson's lap besides his internal organs. A piece of cardboard like poster board, about the size of a sheet of notebook paper, propped up against the Dobson's belly. Written on it in bold black strokes was "#1".

Chapter Eleven

ABOVE THE GENERAL hubbub of hysteria, there arose a cry you couldn't mistake — a shriek, a wail, the horrifying sound of an injured animal in great pain. Rileigh turned, and in the still dimly lit room, she could see someone hurrying toward the stage, knocking people out of her way as she ran, barreling through the crowd. She was as furry as Mitch was, but the fur of her costume was pale blue with big purple splotches of color. She had cast aside the full-head mask with its amiable lantern-jawed face and horns, and was wearing only one of the four-fingered gloves, but it was still clear who she was supposed to be — Sully, from Monster's Inc., whose sidekick, Mike Wazowski, sat on the stage with his guts in his lap.

Mrs. Dobson almost made it to the stage.

The head of security, "something" McCreary, joined Mitch to intercept the screaming woman in the furry monster suit. She ran right at them, knocking people out of her way, shrieking, crying out Hunter's name and sobbing. Mitch grabbed her by one arm and McCreary the other, and she fought them in blind abandon, desperate to get to her husband.

As the Big Bad Wolf and Grumpy the Dwarf fought to subdue her, a different scream rose up out of the crowd, and Rileigh watched in disbelief as another woman came running toward the stage just as Hunter Dobson's wife had done, crashing through the crowd, knocking people aside, shrieking, wailing, sounding like yet another dying animal. Ruby Cunningham, dressed as Mother Goose, her yarn and knitting needles in a basket banging against her side.

A man appeared by Mitch's side as if he had materialized out of the floor. It was Gus, the Headless Horseman, and he intercepted the woman, grabbed and tried to hold on, to keep her from reaching the stage. She fought too, and Rileigh stood there dumfounded, watching the three men fight two hysterical women.

Two hysterical women.

Why would Ruby Cunningham be hysterical at the death of Hunter Dobson?

Ruby Cunningham wasn't merely upset. She was devastated. You don't suppose the two of them were … uh oh. Yup, this was a woman hysterical because the man she loved had been murdered. And so was the woman in the grip of Grumpy the Dwarf and the Big Bad Wolf.

Can you say *awk-ward*?

Mrs. Dobson suddenly became aware of Ruby. She stopped screaming as if you had turned off a water faucet. Rileigh had been introduced to her, but she couldn't remember her first name. Something odd like moon or star. Sky. Skyler, that was it. Rileigh watched recognition dawn on Skyler Dobson's face. And as it did, it was transformed from a mask of hysterical grief to all-consuming rage. She fought even harder to get away from Mitch and the head of security then. But she wasn't lunging toward the dead body on the stage anymore. She was lunging toward Ruby, who was oblivious to the world as she struggled to reach the dead body on the stage.

The room lights finally came all the way up and the people who had run hysterically from the sight of the dead man were now creeping back, trying to get a look at what they had run away from. Mitch called them looky-loos and rubberneckers. But that didn't fit. It was one thing to drive past a wreck and almost cause another wreck because you want to get a look at the dead bodies. It was something else entirely to be standing within ten feet of a man who had been murdered. Rileigh wasn't surprised that they were not only shocked and grieved, but curious.

A large man dressed as the Cowardly Lion — Rileigh couldn't make out who he really was — stepped forward to help the Headless Horseman restrain Ruby Cunningham. But there was no restraining Skyler. Mitch and the head of security might have gotten her under physical control, but they couldn't shut her up.

"You bitch, you whore. *You're* the one. You're who he's been seeing," she screeched. Then she lunged at Ruby, her fingers twisted into claws. "I'll kill you. I'll scratch your eyes out. I'll claw your face off."

Ruby was only a few feet away, but she didn't respond in any way to Skylar's screams and threats. Her eyes were fixed on Hunter Dobson, and there was such desolation on her face that Rileigh felt sorry for her.

Then her husband materialized out of the crowd. Awkward in stereo. Steve Cunningham was dressed as Piglet from Winnie the Pooh. It was an unfortunate costume because it highlighted the profile of the short fat man as he made his way through the crowd to his wife's side as she sobbed hysterically.

Steve looked bewildered and angry. He took hold of his

wife's shoulders and turned her toward him. "Ruby, what's wrong with you? Why are you…?"

She shoved him away and tried yet again to get to the Dobson's corpse. She managed to slip free from Gus and got close enough that Skylar grabbed her arm. Skyler would have ripped the woman's face off if Mitch, Gus, and McCreary hadn't intervened. But even then, Ruby didn't pay her any mind. She just tried to elbow her way to the stage, her eyes fixed on Dobson, calling his name quietly as she sobbed.

Her husband caught up to her again, then turned her around to face him and made eye contact. The two of them held it for a moment, then Steve took her into his arms. She collapsed sobbing on his shoulder. Rileigh realized for the first time that she had stood frozen through the whole event. Might as well have been a mannequin. She hadn't tried to help anybody, not Mitch, not Skyler or Ruby Cunningham. It appeared that the head of security and Mitch were going to have to manhandle Skylar out of the room. She continued to fight and scream and scratch. Mitch turned to a man in the crowd, a big man dressed in what could only have been a really bad recreation of Thomas the Train Engine.

"Harv, can you help me?" Mitch asked.

Harvey Whitaker pushed his way through the crowd to Mitch.

"Help McCreary get her out of here," Mitch said to him. The man nodded and helped McCreary drag the hysterical woman out of the room.

Then Mitch looked from Rileigh to Gus. "I need your help. This is a crime scene. We have to secure it."

Chapter Twelve

MITCH HAD NEVER BEEN in a situation quite like this one, but then he supposed most law enforcement officers hadn't. Investigating a brutal, very public murder while dressed up like the Big Bad Wolf.

It was his job to keep the crime scene as pristine as possible. He couldn't let this big crowd of frightened, chattering, boisterous people disturb any evidence that might have been left by the killer.

He looked at Rileigh, who stood almost rigid, so tight was her grip on her emotional response to the crowd. Then at Gus, whose eyes had grown wide, but of course this wasn't the first mangled dead body Gus Hazleton had ever seen.

"Rileigh, I need you to go find Captain Rowe for me and bring him here. Will you do that, please?" He didn't even wait for her to reply before he turned to Gus.

"Gus, let's see what we've got here."

Mitch spotted a man dressed as one of the seven dwarfs and called out to him. "You're part of the security team, right? McCreary had said all of you were dressed as dwarfs." He hoped that McCreary had told the members of his team that the Big Bad Wolf was really the county sheriff.

"Yes, I am, and so's Joe." The man indicated another dwarf making his way through the crowd toward him. This first dwarf's blue floppy hat identified him as Sleepy. The second dwarf's black hat said he was Sneezy.

"I need you guys to hold the crowd back, can you do that for me? Can you keep them away from the stage?"

"Yes, sir, we're on it."

With the two dwarfs doing crowd control, Mitch and Gus stepped up onto the stage and walked the few steps to the body.

Gus leaned over to get a better look at where the man's gut had been ripped open.

"At least there's no doubt what the murder weapon was," he said, and nodded toward the claw hammer that was buried in the top of Dobson's head. Then he gestured back toward the open wound where Dobson's internal organs had slid out into his lap.

"I'm not prepared to make a definitive judgment about it yet, but from first blush it appears the killer used some kind hunting knife, the kind used to field dress a deer."

"So, you're saying the murderer was a hunter?"

"I'm saying maybe the murderer used a hunting knife to slice this guy open. Whether or not he's a hunter is up to you to figure out."

Mitch pointed toward the piece of cardboard that had been placed in the man's lap with the number one on it.

"Got any idea what that means?" Mitch asked.

"I think it's supposed to mean this is the first of more than one, which is a pretty horrifying thought. But why would a murderer put you on notice that he plans to kill again? That doesn't make any sense at all."

Rileigh returned then with the ship's captain, who had been in the back of the room when the curtains were opened.

"Captain Rowe, I need you to instruct the pilot to turn this boat around and head back to the dock. And I need for you to radio the sheriff's department." He didn't bother to explain that the lake was in a cell phone dead zone because he was sure the captain fielded complaints about it all the time from passengers. "Tell the dispatcher to send deputies Mullins, Rawlings, and Crawford to the dock. Tell her I want them there when I get off the boat, and to have an ambulance waiting as well. Tell her we have a Code 10-27. She'll know what that means."

A Code 10-27 indicated an ambulance was necessary, but that the patient was already dead.

"What happened here?" Rowe asked, shaking his head as he stared at the dead body. When Mitch saw it from his perspective, as a civilian rather than a police officer trying to preserve evidence, he understood afresh what a horrifying sight it was.

"Tell whoever runs the engine to put the pedal to the metal. We need to get to shore as fast as possible."

Rowe couldn't seem to drag his eyes away from the body.

"Why would anybody…?" he began, and his voice trailed off.

"I'll get around to asking that question myself, but right now, there is a whole lot more that needs to be done before it's time to start trying to catch a murderer."

The captain's eyes grew wide then as realization dawned on him.

"The murderer, the killer, it's somebody who's on the boat right now."

"That's right. And I'm going to need your help and the

help of the security team when we get to the dock to keep the passengers on board. Nobody is leaving this ship until I say so. Is that clear, Captain?"

He shook off his dismay and nodded. "Yes, sir, that's clear."

As Rowe left, the head of security returned, having obviously given somebody else the task of holding on to the hysterical Skylar Dobson.

Mitch said to McCreary, "I need for you to cordon off this whole area. Do you have some kind of rope?"

McCreary nodded. "We rope off the dining room, different tables at different times."

"Rope off the entire stage. Then I need you to post a guard, one of your team, make it two of your team here. Their only task is to make sure that nobody disturbs anything on that stage. You understand?"

"Got it."

"Once you've got that all arranged, could you take me to wherever you keep your security footage? I want to see the footage from every camera in this room."

"I'm not sure you're going to find anything that's helpful. Our security system is geared toward keeping eyes on the casino area. We don't have a whole lot of cameras positioned to observe people eat."

"Could there be any footage of the back of the stage?" Whoever committed this crime had gotten onto the stage unseen from the back and left the same way before the lights came up on the body.

"Nope. Sorry. There aren't any cameras at all in that area."

"Eventually, I'll want to see all of the security footage from every camera on this whole boat."

"I'll go get it queued up for you, but you need to know there aren't very many cameras."

Not many cameras? In a casino? Now wasn't the time to go there, so he let it go and turned to Rileigh. She didn't have the same scared rabbit look on her face as she'd had before, but it was clear she was uncomfortable being in this group of people.

"I want you to go around to the back of the stage and look around. See if anything seems to be out of place." She seemed grateful to have something to do. She nodded and walked briskly across the stage toward the back entrance.

Mitch had done everything he could think to do for now. There was just one more matter he needed to attend to. He turned his back toward Gus and said, "Unzip me. I've got to get out of this wolf suit."

"Glad to hear it," Gus said as he ran the zipper slowly down Mitch's back. "It's really hard to take orders from a headless Big Bad Wolf." Gus helped Mitch pull the costume down off his shoulders, and Mitch took it from there. When he stepped out of the costume, looked up and saw that Gus was grinning.

"Uh … don't know if you noticed. You're barefoot."

"Not my fault!" Mitch snapped. "The only wolf costume in the store big enough to fit me was this one — and it has feet." Like a pair of long underwear with feet attached, or a onesie you put a baby to sleep in. "Shoes wouldn't fit inside, and the feet on the costume have hard soles."

"And nice claws, too" Gus noted.

Mitch groaned. "I'd have been better off as Tinkerbell."

Chapter Thirteen

RILEIGH WAS grateful that Mitch gave her an assignment so she could get out of the crowd of people clustered around her. She stepped up onto the stage and walked toward the back, checking the floor for anything the killer might have left behind. The whole back part of the stage was in shadow. The spotlights were on the front lip of the stage, and the house lights didn't illuminate much in the back. There was a door back there, and Rileigh thought before she grabbed the knob — perhaps forensics would want to try to lift fingerprints from that knob. But then she realized anybody on the ship could have come and gone through that doorway at some time during the cruise.

She opened the door and stepped into an anteroom, where the live entertainment acts must have stored their equipment and instruments, maybe even their costumes. There was another door at the back of that room, and she hurried toward it because she didn't like being in this storage room without windows.

That door led out onto the promenade deck at the front of the ship, the bow. This deck, the second deck, had a big promenade area on the front, places where you could put Adirondack chairs and lawn chairs and watch the bow of the boat cut through the water. From the promenade, you could walk around the whole perimeter of the ship on the walkway between the walls and the railing of the ship.

Rileigh pictured the ship's map she'd seen framed on the wall inside. The stage was at the front end of the dining room though she couldn't remember where the kitchen was that served the dining room. It must have been below decks, because the dining room opened into the main deck lounge featuring a beautiful bar with a gigantic mirror behind it and bottles of liquor and wine displayed on racks on the walls.

On the starboard side of the main deck — that was the left side, wasn't it? — was the main deck lounge. A wide staircase led up to the elevators on one side and the bathrooms and a spa on the other. Or you could go straight ahead to the grand saloon and casino, its walls lined with one-armed bandits and gaming tables spread throughout the room.

Rileigh went outside and started down the outdoor walkway, to avoid having to go through crowds, finally entering the casino from the outside door. Much of the crowd had gathered here.

Rileigh had kept her cloak on, had wrapped it around her against the cold when she was outside. Now she pulled the hood back as she crossed the room to where her mother and Millie were still putting chips into the bandit. One look at her mother's face and she knew the news had reached them.

"Oh, Rileigh, honey, they said that man was dead, the man who owned the real estate company who was paying for all this," her mother said all in a rush. "Folks was sayin'—"

Millie interrupted. "This part couldn't possibly be true, but they were saying that somebody sliced him open."

"Oh, no. Surely not," Mama said. You could hear the hope in her voice that something as terrible as that had to be somebody's imagination. Rileigh hated to disappoint her.

"Yes, that part was true, Mama. It was a horrifying sight, as ugly a murder scene as I've ever witnessed." The two old women's eyes grew wide. "But it wasn't the stab wound that killed him. He was already dead when that part happened." Since her mother hadn't already heard that part, she decided against describing the claw end of a hammer buried in his skull. "Somebody hit him in the head with a hammer first."

"There was something else, wasn't there?" Mama asked. "Everybody was talking about it. Said there was a number in—"

"In his lap," Mildred finished for her.

"The murderer left a piece of poster board in his lap with the number one written on it."

"Why the number one?"

"I don't have any idea," Rileigh said. "The only person who knows is the killer."

"And the killer is somebody on this boat. Has to be," Millie said.

Rileigh decided it would be wise to distract Mama and Millie from pursuing that line of thought.

"So, are you winning?" she asked.

Her mother looked at her dumbly. "Winning what?"

Rileigh gestured to the one-armed bandit. "Did you win any money? You've been sitting here poking chips into this slot machine."

"Oh, that. No, and I'm about out of chips. Gonna have to go get me some more."

Rileigh heard the hum of conversation from the gaming tables around her and was mildly surprised that anybody was interested in playing anything after a man had just been murdered. Maybe they were trying to take their minds off what had happened. Or wanted to try their luck before the boat went back to the dock. Rileigh suspected that none of them had figured out yet that they wouldn't be leaving this boat when it docked. Everybody on this paddle boat was a murder suspect and she knew Mitch wasn't going to let any of them leave until he had a better handle on the case.

"You're involved in this, aren't you?" her mother said. "You always get involved in these horrible things, these murders."

"I was a police officer. You know that. Mitch needs all the help he can get."

"Oh, I'm sure he does. I just hate to see you get so wrapped up in something so … ugly."

Mama's world wasn't ugly. She had always been the eternal optimist, unwilling to believe that there were some clouds that had no silver linings, that some clouds gave birth to tornadoes that destroyed everything, left a path of carnage in their wake.

"I just came to make sure you were all right. Now I have to get back."

The look on her mother's face changed between one heartbeat and the next, from concern that slowly melted away to a wide warm smile.

"She's here," Mama said.

"Who's here?" Millie asked.

Rileigh didn't have to ask.

"Mama, let's not do that right now."

"Not do what?"

"You know what."

"I was just telling you, I know she's here." When Mama saw her reaction, she reached out and put her hand on Rileigh's arm. "Now don't be like that. A mama knows. I can feel her presence. She drove up here from Atlanta. She got all dressed up in some costume and she's here. I promise she's here. I've been looking and looking."

Rileigh held her hand up and Mama stopped.

"I can't do this right now, Mama. I've got other things on my mind and I can't deal with your…" She almost said delusions, but didn't. "Your suppositions about Jillian."

She turned to leave and her mother called after her. "Look for her. You're going to be out where everybody's mingling, seeing everybody. Look for her."

Rileigh didn't think Millie knew exactly what her mother was talking about, but she weighed in anyway.

"Hard to find somebody in a crowd where everybody's wearing masks," she said. "How would you know?"

"Her eyes," Mama said. "Jillian had the most incredible eyes. Even with a mask on, you can see a person's eyes."

Rileigh kept walking. Her mother continued to talk, trying not to hear the words. But, of course, she did hear them. They hung like a fishhook in her mind. *Look for Jillian.*

Dammit, Mama!

Look for Jillian.

Rileigh hurried out of the casino through the archway into the area that contained the elevators and the restrooms. Off to her left, she caught sight of Charlie Hayden coming in from the promenade deck. He had obviously paid a hell of a lot of money for a custom costume of the Mad Hatter. On his head was a big top hat with an ace of spades tucked into the purple band. Below the hat was a curly red wig that hung all the way to his shoulders. He wore a vest checkered like a checkerboard. The suit jacket over it was multicolored, looked like paint had been splattered and spilled on it in every color. And below that were black pants and high-top boots. His face was covered in white clown makeup with big red circles around his eyes and bright red lips. The makeup accentuated the hollows in his cheeks, just as the baggy jacket accentuated how thin he was. He looked more like the scarecrow from The Wizard of Oz than the Mad Hatter.

Rileigh called out to him. "Hey Charlie, you got a minute?"

He turned and stopped, but just stood there. Waiting for *her* to come to *him*. He wasn't going to make this easy.

She went to where he was standing, ready to extend an olive branch.

"About the other night at the zoning board meeting …" she began, expecting the usual gush of charm, insincere though it was.

"If you came over here to hit me again, you need to know that my mama did not teach me not to hit a girl."

Wasn't expecting *that*.

"I over-reacted. I'm sorry."

"As you should be."

She'd been about to parrot the usual, "Please accept my apology." But she didn't have time before he turned on his heel and walked away from her.

Something was wrong, bad *wrong*, with Charlie Hayden.

She didn't want to go through the main lounge and the dining room, so she went back out onto the walkway on the side of the ship. A blast of cold hit her in the face as soon as she opened the door. It had been cold when they arrived, but it had gotten colder. That storm that'd been predicted on the news — apparently it had struck. It began to drizzle, and she could see a thin layer of ice forming on the railing of the boat.

She hurried back down the walkway outside the dining room toward the bow of the boat. She was halfway there before it occurred to her that the boat wasn't moving. She heard Mitch tell the captain to return the boat to shore, but out here where you could see the water, it was apparent the boat wasn't going anywhere. It was sitting dead still, slowly being encased in a cocoon of ice.

Chapter Fourteen

RILEIGH STARTED up the wide stairs from the deck to the promenade area on the bow of the boat. The door there led into the dining room.

She wrapped her Little Red Riding Hood cloak around herself against the cold wind and gritted her teeth to keep them from chattering. Rileigh had never liked the cold. She was born and raised in Tennessee. She'd never had to brave the kinds of winters that fellow soldiers from Maine and Michigan and Montana had told her about. Rugrat, a soldier from Michigan who was killed by an IED in Afghanistan, had talked about how much he hated climbing up on the roof in the wintertime to shovel the snow off.

Rileigh had said, "Off the roof? What for?"

He'd looked at her as if she were TDFW— too dumb for words.

"You know how heavy snow is, sweetheart? Leave it up there and you're gonna have it in your living room."

She smiled as she thought about that, and almost missed the sound. It was a small sound. She could almost have thought it was the wind sighing through the deck railings, but it was a sob, and it had come from the darkness off to her left. She stopped, stepped over to that side of the stairs, and looked down. Hunkered there in the lee side of the staircase, out of the wind and freezing rain, was a figure wrapped up in something furry with a hood on it. The hood was up, so she couldn't see the face of the person sitting there in the darkness, but she could tell that it was a woman crying.

Rileigh turned and went back down the stairs and into the puddle of darkness Ruby sat on a pipe with her elbows on her knees, her face in her hands.

Rileigh opened her mouth to ask something lame like, "Are you alright?"

But it was clear Ruby Cunningham wasn't alright, and Rileigh could understand why not. She could also understand why she had sought a private place, even if it was outside in the cold, to shed tears for a man who was married to somebody else —Dobson had been murdered such a short time ago that his body might still be warm.

Rileigh got down on one knee so she was on the same level as the woman's face and said nothing, just sat for a few moments. Eventually Ruby lifted her face.

"I loved him," she said in a tear-clotted voice. She barked a harsh laugh. "Yeah, I know the other woman isn't supposed to fall in love, but I did. I couldn't help it."

In circumstances like this where you have no idea what you ought to say, what you ought to say is absolutely nothing, so Rileigh said exactly that.

Ruby drew in a shaky breath. "I met him for the first time at a Chamber of Commerce dinner. Can you imagine anything less romantic than a Chamber of Commerce dinner?"

Rileigh could not. Chamber of Commerce dinners

were populated by two kinds of people. One, business owners with a genuine desire to see the town and the county prosper. That's what a Chamber of Commerce was for, right? The second kind of people was assholes like Charlie Hayden. He'd once been president of the Chamber of Commerce. People like Charlie weren't interested in seeing the town prosper. They were interested in seeing themselves prosper. They were the ones who always lobbied for new development and new tourism strategies and new anything that would get more human beings into the county so that Charlie could sell them a house.

"It was about a year ago," Ruby said, "and it might have been the first time he came to present his development proposal."

Suddenly it made sense. Rileigh had been wondering why in the world a woman like Ruby Cunningham would volunteer to serve on something as dry and boring as the zoning board.

"It was just random seating. Steve was where he always is — not home. And Hunt's wife was off doing something that cost a whole lot of money. Skyler Dobson never did anything that wasn't expensive. So neither of us had anybody to talk to but each other."

Ruby reached up and wiped tears off her face with the back of her hand. "He was so easy to talk to. He didn't judge. He didn't dominate the conversation. He asked questions. He acted like he was interested in me. Do you have any idea how rare that is? How long it's been since a man has been interested in what I thought about something? Steve never asks for my opinion anymore. He used to in the beginning, but after he realized I wasn't going to rubber stamp everything he wanted to do and agree with everything he said, he stopped asking me what I thought."

Ruby drew in a long, deep breath and let it out in a sigh.

"Hunt came here and rented a small studio apartment when he realized how much opposition there was going to be to his project. He knew he had to get to know the people, and he tried. He really tried." She paused. "But you know what that's like."

As a fellow homie, yeah, Rileigh knew what that was like. If you were from Away From Here, you were stuck with that label, and even someone like Mitch, whose job forced him into the private affairs of all manner of local residents, at the end of the day and he was from Away From Here and not to be trusted.

"It was just chance meetings in the beginning." Ruby smiled then, a sad smile with lips that were trembling. "We both admitted later that most of the meetings weren't chance. He'd show up at the grocery store Thursday mornings because he knew I always went on Thursday mornings and …"

She let the 'and' dangle. Suddenly, she reached out and grabbed Rileigh's hand. Her fingers were like popsicles, but her grip was strong.

"I meant what I said. I loved him. I didn't mean to love him. I didn't plan to love him. I certainly didn't want to love him. It just happened." She made a snuffling sound.

"And you're probably not going to believe this, but Hunt loved me too. He did. His wife was your basic trophy wife. She was pretty. She was splashy. She showed well, made an impression on people, and when you were a man like Hunter Dobson who needed to be recognized, having a wife like Skylar was an asset. But she was only an asset when they were out in public. In private, she was a witch. She was shallow and self-centered. Nothing mattered to Skylar Dobson but Skylar Dobson. She had flatly refused to move to Yarmouth County with her husband when he rented the studio. Said there was no amount of money he could spend on her to make her move to some little backwater town where there wasn't even a Walmart, for crying out loud."

Ruby snuffled again and wiped her eyes. Rileigh spoke for the first time then. "Did your husband know?"

"I think he suspected after a while. It was hard to keep coming up with excuses to be gone every evening. At first, he didn't notice because he wasn't home either. But eventually... If I'd only gone to see Hunter occasionally, it would have been easier to keep up the ruse. But I couldn't stay away from him. I couldn't stand being out of his presence. Rileigh, when he put his arms around me and held me close, I never felt feelings like that. I would have done anything for him. Up to and including leaving Steve, getting a divorce."

Then she hurried ahead, maybe explaining to Rileigh, maybe trying to convince herself.

"He would have divorced Skylar in a heartbeat. But she was such a witch. If he'd dared to even mention divorce, she would have hired a panel of the most expensive lawyers in the state and gone after every dime he had. She would have bankrupted him. So he didn't dare."

"Did she know about—"

"Oh, she was the jealous type. She'd been accusing him of cheating on her for years. In fact, she might have been glad that eventually her suspicions were confirmed."

Rileigh was so cold she couldn't keep her teeth from chattering. She wasn't sure she would be able to stand up if she tried, suspected that her knees and hips were frozen in place in a squatting position.

"Ruby, you really need to get inside. You've been out here too long in the cold."

She barked out a sardonic laugh. "I hadn't noticed."

Rileigh stood and offered her hand to pull Ruby to her feet. But Ruby waved her off.

"You go on. I'll be in in a minute. I need to get myself together first."

"Do you promise you'll come in? Because if you don't, I'll come looking for you."

"I'll come in."

Rileigh turned to go but stopped when she heard Ruby's whispered voice.

"We had plans, not now, not this year, and maybe not even next year. But one day Hunter would be fiscally solvent enough that he could take the hit when Skylar divorced him. We were determined to be together."

For the first time, Ruby showed an emotion other than grief. Her eyes shone with anger. "But those monsters, those Ku Klux Klan hooded monsters, killed him before we had a chance."

Rileigh had suspected that was the lily pad of consensus that most people would hop onto, that some vigilante in the Save Gum Tree Hollow Association had murdered Hunter Dobson. Rileigh didn't think so. She did think that the whole thing had been staged in such a way to make you think the Save the Gum Tree Hollow Association was responsible. It was the obvious.

And while it was true often the obvious was just that, obvious because it was the truth. She remembered what one of her sergeants said when she was explaining some situation and drawing all manner of conclusions about it. He'd stopped her in mid-supposition and said, "Rileigh, when it comes to crime, always think horse, not zebra."

In this situation, the Gum Tree Hollow Association was the horse, but Rileigh's gut was telling her that the real explanation was a zebra.

Chapter Fifteen

RILEIGH WAS grateful to get back inside the boat where it was warm. The doors were heavy and sealed tight — had to be, to keep the indoors air conditioned in the summertime, but it helped keep the cold outside now. It felt like the temperature had dropped ten degrees while she was talking to Ruby. The fine drizzle had turned into freezing rain, the pellets pecking against the side of the boat. She'd gotten chilled squatting beside Ruby Cunningham as she poured her guts out. Rileigh felt sorry for the woman, she really did. Even though the old Puritan principles of being faithful to your wife and to your husband still formed the skeleton of her own morality, that didn't mean she couldn't feel sympathy and compassion for somebody who'd broken those rules.

She went back in via the door she had come out of, passed through the anteroom that was probably for storage of instruments, and opened the door to the stage. But the stage was dark now. Mitch must have pulled the curtains to hide the body that she was sure still sat right where it had been when she left. He wouldn't have moved anything, but pulling the curtain didn't mess with any evidence. There was no reason not to hide the gruesome sight from all the guests.

She wanted to let him know that Ruby had admitted her affair with Dobson. Though it was clear from Skyler's behavior that she'd suspected, but that she'd had no clue the affair was with Ruby. But more importantly, she needed to tell him that the boat wasn't movin, which was more obvious when you were outside the boat than inside.

As she approached Mitch from one side, the captain came rushing toward him through the crowd.

The captain was dignified and professional, but Rileigh could tell he was rattled.

"Sheriff Webster," he said quietly enough not to be overheard, "we have a problem. I was on my way to the communications room — I wanted to talk to the sheriff's department and deliver your message personally — when I heard from the communications officer that somebody had disabled the ship-to-shore radio. I confirmed that for myself, and I think it's something you'll want to see."

Mitch was already moving. Rileigh trooped through the narrow passageways after the sheriff and the captain. When they got to the communications room, they found the communications officer sitting in front of a radio that looked like somebody had smashed it with a sledgehammer. There was a red phone on the wall, except it wasn't on the wall anymore. It was dangling by several cords — somebody had ripped it off.

"Sheriff Webster," the captain indicated the communications officer who was sitting in front of the shattered radio, "This is Sanjay Patel. He is—"

Before the captain could finish his sentence, Patel looked up into his face and blurted out, "Excuse me, I'll be right back." Then he leapt to his feet and rushed out of the room.

The man hadn't looked good. His face was pale and drawn, his skin had an ashy quality to it, and he was sweating, though the room was not warm.

"He's sick," the captain said. "That's why he left the radio unattended, which he is never supposed to do. He said he was gone only a few minutes, but it doesn't take very long to slam a hammer into a radio and rip a phone off the wall."

The captain looked like he had more to say. Rileigh could see it and so could Mitch, who voiced what they both were thinking. "And …"

The captain let out a breath. "And he's not the only crew member who's sick. We've got several men down. I'm wondering now if somebody did something to their dinner tonight."

The crew didn't eat in the dining room with the guests; they had their own dining area, their own kitchen, and their own cook.

"Tonight's dinner was chili, a big pot of chili, which means everybody ate the same thing."

"And with everybody's meal in one spot, it would be a whole lot easier to slip something into it," Mitch said.

Patel returned from the head then, looking green around the gills, his face even more pale.

"When did you start feeling sick?" Mitch asked him.

"Soon as I finished dinner, I barely got back here before I had to–" He shot a glance at Rileigh and then back at Mitch. "You know, I had to … *go.*"

Rileigh put him at ease by telling him, "My aunt Daisy used to call that kind of problem the screaming squirts."

Patel managed a weak smile.

"As soon as I got back here and saw the mess–" He

reached to the desk and picked up a walkie talkie. "I got on the walkie talkie and told the captain what happened." The man looked apologetic as well as sick. "I swear I wasn't gone 10 minutes and there was nothing I could—" He stopped then, got a desperate look on his face and leapt to his feet. "Excuse me, please," he said and rushed out of the room again.

In the silence that followed, Mitch looked around the communications room. There had been no finesse to the damage. Whoever had destroyed the radio used some kind of blunt object. Rileigh had thought at first it was probably a sledgehammer. But now it seemed more likely that maybe it was something closer to hand. She glanced around the room and then pointed to the fire extinguisher that was lying on the floor in the corner.

"Maybe that's the radio murder weapon."

Mitch stepped over to take a look at it. But he didn't pick it up.

"That would make some serious blunt force trauma. It's got scratches on it, too."

Mitch turned to the captain.

"So the ship-to-shore radio is disabled. How else do you communicate with the shore?"

"WE USE LIGHTS. Ship to shore lights." Rowe gestured with his chin toward a cabinet on the far side of the room. "They're in there. But in practical terms, we've never had to use the lights. And I'm not completely certain the guys on the docks could read a message if we sent one."

"You won't find out tonight," Rileigh said. "Even if there was somebody on the dock looking this way, they wouldn't see the lights. Have you looked outside?"

She went on without waiting for an answer. "That ice

storm they were predicting on the radio while we were on our way here, well, it's here. When I was outside, ice was beginning to form on everything. And the freezing rain came at me like birdshot from a shotgun. I'd say visibility's down to thirty feet, if that."

Mitch turned to the captain again. "Besides the radio and the lights, isn't there some other way you can communicate with the shore?"

Rileigh watched the captain shoot a look in the direction that Patel had gone, obviously reluctant to deliver more bad news.

"We have four handheld ship-to-shore devices on board. One in the captain's quarters. One hangs on the wall in the pilot house. The head of security has one in his office." He gestured then to an empty hook on the wall. "And Sanjay has one … *had* one."

Rileigh didn't like where this appeared to be leading.

"The person who destroyed the radio must have taken the hand-held off the wall. I radioed Belle right before you got here, and she said she'd noticed the one in the pilot house was missing a little while ago, but she figured I sent somebody for it."

"And the other two?" Mitch asked.

"I have someone looking for Jack's. Jack Winston is the head of security. His should be locked up in his quarters. But mine is missing."

Rowe's voice was tight and controlled.

"I noticed mine was missing right before we left the dock. I thought I might have misplaced it, or — it's an expensive piece of equipment. You could sell it to a marine equipment store."

"Or on eBay," Rileigh put in. "You can sell anything on eBay."

"You thought somebody stole it?"

"I was pretty sure somebody … *took* it. I keep it in a cabinet with some other gear and … my mama raised me to put things back where I found them."

Rowe paused again. "I should have delayed departure until I could locate it. But I radioed Belle to make sure she had hers. That's why she thought I'd taken it when she saw it was gone later. And Sanjay had his, so I let it ride. A private charter doesn't come along often, and certainly not one that's as grand as this one."

Rileigh couldn't begin to imagine what it had cost Hunter Dobson to rent out this whole riverboat, including the crew, to pay for dinner and drinks and cabin accommodations. Had to be hundreds of thousands of dollars. It seemed a foolhardy expense to her. She'd thought so when she first heard about the cruise. Was Hunter Dobson so naive that he thought he could sway the minds of the whole community by wining and dining them for one lavish glamorous masquerade party?

"I knew the big bosses further up the food chain than I am wouldn't take kindly to this one getting off to a bad start because I lost my hand-held radio." The captain shot another glance at Sanjay Patel, who had just returned, and said, "So over Sanjay's objections — he thought we should delay — I said we'd leave without the full complement of handhelds."

"But there could still be one in the security office, right?"

"Yes ma'am, we're checking."

You could hear the dread in his voice. Who destroys a boat's radio and then steals only three of the boat's four other communications devices?

"So, there isn't any other way to communicate with the shore?" Mitch asked.

"Not unless somebody has coverage on their cell phone."

Rileigh burped out a grunt of derisive laughter. "Right. Cell phone coverage on Big Puddle Lake. If I got more than one bar here, I'd start looking up at the sky and waiting for it to start raining frogs, because that would be one of the final signs of the second coming."

At that moment, the captain's walkie-talkie crackled in his pocket. He took it out, hit the receive button.

Captain, it's Heck. You need to get down here."

Who's Heck?" Mitch asked.

He's the chief engineer ... in the engine room."

As they hurried out into the passageway, Rileigh had a sick feeling that they were about to find out why the boat wasn't moving.

Chapter Sixteen

RILEIGH HUNG BACK behind Mitch and the captain as they rushed down yet another nearly-identical passageway. It felt a lot like a hospital to Rileigh, where one hallway leads into another, and they all look alike, so you're lost in no time.

Finally, they came to a door, and on the other side was a metal staircase leading down to the deck below where the engine room was located. They clattered down the stairs and across an open space with several unmarked doors to one above which were the words "Engine Room" in black letters.

Rileigh had time to think that the metal stairs and floor must be murder on Mitch's feet before the captain rushed inside with Mitch behind him. Rileigh was slower to enter, reluctant to enter the room until she could see how big it was. She was relieved that the engine room itself was a huge room full of machines she didn't know the function of. Standing inside the door was an older man, holding the receiver of a red wall phone in one hand and pressing a rag to the top of his head with the other, staunching a wound, Rileigh suspected. Thin and wiry, the kind of guy who likely got called scrappy when he beat the shit out of kids twice his size. He was bald, with a gray mustache and a well-groomed beard, and instead of being dressed like a storybook character, he wore a blue jumpsuit with the words "Chief Engineer Hector Quiñones" above the pocket.

The man hung up the phone. "Just telling Belle to stand down, we ain't going anywhere."

Rowe rushed over to the man. "Heck, what happened? Are you hurt?"

"It ain't bad, just a bump on the head."

"Bumps on the head are bad," Rowe said. "Come into the office and sit down."

The other squeezed into a small office off to the right — Heck and Rowe on a small bench while Mitch stood at the center of the room. It was far too crowded for Rileigh's tastes, so she stood outside in the doorway.

"Let's have a look at this." Rowe pulled Heck's hand away, along with the rag he was holding against his scalp. Blood poured from a pretty nasty-looking wound above his eye. "You might need some stitches to close this."

"Like I said, it ain't nothing."

Rowe looked up at Mitch and said, "The answer to the question you're not asking is, no, we don't have a doctor on the boat. But we never leave the dock without Gustov or Emilio. Gustov is a cook and Emilio is a deckhand, but they're both paramedics." He turned back to Heck. "You're going to see Gustov." When the man started to protest, Rowe added, "That wasn't a suggestion."

Heck nodded and said, "Yes, sir."

Mitch spoke for the first time then.

"My name is Mitch Webster. I'm the Yarmouth County Sheriff. Feeling up to a few questions?"

Heck pointed to Mitch's feet. "You ain't got no shoes on. It's against regulations to be in this engine room without metal-toed shoes." He looked up at Mitch's face and continued, "Don't believe I've ever met a barefoot sheriff."

Rileigh could see Mitch's face flush a bright red. "I was dressed in a costume for the party upstairs. Unfortunately, my costume had feet in it, so when I took the costume off —" Mitch shrugged amicably. "—I was barefoot."

Heck studied Mitch's feet, sized them up.

"Gunther's got big feet like you. He's a stoker, shovels fuel into the firebox. The man's a beast." He cocked his thumb toward a cabinet in the corner. "There's a pair of his shoes in there if you want them."

Mitch's face lit up. "I'd appreciate that. Now can you tell us what happened to you? Who hit you on the head?"

"Hell if I know. Somebody came up behind me. And they was as silent as a mouse in house shoes walking across a cotton ball, quiet as it was in here without the engine running." Rileigh imagined the sound of the huge engine was deafening — another reason for the tightly sealed outside doors on every deck. With the doors closed, sound wouldn't carry from one deck to another. "One minute I was standing there reading the pressure gauge, and the next minute I was on the floor looking up at the ceiling."

He gestured to a spot on the shiny metal floor, where there was a smear of blood in front of the pipe that held the gauge.

"Didn't knock me all the way out, I's just stunned, you know, my head swimming. Everything was a blur, and by the time I come back around, it was all done."

He gestured around at the room as if everyone would know what he was talking about.

Rileigh certainly didn't, and neither did Mitch.

"What was all done?" Mitch asked. And before the man could answer his question, Mitch said, "I don't know jack shit about the functioning of a steam-powered engine. So keep it simple."

"Oh, it's simple, all right. The engine's dead. Somebody let off all the pressure in the boiler." He pointed to a big gauge with numbers you could read from where he sat, sectioned off in zones colored blue, yellow, orange, and red. The needle rested in the far end of the blue zone. "They also closed the damper and killed the fire in the fire box."

Rileigh asked, "And what did that do?"

"It killed the engine, that's what," the engineer said testily. "And you are?"

He was one of those. Rileigh could spot them a mile away. Most women could, and most men couldn't. When she pointed it out, other men always looked surprised and confused, like they hadn't noticed. Clearly, Mitch and the captain didn't catch the attitude that wafted off the man as surely as heat had wafted off the boiler before somebody let off all the steam.

Sexist. Misogynist. Chauvinist. Pick your preferred descriptor.

"My name's Rileigh Bishop, and I'm helping the sheriff in the investigation."

The man made a humph sound in his throat. "Investigation of what?"

"Of the murder."

"What murder?"

She had assumed that every person on the boat knew about the body sitting in a chair on the stage with his guts in his lap. Apparently not. And when she thought about it, it made sense. It's not like they'd have put out an announcement on some kind of public address system. "To all hands, there's been a murder in the dining room."

As Mitch filled the chief engineer in on what had happened earlier in the evening, Rileigh's gaze fell on a plaque on the wall just outside the chief engineer' office.

She'd seen others scattered around, explanations of interesting features of the boat.

"The paddle wheel on the Queen of the Smokies is made of oak and steel, weighing over 26 tons. There are four steam cylinders, one high- and one low-pressure cylinder on each side of the paddlewheel. Steam is expanded twice within the engine. The high-pressure cylinders receive 'live' steam from the boiler to move their pistons down the cylinder bore. After the steam is expanded in the high-pressure cylinder, it is exhausted into the low-pressure cylinder. The steam then expands again, allowing more work to be performed than in a single expansion engine. The engine lies flat rather than standing on end so that its weight is distributed over a larger area of the hull, reducing the vessel's draft in shallow water."

She tuned back into the conversation after she read the plaque, heard Heck explain what he'd meant by "killed the engine." It was a fairly technical explanation for all Mitch's request that he keep it simple. But Rileigh got the gist of it anyway. Apparently, someone had come into the engine room, knocked the chief engineer senseless, then released the pressure on the steam in the boiler. That was bad enough, the chief engineer said, but what was worse was that they'd also put out the fire in the firebox.

She didn't know why that was such a big deal, but that was a dumb-blonde question and she wouldn't ask it.

Thankfully, Mitch did.

"Did putting out the fire damage the engine somehow?"

"Nope, the engine's fine. We can rekindle the fire and we'll be back in business."

The captain rolled his eyes. "In six, maybe seven hours."

"Could take eight," Heck put in. "Just depends."

"Eight hours to—" Mitch began.

"To get the fire box hot enough to heat the boiler hot enough to produce the steam it'll take to power this boat back to the dock," Heck said.

"Six to eight hours!"

"Maybe more than that, maybe nine. Hard to tell."

"Where are Curtis and C.J.?" Rowe asked, then added, "Curtis and C.J. are the assistant engineers."

"They've been in and out of the head ever since dinner. Guess it's a good thing I didn't eat."

"I'll send someone to find them." Rowe stood.

"Aw Capt'n. I don't want them yahoos fooling around my engine 'thout me here to keep an eye on 'em."

"One of them needs to be here to start building the fire in the firebox while I take you to see Gustov." Before Heck could protest again, Rowe said, "If he says you're okay, you can come back down here and take charge."

Then Rowe tried to take Heck's arm for support, but Heck brushed him off. "I can walk by myself, thank you, captain."

And he proceeded to do just that without wobbling at all.

"Them shoes is on the bottom shelf in that cabinet, socks is stuffed in them," Heck told Mitch. "I doubt them socks is clean."

"I'll survive a pair of dirty socks. I'm just grateful to have something on my feet." He looked down at them and then everybody else did, too. Rileigh thought they looked blue from the cold of the metal deck.

Mitch headed toward the cabinet, but stopped when he heard the captain's walkie-talkie crackle. Rowe put the walkie talkie to his ear so they couldn't hear the person on the other end, but they didn't need to hear the words to know it was bad news. That was evident on the captain's face.

He clicked the device off and told Mitch. "The hand-held's not in the security office. They've turned it upside down looking."

It wasn't surprising news, but it was still sobering. There really was no way to contact anyone on shore.

"Find McCreary. I want somebody on the security team stationed here in the engine room."

"I'll call him," the captain said, putting his walkie-talkie to his ear.

"Those walkie-talkies — don't suppose anybody on the dock has one you could call, huh?"

Rowe shook his head.

"They're supposed to have a range of half a mile, but good luck with that. If both the sending and receiving units are outside, they're reliable. But if either of them is some-where inside the boat, all bets are off."

"Who on the boat has walkie-talkies?"

"We have a dozen of them scattered among the crew, some of them operational and some not. Me, McCreary and all the members of the security team, the first mate, the bosun, the pilot, the chief engineer, the communica-tions officer, the cook—"

Mitch stopped him before he could recite them all. "I'd like to borrow one, if I could."

"I'll bring one to you in the dining room after I get Heck settled with Gustov."

"I don't need no damned security guard," the engineer snarled. "Ain't nobody gonna get the jump on me a second time."

Rileigh figured he was probably right on that score.

"We'll see what Gustov says."

As Rowe led Heck out, Mitch went to the cabinet for the pair of shoes. Rileigh wandered around the huge engine room as he put them on. There was a big open area in the center of the room behind the temperature gauge. All manner of pipes and gauges lined the walls and sprouted out of pieces of equipment.

"Look how clean everything is." The floor in the big open area was painted red and was so shiny you could see reflections in it. "I guess I thought all engines were as dirty as the engine under the hood of my car."

"Dammit!" Mitch said.

Rileigh went back to the office doorway and saw him sitting on the bench where the engineer and captain had been sitting. He had put on socks — one black and one a white gym sock with red stripes — and was struggling to get a shoe on his right foot. She watched for a moment.

"Ever heard the phrase 'you can't put ten pounds of mud in a five-pound sack?' I think it's what Dolly Parton said once when she had a … revealing wardrobe malfunction."

He struggled to get his foot into the obviously too-small shoe for a little longer, then sighed. "Apparently, my feet are ten pounds of mud." He went to the cabinet and put the shoes back on the shelf. "I'm keeping the socks. They're better than nothing."

The engine room door opened and a man wearing a blue jumpsuit like the engineer's came in. The name above his pocket was "C.J. Crockett." He didn't look like he felt a whole lot better than Sanjay Patel.

"I guess you've come to crank up the fire in the fire-box," Mitch said, standing in the office doorway in sock feet.

"Yes, sir," the man replied.

"We'll leave you to it," Mitch said and started for the door with Rileigh. Then he turned around and asked the man, "Tell me, does everybody on the crew of this boat know how to operate this steam engine?"

"Oh, no, sir. Just the engineer, me, and Curtis. Oscar knows, too, but he's off tonight."

"So you're saying the rest of the crew wouldn't have known how to disable this engine?"

"Well, some could. You'd have to ask the captain who, though. "

Rileigh walked with Mitch out the engine room door.

"You think any of the passengers knew how?" she asked.

"Not likely."

Chapter Seventeen

MITCH AND RILEIGH climbed the metal steps to the main deck one floor up. Rileigh watched Mitch's face, watched him pretend that the metal stairs on his only-socks-on feet wasn't cold. Rileigh would not have been able to stand it. Rileigh always had cold feet, always. She suspected it had a whole lot more to do with blood circulation than it did with temperature, or simply that the sensation of cold feet just annoyed the hell out of her. But she did know that if she'd been walking around tonight with nothing but socks on, she wouldn't have been able to feel anything below her ankles.

"Your feet are cold, aren't they?"

"I'm good."

"No, you're not. Your feet are cold."

"No, they're not." He held up his hands before she could argue with him. "Look, I'm trying to ignore how cold they are, and it doesn't help when you keep pointing it out every ten seconds. I don't want to be thinking about my cold feet. I want to be figuring out who wanted to strand this boat in the middle of a lake, unable to communicate with the shore, and why."

As they made their way down the interior corridors, Rileigh felt like the walls were closing in on her. But the engine was in the stern of the ship, and the dining room, where Hunter Dobson's cold corpse sat behind closed curtains on the stage, was in the bow of the boat. If she had been going from the engine room to the dining room alone, she would have gone out a door and walked around the walkways on the outside of the boat. But it wasn't just cold out there anymore. It was freezing rain and ice. Mitch couldn't walk out there in sock feet.

When they got back to the stage, Rileigh was relieved to see that the area had been roped off as Mitch had directed and that two security team members were standing watch to make sure nobody disturbed anything. The security team members were still dressed as dwarves, but they'd taken off their bearded masks, so their dwarf costumes just looked like baggy clothes.

Rileigh still wore the red dress she and her mother had made as her costume. She wasn't wearing pants under the floor-length skirt. The Red Riding Hood cape and hood were warm, and she kept them clutched around her. As she glanced around the room, she saw that other people had taken off whatever part of their costume they could. It didn't feel like a party anymore.

As Mitch and Rileigh crossed the dining room together, they saw Captain Rowe approaching. He had taken off his pirate's three-cornered hat and eye patch and he held a walkie-talkie in his hand.

"How's Heck?" Mitch asked. "What did the paramedic say about his wound?"

"Gustov wouldn't let Heck pass it off as 'no big thing,' but he said it wasn't serious. He put a butterfly bandage on it and gave the okay for Heck to go back to work, kick out his assistants, and coddle his precious engine. We don't have much of an infirmary here, just a glorified examining room with an exam table, but there's a room next to it with a cot. If Gustov had been concerned, we'd have made Heck go in there and lie down."

The captain held out a walkie-talkie to Mitch.

"I got this from one of the cooks, saw him in the hallway on the way to the head, and he clearly wasn't going to be using it."

"Yeah, about the crew getting sick," Mitch began.

"I'm on it," said Rowe, "but until we can get to shore and perhaps get the chili tested to see if something was put into it, there really isn't any way to know."

The captain glanced down and noticed that Mitch was in socks. "I thought Heck found an extra pair of shoes for you to wear."

"They were a couple of sizes too small."

The captain groaned.

"I want to talk about disabling the steam engine," Mitch said. "The assistant engineer who came in after you left said that not everybody on the crew knew how to operate the engine. He wasn't sure exactly who did and who didn't. Said I should ask you."

"It's not like it's some big mystery. The functioning of a steam engine is pretty standard and these guys on the crew have been working with it and around it for years. But if you're asking who knew specifically how to let the steam off without getting scalded and how to close the damper to put the fire in the firebox out without getting burned, that's a different matter. I'd say … Dimitri, the first mate, the bosun, the pilot." The captain was ticking them off on his fingers. "The chief engineer and his assistants. Those are the only ones I know for sure. Maybe some others did."

"So there's a finite number of people who would know how to disable that engine," the sheriff said.

Rileigh hated to put her two cents worth in, but …

"Well, yeah, and my two good friends, Google and YouTube."

Mitch shook his head.

"Come on, you know as well as I do that you can find a video to show you how to do anything. I bet I could have disabled that engine if I found the right YouTube video to show me how."

Mitch picked up the ball and ran with it in a different direction. "Let's leave off who knew how to disable the engine for a minute and consider the more pressing and important question. Why would anybody want to? Why did somebody commit a murder, then disable the ship so that it was dead in the water and couldn't communicate with the shore?"

"You're putting the two of them together. The murderer is the same person who disabled the radio and the engine?" the captain asked.

"It seems to me that it's stretching the bounds of coincidence that they'd be unrelated incidents."

"Why would somebody want to keep this boat right where it is, unable to communicate with the shore?" Row asked.

"Well, the unable to communicate may be related to disabling the engine," Rileigh said. "If somebody was determined that this boat was to sit here dead in the water for whatever reason, they'd have to keep you from simply radioing for help. The central question is why keep the boat out here? How does it help them get away with Hunter Dobson's murder?"

Mitch held up his hands before she could continue.

"Yeah, I need to give Dobson's murder my full attention, but first I have an unpleasant task to do."

"And that is?"

He turned to the captain. "Can you gather all the passengers for me in one place? It's time they found out what's going on."

Chapter Eighteen

BEFORE MITCH DID ANYTHING ELSE, he had to do the thing he least wanted to do: talk to the passengers. They had a right to know what was going on, and it was his job not only to protect them but to reassure them. Often the reassuring part was a whole lot harder than the protecting part.

But the longer he waited, the more frightened they'd become, not by what was actually happening, but by what they were telling each other was happening. And the story would get bigger and bigger, until it was out of control.

Elijah had gotten the crew to set up a microphone for Mitch on the small stage in the casino in the stern of the boat, as far as it was possible to get from the stage in the dining room where Hunter Dobson's body remained untouched behind drawn curtains.

Dobson had said he didn't want a microphone, that he could talk loud enough that everyone could hear him. And that it would spoil the whole experience of being read a story. Mitch didn't know Hunter Dobson at all, but he had heard a few good things about him in addition to all the bad. That he appeared, at least from what the people on the County Council could see, to be a straight shooter, owning up to the fact that his development would put a whole lot more traffic on the streets that already had too much traffic. And there wasn't anything he could do to make the streets wider. That was up to the state of Tennessee.

But whatever Mitch might or might not think of the man, he certainly didn't deserve to die that way. Nobody did. Mitch was determined that he would find out who had done it and lock their asses away for a long time.

As soon as he got the nod that everyone had been gathered, he stepped up to the microphone. He didn't bother with the tacky "testing, testing, testing," he just assumed that a boat somebody had spent millions of dollars on wouldn't have a squawking sound system with feedback.

"May I have your attention, please?"

Mitch kept his eyes focused outward on the crowd, making direct eye contact with as many people as he could. Well, that was one reason he looked out into the crowd. The other reason was that he didn't want to look down and direct anybody else's attention in that direction.

Though he was in uniform — with a badge and his sidearm strapped on his hip — he was wearing no shoes. Just socks, and they didn't even match.

He cleared his throat and conversation silenced.

"I know there are all kinds of stories going around about what's happened on this boat, and I wanted you to have correct information straight from me. You know, of course, that Hunter Dobson has been murdered."

A groan washed across the crowd like a wave across the sea. They had pulled the curtains on the stage, but everybody knew the body was still right where they'd left it. It was a crime scene and it couldn't be disturbed. The crowd had come to the party for a dinner cruise, but you couldn't expect them all to sit down in the dining room and eat a meal with a dead body— a gruesomely murdered dead body— in the room. Fortunately, there was a buffet-style restaurant on Deck 3, so guests had been diverted there to eat. Mitch didn't know how many had actually had dinner. He suspected most of the people who'd been present when the curtains opened on a dead Hunter Dobson earlier— and that was just about the whole crowd— had lost their appetites.

"What I'm sure you're also aware of by now is that the boat is not moving. Immediately after Hunter Dobson was killed, I instructed the captain to return the boat to shore and to radio the sheriff's department, requesting that my deputies be waiting on the dock, as well as an ambulance. Unfortunately," he cast a glance over at the boat's captain, "Captain Rowe was not able to comply with either request. Somebody has destroyed the boat's ship-to-shore radio and sabotaged the boat's engine."

A a cry rose up in the crowd, and people started hollering questions at him.

"Hold on, hold on, I'll answer questions when I'm finished talking."

There were more histrionics from the crowd, but Mitch stood mute, and when they realized he wouldn't tell them anything else until they were quiet, they settled down.

"I don't know how much you know about a steam engine, but someone knew how to let off the pressure on the steam valve and kill the fire in the firebox. That does *not* damage the engine in any way — it still functions."

Relief rippled through the crowd. Mitch cut it off mid-sigh.

"However, it takes from six to eight hours to get the fire in the firebox hot enough to build up enough steam to run the paddle wheel."

The crowd erupted again.

"Eight hours!"

"You saying we're stuck here?"

"You gotta do something."

All manner of suggestions that Mitch had already considered and discarded, were shouted out to him from the crowd, but he held out his hands and motioned for silence. The rumble dampened down.

"Get somebody to come out here and take us off this boat," somebody called out, and Mitch latched onto that one.

"We can't get anybody from shore to help because we can't communicate with them. As I said before, someone destroyed the ship's radio, took a hammer to it."

"Like somebody did to Hunter Dobson's head," someone called out, and was shouted down by the others.

"Isn't there some other way to communicate with the shore?" asked a woman down front who was dressed as Cinderella.

"There is," Mitch said. "The boat could communicate with the dock using lights." He heard the groan go through the crowd. "Yeah, that's right. In this weather, nobody's gonna see any lights."

Someone else hollered out, "So you're saying we can't talk to the shore, and we got no engine to get there?"

"That's exactly what I'm saying." Mitch heard snatches of phrases popping up out of the crowd in their emotional outburst. It was clear most of them blamed the Save the Gum Tree Association for Hunter Dobson's murder and assumed that whoever had killed him had also disabled the engine and the radio.

"Why would somebody do that?" a man in the back hollered out. He was dressed as a soldier from the

Nutcracker, but he had taken off his helmet and wore only his uniform.

"That's a really good question," Mitch said, and the crowd hushed to hear his reply. "Why does somebody want to keep us stuck out here in the middle of the lake, unable to call for help?"

Before there could be a roar of response, Mitch held his hands out. "That was a rhetorical question. I don't know the answer, but I will find out. What you need to know right now is that this boat is not going anywhere for a few hours, but as soon as we can build up a head of steam, we'll go back to the dock."

More consternation roiled up from the crowd, and Mitch just let them vent. When most everybody had had their say, he held up his hand and continued. "I know you're all concerned, you're scared."

Before he could continue, he heard the question he'd been dreading.

"What about that number one that was laying in Dobson's lap?" The question came from Eduardo Gomez, one of the pharmacists at Main Street Drug Store. "Does that mean he's the first? Because if he's the first, who's the second?"

Another rumble of emotion arose out of the crowd. Mitch had been dreading that question because he didn't have an answer for it.

"Mr. Gomez," Mitch said, "I don't have any idea what the number one meant, but I do believe that everyone needs to take reasonable precautions. Stay in groups. Don't wander off by yourself."

A younger voice cried from the back of the room, "Don't be like the idiot in a slasher movie who hides behind the knife rack."

There was a little titter of laughter before Mitch

continued, "The best defense you have is to stay together. If you need to pee, take three people with you."

Then he looked up and swept his eyes over the crowd, picking out some of the zoning board members, and spoke to them.

"Of course, I want to give a special warning to the zoning board members here tonight." He hurried on before anyone could speak. "I am *not* saying Hunter Dobson was killed because of the Gum Tree project."

"What other reason was there?" someone asked, and Mitch heard a soft response, "Well, he was cheating on his wife," but that person was right down front, and Mitch didn't think the whole crowd heard it.

Mitch continued, "What I *am* saying is that there is safety in numbers. Stick together."

It was time to end this, because otherwise the discussion would go on and on without going anywhere useful.

"That's all I have to say right now," Mitch said. "If there is more information to divulge, I will call you back together and give it to you. Thank you."

Then Mitch turned and walked off the stage with as much dignity as he could muster in sock feet. He had not known that Dmitri Mikhailov, who was the second mate, had stepped to the microphone after him until he heard the man begin to speak. Mikhailov was the man whose job was overseeing the casino.

Mitch couldn't stop him now, but he would speak to the captain about it. Mitch wanted to be the only person dispensing information to the passengers, and he had no idea what the second mate intended to tell them now.

Chapter Nineteen

RILEIGH HAD BEEN STANDING on the side of the stage while Mitch spoke, out of the crowd of people. She thought he did an excellent job quieting the rumors, and people's nerves. When he stepped away from the microphone, she was surprised to see the first mate step up behind him and begin to talk.

Dimitri Mikhailov had just the whisper of a Russian accent and Rileigh decided even that much was fake, an affectation like those who leaned into their southern accents, tossing out "ya'lls" and "Bless-your hearts" like throwing feed to chickens in an effort to charm the tourists. Raleigh thought it made men sound like toe-in-the-sand rednecks and women sound like witless twits.

But she did harbor a grudging admiration for the few, and there were only a few, who could pull it off to their advantage. She'd worked her ass off when she first went into the military, listening carefully to how other soldiers pronounced words and practicing at night in front of a mirror until she'd effectively wiped out her Tennessee accent. Oh, she could crank it up and slather it with molasses if the need arose. Any southerner could.

Dimitri's Russian accent just didn't ring true, it clanged in some way Raleigh couldn't put her finger on. She was certain he was third or fourth generation American and that "the old country" meant nothing more to him than "that place we used to live in New Jersey."

He obviously knew the accent made his speech "exot-ic." People listened a little closer to what he said because of it. So he was milking it for all it was worth.

He told the crowd that everybody would be issued a hundred dollars in money chips to play in the machines, and an equivalent value in house chips to play at the game tables. House chips had no monetary value, but could be redeemed in the restaurant, the snack-bar, the gift shop, or to purchase future excursions on the boat. What he said at the end actually got a rumble of approval from the dour crowd.

"For the rest of the eve-nik, drinks will be hef price."

She saw Mitch wince at that. If dealing with frightened people was herding cats, the only thing worse was herding drunk cats.

Mitch came down the two steps from the stage and walked back to where Rileigh was standing off to the side.

"I saw you cringe when that Dimitri told everybody drinks would be half price," Rileigh told Mitch, trying not to grin. "You look like you wanted to strangle..."

She trailed off because she saw that Mitch wasn't looking at her, he was looking over her shoulder at the few people in the dining room. When she followed his gaze, she groaned out loud. That's all Mitch needed right now. Yarmouth County Mayor-for-Life, J.P. Rutherford, was barreling down on them like a torpedo heading for a battleship.

Mitch had last crossed horns with him last summer when he was working on the case of the tourists murdered by Angus Park and his crazy sister, Sarah. The mayor had not wanted Mitch to make waves about the case, wanted him to keep it quiet because he feared that tourism in the county would drop if people read in the newspaper that somebody in Yarmouth County was splashing tourists with gasoline and setting them on fire. At the time, it had reminded Rileigh of the scene from Jaws where the mayor of that little town, wherever it was, didn't want the sheriff to warn the tourists to stay out of the water because there was a great white shark out there eating people.

Mitch hadn't done what the mayor wanted, of course, and the mayor had fired him. But Rileigh put a bug in the ear of Melissa Mendosa, WATE 6 News, and Mendosa did a story about the sheriff who had warned the public when the mayor didn't want him to, then caught the bad guys even after he'd been fired, saving the county. It was a heart-grabbing piece, and the mayor had shown up at Mitch's house the next day making amends, saying it was all a big misunderstanding, that he hadn't really meant to fire him, and gave Mitch his job back. After that, the mayor cut a wide path around Mitch, which suited Mitch just fine.

Rileigh's heart had sunk when she'd glanced across the dining room earlier and seen the mayor dressed as the Wizard of Oz — another con man, so it was fitting. His wife was Glenda the Good Witch. But it was too much to hope that he wouldn't be invited or that he wouldn't show up.

J.P. Rutherford was a used car salesman to the bone, and not because it was his former profession. He'd simply decided to do for a living what he was so naturally gifted at doing, which was smiling his big toothy smile and wringing the last dime out of his unsuspecting customers.

He actually looked better as the Wizard of Oz than he looked most normal days, with his too-long hair swept back in a style that was last popular in about 1985, his too-colorful suits, and those shiny black patent leather shoes. Made him look like a cartoon character far more convincingly than the Wizard of Oz costume did now.

"Mitchell, my man," Rutherford bellowed from ten feet away. He didn't bother to reach out his hand or perform his usual good ol' boy routine, claiming that "me and Maggie been meaning to have you over to the house for supper" and other inane lies with which he peppered most conversations. Tonight, he cut right to the chase.

"I've been hanging back, as I'm sure you're well aware, because I've always believed that you hire the right people, then you get out of their way and let them do their jobs." The mayor had not hired Mitch, but would take credit for having hired him if that made him look good, just like he'd point out that he hadn't hired him if the reverse were true. "So I haven't been a backseat driver."

Rileigh thought, here comes the *but*.

"But as the chief executive officer of this county, I am responsible for the people on this boat and their welfare, and it's my duty to make sure that what's going on here, this terrible, terrible circumstance comes to an end, a favorable end, as quickly as possible." He gestured toward the microphone that now stood empty on the stage.

"Now you tell us that the engines and the radios are broke, and we're gonna be sitting here for the next eight hours. I want to know what you're gonna do about that!"

"There isn't anything I can do about it," Mitch said calmly and quietly as Rileigh stood back, grinding her teeth. "The engineer is working as hard as he can to fire up the firebox and get the water boiling in the boiler, but as I'm sure *you're* well aware, you can't make water boil any faster no matter what you do. It will take as long as it takes for that water to get hot enough to run that paddle wheel. Until then, we are stuck here."

"And you're telling me there's no way to get anybody to come out here and help us?"

"Yes, sir, that's what I'm telling you. We have no means of communicating with the shore."

"Hot damn!" the mayor said, then looked at Rileigh. "Excuse my French, little lady. Then back at Mitch, "What the hell happened to the radio?"

"It looked to me like somebody took a hammer to it. They also ripped off the wall phone that allowed the engineer to speak to the pilot and the captain."

"And you can do nothing? You can't use your radio to call the shore?" Mitch didn't even dignify that with an answer, just looked at the mayor. "All right, I guess your radio is in your car."

Then he puffed himself back up again.

"Well, I've just got one thing to say to you, Sheriff Webster, and this is it: you fix this, you get these people back to shore and off this boat, and you make sure you find whoever it was that killed Hunter Dobson, arrest him, and throw him in the clink."

Mitch didn't avail himself of the teed-up shot at sarcasm: *Why I never thought of that.*

"I'm doing the best I can, sir." He nodded and tried to extricate himself from the conversation by turning and walking away, but the mayor wasn't through.

"Sheriff Webster." He pointed toward Mitch's feet. "For the love of God, man, put some damn shoes on."

With that parting shot, he walked away.

Rileigh could hear Gus chuckling as he walked toward them, watching the mayor flounce out of the room.

"Well, I guess he told you."

Mitch rolled his eyes.

At that point, Gus sat down on the nearest chair and started taking his shoes off.

"I can't keep walking around in these shoes when my friend is about to get his ass fired because he's barefoot," Gus said. He pulled off the first shoe and the sock beneath. "They're big enough for you, all right. Surely to God, your shoe size isn't bigger than twelve and a half."

"As a matter of fact, that is my shoe size," Mitch said, "but I couldn't take your—"

"The hell you can't! You need them more than I do. It's damned hard to take a man seriously when he's standing there with mismatched socks."

Mitch sat, pulled off the dirty white gym sock and held it out to Gus.

Gus wrinkled his nose. "No thanks, I'll pass."

Mitch pulled off the other sock and handed them both to Rileigh. "Do something with this," he said, and she stuffed it into the pocket of her cape.

"Try not to scuff up my shoes," Gus said. "Now, let's you and me and Rileigh go find us a quiet corner somewhere to get a drink and talk."

Chapter Twenty

MITCH, Rileigh, and the now-barefoot Gus went up the stairs to Deck 3 to the buffet-style restaurant. It's where most of the guests had eaten dinner, if they had eaten dinner at all.

"Damn, you didn't mention how cold the floor is," Gus said, "especially those metal stairs."

"Hey, you can have the shoes back any time."

"I didn't say I wanted the shoes back, I was just commenting about the fact that it never occurred to me I might get frostbite in Tennessee."

The three of them went through the serving line of the buffet. Mitch and Gus just grabbed coffee, Rileigh snatched a bagel off the tray, too.. Then they found a table near the windows, away from all the other guests, and sat down together.

The view out the windows was bleak. Ice was forming everywhere now: on the railings, on the deck itself, on the gingerbread that hung down from the roof outside. Visibility was probably 10 feet beyond the boat.

"Wouldn't want to have to negotiate my way back to

the dock in this weather, even with a full head of steam," Gus said.

"Yep, this was a made-to-order night for whoever wanted to strand a boat full of people out in the middle of the water." Mitch took a big swig of his coffee and set the mug down, spread his hands out on the table and said, "Okay, we're stuck here. There's a dead body downstairs and a murder scene cordoned off. We're not going to get any help for hours. I'm going to see if I can't make some progress on this case. Know anybody who's be willing to join me in this largely futile effort?"

"I'm a fan of futile," said Gus.

"Futility is my spirit animal," said Rileigh.

Mitch held up his fist, they bumped,

"In any murder investigation, you look for three things," Gus pontificated, as if the other two people at the table didn't know that as well as he did.

"Motive," Rileigh said.

"Opportunity," Gus added.

"And means," Mitch finished.

"We can pretty much scratch out opportunity if we're trying to eliminate any of the people on this boat, because everybody on the boat had an equal opportunity to sneak onto that stage and bury a hammer in Hunter Dobson's head," Rileigh said.

"True that," said Mitch. "Think about all the people who were standing around us as we waited for the curtains to be opened. Any one of them could have been the killer. Just do the do and go back out the door you came in, then mingle with the crowd."

"I'm wondering about blood splatter," Gus said. "Clocking somebody on the head is not a bloodless event. Head wounds bleed like a son of a bitch."

"And whoever hit him, hit him twice," Mitch added.

"How did the murderer slice him open and not just get covered in blood?" Rileigh asked.

"Well," Mitch offered, "If you stood behind the body after you killed him, you could lean over his shoulder to make the incision. The blood would run down his lap and legs, and you wouldn't necessarily be covered in it."

"Just your hands," Rileigh said. "If you planned ahead, left a towel or something back there and then took it with you."

"So you're walking around with a bloody towel?" Gus said.

"We need to check all the trash receptacles around the back of the stage," Mitch said.

"You could wipe most of the blood off on a towel, enough so nobody'd notice until you could wash your hands," Rileigh said.

"So, the process of elimination really hasn't eliminated anybody at all, because the whole crowd had the opportunity to kill him."

"Next up, motive," Rileigh said.

Mitch let out a short burst of laughter. "Right. And you could say that we can't eliminate anybody in the room over the motive either. Just about everybody in the room had something against Hunter Dobson."

"So you think this is all about the Gum Tree Project," Rileigh said.

She didn't mean to say it in a challenging way, but it had come out like that. She hoped Mitch hadn't picked up on it.

"Well, that's the elephant in the middle of the room, isn't it?" Gus sipped his coffee. "A guy comes to town to bulldoze his way into millions, clog the county's roads, and disfigure the mountains. He didn't lack for would-be assassins."

"But the Save Gum Tree Hollow Association members aren't violent," Rileigh said.

"Maybe not violent, but they're destructive," Gus said. "They spray-painted slogans on walls and vandalized all that earth-moving equipment."

"You don't know they did that," Rileigh said. And she saw that Mitch picked up on her tone this time.

"Sounds to me like you're hell-bent on defending them," he observed.

"No, I'm not. I just... Let's not go around hanging labels on people. Nobody knows who the members of the Save Gum Tree Hollow Association are, other than Georgia's brother, Ian."

"I'm planning to have a conversation with Mr. McGinnis about his involvement in all this," Mitch said.

"A conversation or a confrontation?" Rileigh said. "Because if what you want is information, I need to be the one doing the questioning."

Mitch started to protest, but she held up her hand and went on. "Come on, in ten seconds, the two of you will be going at each other — both of you with very high levels of testosterone — seeing who can out-macho who. You won't find out anything that way. I know Ian, and I'm the person who needs to talk to him."

She could tell that though he didn't like it, Mitch agreed.

"I think it's safe to assume that all the people in their little 'secret society' are just garden-variety folks who are bound and determined to save their mountains. That shouldn't make all of them murder suspects," she continued.

"I think Rileigh's right on that point," Gus said. She was properly surprised. "Only because of the violence in the murder. The person who committed that murder was one sick son of a bitch. And it all seems too... well, too pat to me. If you're killing the guy just to get him out of the way, you could do that by running over him some night when he goes out to walk his dog. Why wait until he's on a stage in front of 250 people to crack his skull open and spill his guts out on his lap. That's pretty flamboyant. That's sending a message of some kind. I'm just not sure what it is."

"Gus has a point," Mitch said. "Why *here?* Why *now?* This would appear to be an inopportune place to commit a murder, if your objective is merely to get rid of Hunter Dobson. I think whoever killed him had a bigger agenda than that."

"Yeah," Rileigh said. "And the number one. That's pure melodrama. That's begging for the spotlight. I can't imagine why someone who merely wanted to keep Hunter Dobson from building that development would have done that."

"Fine then," Gus said. "So it's not somebody pissed off at him because he is about to rape Gum Tree Hollow. Who else?"

"His wife," Mitch said. "He was having an affair with Ruby Cunningham."

"Or Ruby's husband, for the same reason," Rileigh said.

"But we all saw their reactions to the murder. It's hard to believe that Skylar Dobson could whack her husband over the head with a hammer, cut him open, and a few minutes later come screaming toward the stage in hysterics."

"Same goes for Ruby Cunningham's husband," Rileigh said. "If ever somebody looked dumbfounded, it was that guy when he saw his wife's response."

"And how about we toss into the mix of complicating

factors that somebody, disabled the engine so the boat couldn't go back to the dock, and disabled the radio so we couldn't summon help," Gus said.

"Those are the kickers," said Mitch. "Why would the murderer want to strand the boat in the middle of the lake? You'd think they'd want the boat to go back to shore as soon as possible so they could get off the boat and get away."

"And there's opportunity rearing its ugly head again," Rileigh said. "Somebody committed a murder, washed the blood off their hands, and rushed down to the hold to—"

"Not just disable the communications and the engine," Mitch said. "Somebody put something in the food the crew had for dinner. So, you're talking somebody who knows where they eat, when they eat.–"

"Somebody whose presence wouldn't be noted," Gus said. "Somebody went into that galley — and I don't even know where it is — and nobody noticed them there. If it's one of the passengers, and they're dressed up like Tinker-bell, I think somebody would have mentioned it."

"Sounds like we're working our way around to believing that either a member of the crew is the murderer or there's more than one person involved in all of this," Mitch said.

"That makes sense in practical terms," Gus agreed, "in the getting-from-point-A-to-point-B aspect of it all. It's certainly easier to believe that two people did it than to believe one person managed to pull it all off by themselves."

"I've been thinking about the crew angle," Rileigh said, "and I can't see any way around it. Maybe the killer paid off somebody on the inside to destroy the communications equipment and disable the engine."

"Which leads us right back around to why," Mitch said.

"What for? How does it benefit the murderer to strand this boat out here in the middle of the lake with no communications?"

"Don't you just love circular reasoning?" Gus said, "where you put your best mental energy into solving a problem and work your way right back where you started in the beginning?"

"So where do we go from here?" Rileigh said.

"We can't eliminate by motive or opportunity," Mitch said, "so we have to eliminate by means. Anybody on this boat could have killed Hunter Dobson with a hammer. Anybody on this boat could have destroyed the communications equipment the same way. But there are a finite number of people on this boat who could have disabled the engine. Only a handful would know how."

Gus and Rileigh nodded agreement.

"The captain said that he, the first mate, the bosun, the pilot, and the engineers were the only people he knew for sure would have have the knowledge. Not just who understood the general functioning of it, but the ones who knew exactly where the valve was to let the steam off the boiler and knew how to put out the fire in the firebox. Only those people had the means."

After Mitch said that, they all sat quietly looking at each other or into their coffee, until he spoke again.

"Moving forward, we need to go out and start questioning 'suspects.' Rileigh, would you go have a talk with Skylar Dobson, and see if there's something we missed about her involvement in all this? Then we'll start with the crew. You talk to bosun and the pilot about disabling the engine. I'll ask the first mate and the captain the same thing, and I'll have a talk with Steve Cunningham."

"So I don't get to go out and interview anybody?" Gus said.

"Would you know what to ask?" Mitch said.

"It's pretty obvious, isn't it?"

Rileigh raised an eyebrow. "You think so?"

"Sorry, didn't mean to diss on you, like anybody can do what you do. I'll just wander around, eavesdropping on conversations. I'm a lucky guy, after all — maybe I'll overhear somebody confessing." He paused. "Mostly I just want to get back downstairs where there's carpet on the floor."

Mitch stood. "Before I do anything else, I'm going to go have a look at the security footage." He said to Gus, "Why don't you come with me? Maybe you'll spot something I miss."

Chapter Twenty-One

MITCH USED his newly acquired walkie-talkie to call Donovan McCreary and tell him that he was ready to see the security camera footage of the dining room. McCreary said he would come up to the restaurant for him.

"It's a pretty straight shot to the security room from the restaurant on the third deck, but I'll come get you anyway. Wouldn't want you to get lost."

McCreary arrived before Mitch and Gus had finished their coffee. Rileigh had left to go talk to her mother before she went looking for Ian.

The security room was in the bottom deck of the boat, what the crew called the hold, the part that would have been underwater if the boat had been a sea-going craft that operated in deep water. But on the paddle-wheeler, the hold was deck one, and the main deck, where the dining room, casino, and lounge were located, was deck two.

The security room was down a passageway from the area where Mitch had come through earlier on his way to the engine room. There were several closed doors marked *Employees only*.

They passed a big window that revealed a darkened room which appeared to be some kind of children's playground. No children on the boat tonight. He could see through the window, across the room and out the window on the other side that showed the deck out there. And his eye was caught by what appeared to be a giant green frog with a plume of ice sticking out of his mouth like an unlit cigarette.

Then they entered a brightly-lit room where a crewman sat in front of a bank of computer monitors. Each one showed a view from a different security camera, and Mitch was struck immediately by how few views there were.

"Is this all?" Mitch asked. "These are the only security cameras you have?"

"It's the only security cameras that are turned on right now. We have several others in the parts of the boat that are closed up, but I warned you there wasn't a whole lot of security footage to look at."

Mitch and Gus examined the views in the various monitors where the crew member was overseeing real-time camera footage of what was going on in the boat.

Each of the monitors was labeled according to the camera it connected to, and the ones that were currently off would have been trained on the viewing area on the stern, where people stood to watch the paddle wheel, and the deck on the bow.

It was not surprising that most of the cameras were in the casino. There were cameras in the ceiling above the gaming tables, one above each table. There was a camera in the ceiling above both rows of slot machines. And there were additional cameras that showed different views of the whole room from different corners of the room.

There were also monitors that showed the dining

room. But there were only four views, one from each corner of that room. None of them showed the back of the stage, which is what Mitch was hoping to find. They only showed the eating area and the tables set. The room was virtually deserted now, just a few people talking, and nobody eating.

There were three cameras that showed the lounge, two in the ceiling above the bar, and one that gave an overall view of the whole lounge. In the diagram of the boat between the lounge and the casino, there was an open area containing the elevators and stairs, more restrooms, a spa. There were no cameras at all in that open area.

THERE WERE ALSO VIEWS of the library and the video game room on the third deck. People had retreated to those places for calm and privacy. There were probably more people in the library now than on most cruises.

Other cameras showed the gift shop, the theater, and the small lounge and bar on deck four. The security cameras on the fifth deck were mounted on poles, looking down on the sunbathing area that right now was frozen over with an inch layer of ice. The walking track around the deck was a skating rink. One of the cameras on the pole showed a view of the front of the building where the pilots steered the boat. The big glass window in front was clear of ice. There was a light on in the room behind it, but the pilot wasn't at the wheel.

Mitch stood for a time studying the live feed cameras, asking questions about when they were turned on and who monitored them, and how many of them had been out of service tonight. Even though there were far fewer cameras than Mitch was expecting, closely examining the footage from even one of them would take an enormous amount of time that Mitch didn't have right now. He hadn't really expected to come down and look at it all, just wanted to see what was available when he did have the time and resources to examine the footage. But the small number of cameras brought up a question that had been itching in the back of Mitch's mind all evening.

"There are only seven men on the security team for tonight's cruise," Mitch asked.

"That's right. I'm not the head of the security team. It's just that the guy who is didn't show tonight and I got called in." He made a grunting sound in his throat and a wry smile took over his face. "Yep, I get called in to oversee security on the night there's a murder. Lucky me."

"I don't understand the size of the security team," Mitch said. "I would have thought you would have at least a dozen, probably more than that, given the amount of money that's bound to be socked away somewhere on this boat."

Gus, who'd been examining the different views that were showing real-time views of the activity on different decks, looked at him then. "Money?"

McCreary didn't seem surprised by Mitch's question.

"You're thinking about the gaming commission's requirements," he said, then turned to Gus to explain. "Even small casinos in Las Vegas have five, maybe as much as seven million dollars in cash available at all times." Gus's eyebrows shot up. "Because the gaming commission requires that they be able to pay out every chip that's in play in the machines and on the game tables."

Gus gave a low, soft whistle. "Seven million dollars. Damn."

McCreary chuckled. "And that's for a small casino. The big ones — Caesar's Palace, MGM Grand — $150 million, maybe $200 million."

"No wonder Danny Ocean was drooling."

"But the Queen of the Smokies ... not so much. As we say in this part of Tennessee, don't get your panties all in a wad over it, because this is a *mini* casino. We only have a dozen slot machines and half a dozen game tables — roulette, blackjack, poker, craps, baccarat, and big six wheel. And it's at the *gaming tables* in Las Vegas where the big money is won and lost. Some have ten, twenty-dollar minimum bets and the pot gets big quick. An unbelievable amount of money changes hands every night on those tables, and the casino has to have enough cash available to pay every chip at every table and every chip in every slot machine."

He smiled. "But we get around that huge money requirement because we don't use monetary chips at our game tables. When you play blackjack on the Queen of the Smokies, you're playing to win a free week in the honeymoon suite, or dinner with the captain, or a gift certificate for the gift shop. The chips on our game tables have no monetary value, so we don't have to carry cash to cover them."

He pointed to a monitor on the bottom left of the screen that showed a small room, devoid of furniture, with a metal door on one wall.

"The cash we do carry is in the safe, which is kept in the vault room. It takes three keys — the captain's, the first mate's and the pilot's — just to get into the room, which has all kinds of alarm systems: movement sensors, infrared, that kind of thing. I don't know how you open the safe itself, you'll have to ask the captain."

Mitch's attention returned to the live feed from the cameras, and he stood for a time, his eyes going from one screen to another.

Then he turned to McCreary. "I've seen all I need to

see for now. I want you to secure the footage from every camera that was operating on this boat from the moment it was turned on. I want to see all of that at some point. But right now is not the time."

Gus followed Mitch back out into the passageway, past the children's playground, the engine room, and the unmarked, closed doors, back to the metal stairs that led up to the main deck. Gus leapt up them, taking them two at a time, making little squeaking sounds all the way.

When they got to the top of the steps, Mitch said again, "Hey Gus, I'm glad to give you your shoes back—"

"Nope, I'm good to go. You need them more than I do. A shoeless sheriff reinforces all the stereotypes about Tennessee hillbillies and we can't have that, can we? But I do think I'll just hang around on the main deck from now on. The carpet's warmer than the hardwood floors, and a hell of a lot warmer than the metal stairs."

Chapter Twenty-Two

WHEN MITCH DIVIDED up the crew-members-who-could-disable-the-engine list, Rileigh took the pilot and the bosun's mate. It wasn't reasonable to believe that either of those people had anything against Hunter Dobson or were involved in his murder. But it was possible one or the other of them had been paid off by whoever did kill him, or maybe they knew who had been paid off, or suspected something. Anything was better than nothing, and nothing was what they had right now.

The more convoluted the scenario got, the harder it was to believe that only one person was responsible for all of it. Someone killed Hunter Dobson without getting caught, then had somehow managed to slip something into the chili to make the crew sick, then took a hammer to the ship-to-shore radio, clocked the engineer on the back of the head, let off all the steam pressure, closed the damper and killed the fire in the fire box. That was a pretty tall order for only one person. The more they talked about it, the more it seemed reasonable that somebody who knew the operation of the boat had to have been involved.

Rileigh was glad to help question the "possibles". They were far removed from suspects at this point. What she wasn't glad to do was make her way down the internal passageways of the boat. She managed her discomfort in small places during the boat trip by spending as much time as she could going from point A to point B *outside* on the walkways of the boat rather than inside through the passageways. That was becoming more and more problematic as the weather worsened, and besides, there wasn't any way to get to the crew's quarters by way of an outside walkway.

The crew's quarters, like the crew's mess, the crew's kitchen, and the other mechanics of the ship, were in the hold, one deck below where all the festivities had happened. McCreary had told Rileigh that she could find the pilot in her quarters. Rileigh didn't have a problem until she started down the passageway with doors opening off it to the quarters of the crew. It wasn't as wide as the passageways upstairs between the cabins for guests. It wasn't as well-lit either. Rileigh was instantly uncomfortable. She felt her heart begin to pound and struggled to keep her composure.

She knocked on the door of Cabin 3 and a voice from inside called out, "Come on in, but shut the hell up until I'm finished."

Rileigh opened the door and stuck her head into the cabin, where a woman on the other side of the small room was engrossed in a video game. The walls of the room were covered with architectural drawings ... no, floor plans, of paddlewheel boats. She saw the three-decked Belle of Louisville, the four-decked Cincinnati Star, and the six decks of the gigantic American Queen. Then she spotted the plans for the five decks of the Queen of the Smokies. The plans proved she hadn't imagined it — the passageways on the boat were a rabbit warren.

The woman playing the game never even looked at her, just hollered over her shoulder, "I'm about to beat this son of a bitch and I'm not quitting now. Whatever you want, it can wait."

Well, the pilot might not mind waiting, but Rileigh did. The room was small and stuffy, even more cramped than the passageway outside, and Rileigh wasn't sure how long she could stay here without freaking out. She hated to interrupt the woman, but she didn't have any choice.

"I'm sorry, Ms. Watson, but I have to talk to you, and I have to talk to you right now,"

The pilot whirled around.

"Who the hell are you?"

Then she turned back to the game, issued a mouthful of some of the most colorful expletives Rileigh had ever heard, and slammed her hand down on the switch to turn off the video game.

"My name is Rileigh Bishop, and I don't have very long," Rileigh said. She didn't tell her why she didn't have very long. "I'm helping Yarmouth County Sheriff Mitchell Webster with the investigation of the murder that happened upstairs earlier this evening."

The woman's eyes grew wide. "Why in the world would you think I know anything about that?"

"I just have a few questions to ask, Ms. Margely—"

"Call me Belle, everybody does." She paused. "Or Large Marge. I prefer Belle."

"Belle, then. I won't take long, and then I'll leave you alone."

The woman eyed her carefully, and to Rileigh's utter surprise said, "You don't like it in here. You're one of those."

"One of those what?"

"One of the closet people. That's what we call them."

"Closet people." Rileigh mulled the words over as she said them.

"That's the ones that can't stand to be in tight places. They never last long, and you're one of them. I can always spot 'em."

Rileigh didn't know what to say, never dreamed that she would be outed instantly, but she didn't see any hostility in the woman's eyes, and didn't see any other option but to be honest.

"I had a very, *very* bad experience with closed-in spaces a couple of months ago, and I'm still working through it."

"Didn't try to squirm out of it. I like that."

Belle got up out of the chair and walked the few steps from the chair to the doorway. She gestured at all the plans decorating the walls. "One of these days, I'm gonna build my own paddleboat."

Then she pointed at the door.

"Come on. Let's go sit down in the crew's mess. Nobody's in there right now, and it's a bigger room." She stepped out into the passageway and went purposefully down it with Rileigh trailing along behind her.

Rileigh didn't know much about the pilot, but she would bet that Belle was one of only a handful of boat pilots who had two X chromosomes.

Belle led the way through a door into a small dining room that had several tables, and it was indeed much larger than her cabin.

"Have a seat." She pulled out a chair and sat down opposite Rileigh.

That was the first time she'd had an opportunity to get a good look at this woman who was the pilot of the Queen of the Smokies.

She was a big woman, not fat, just big and tall and broad —at least 6'2", maybe 6'4", with short cropped gray hair and the shoulders of a lumberjack. Her face was weather-worn and there was a web of spider wrinkles around her eyes, put there—Rileigh was sure—by a career squinting into the sun reflected off the water.

Feeling less stressed out over the closed spaces, Rileigh managed to relax enough to be curious.

"So, tell me, what's the job of a pilot on a paddlewheel boat?"

"I steer the boat," Belle said. "The other boats know to give the Queen of the Smokies a wide berth because she's got a woman driver." Then she chuckled and it was a deep sound, easy and relaxed, the kind of laugh that made you want to laugh too, even if you didn't know what was funny.

"I communicate with the engine room, give them changes in speed or direction, tell them forward or reverse. I'm making this really simple, because it doesn't look to me like you know a whole lot about the duties of the crew of a paddleboat."

"I know absolutely zip," said Rileigh.

"What I don't understand is what you want to talk to *me* about. I get it that there's been a murder and the captain said that the whole crew was to cooperate with the investigation. But what is it you think I can tell you that you don't already know?"

Her eyebrows went up then and she said, "I'm not a suspect, am I?"

"No, you're not a suspect."

That was probably true, but …

It appeared to Rileigh that the woman valued honesty, so she said, "Actually, that's not entirely true. Everybody on this boat who knew how to disable that engine is a suspect. And that's a small group of people."

"Hell yeah, it is. But why would being able to disable the engine make you a suspect in a murder?"

"Because it would be way beyond the bounds of coincidence that there happened to be a murder upstairs at the same time that the engine downstairs was suddenly disabled and the ship to shore radio was destroyed. It's all connected. Has to be. I don't know what the connection is right now, but—"

"You think somebody on the crew is helping a murderer." The woman's face darkened like a storm over the water. "Are you accusing us of—"

"I'm not accusing anybody of anything. But facts are facts. Somebody disabled that engine and none of the passengers knew how. It has to be possible that—"

"Let me tell you what's possible and what ain't. The crew on this boat is tight. We've worked together, some of us for years. Boat crews kind of make the rounds of boats, you know, but it don't matter what boat you're on, you know each other, help each other out when you can." Belle paused, "Not saying there ain't been new hands — those is mostly jobs that don't require you to have experience on boats, in security and the like. There ain't enough money anywhere to bribe somebody on this crew to commit cold-blooded murder. And you're wasting my time and yours asking questions about it."

Rileigh agreed—it was a waste of time. Belle Margely was a person you could trust. But even though she didn't believe any crew members would take a bribe, there had to be somebody on this crew who wasn't worthy of the woman's trust.

Rileigh stood. "Thank you for your time, Miss Margely." She stopped herself. "Belle." She held out her hand. "It was good to meet you."

Belle took Rileigh's hand in her large one, shook it, and then held on and spoke quietly.

"I've known quite a few people who got the same problem you got. You run into them on a boat or a ship because the quarters are so small. That kind of thing can cripple you or you can work through it. I've seen some of both. Appears to me you got the stones to make it all the way to the other side."

She let go of Rileigh's hand, and Rileigh stepped out of the room and made her way as fast as she could down the passageway, up the stairs, and out onto the cold deck, where the freezing rain hit her in the face like buckshot. She took great heaving lungfuls of cold air, grateful to be out in the open again.

Rileigh stood for a while in the cold, shivering, hunkered against the wall out of the wind until she had relaxed enough that she was willing to go back down into the rabbit warren of passageways in the hold and pay a visit to the bosun. She'd ask him the questions she'd asked Belle and hope maybe the guy knew something, or maybe she could catch him in a lie. She took a deep breath, went back inside, and a few minutes later was knocking on the door of the cabin of the bosun's mate.

Rileigh rapped her knuckles on the door. "Mr. Peterson, my name is Rileigh Bishop. I need to speak to you, please."

She heard a grunting, groaning sound and then another sound that was universal and unmistakable — the sound of somebody heaving. The retching went on and on for a few seconds, and then there was silence.

"I can't talk to nobody," came a weak voice from the other side of the door. "I'm sick as a damn dog."

Well, that pretty much crossed his name off the list of possible suspects. Since he was among the crew members who had eaten the chili that made them sick, it wasn't likely he was the guy who'd spiked it.

"Sorry to have bothered you, sir," she called through the door. She heard more retching sounds as she turned and went back down the passageway.

Maybe Mitch would find something useful in the security tapes.

Chapter Twenty-Three

RILEIGH FOUND Skylar seated at the bar in the lounge between the dining room and the casino. She had taken off her blue-and-purple Sully costume.

Apparently, she had intended to ditch the blue fur costume all along, because she was dressed in a sexy, slinky black dress and spike heels. Though the Sully costume was a full head costume with horns on top and a cutout for the face, somehow she'd managed to come out of it without hat-hair, a feat of pure magic. Her hair was long, appeared to be naturally blonde, and flowed down her back and around her shoulders in the current style that Rileigh had seen on every female news anchor from CNN to CBS to Fox News. Skyler was petite, but had curves in all the right places and a bust just a little too big, likely courtesy of a splash of silicone.

The slinky black dress was cut low in the front, exposing ten miles of cleavage, and she wore a necklace that dipped down between her breasts provocatively, a pendant that had a rock on it that, if it was real, was worth more than it would cost to cut down every tree in Gum Tree Hollow.

She was striking woman, a woman who literally turned heads. But she was only pretty, not beautiful, despite her expertly-applied makeup. Her most memorable feature was a heart-shaped mouth with full lips that might or might not be collagen-enhanced. She looked as good as it was possible to look given the materials at hand. That's what money could buy.

As Rileigh approached, she saw Skylar say something to another woman who had approached, and the other woman had backed off. Clearly, she wanted to be alone. Sorry about that.

Rileigh walked up and seated herself on the stool beside Skylar. Skylar didn't even look at her when she said, "There are three other empty stools. Pick one."

"Mrs. Dobson, my name is Rileigh Bishop, and I'm sorry for your loss." When she said that part, Skylar winced. "I'm helping County Sheriff Mitch Webster in the investigation of your husband's murder."

"Well, good for you. So go, go find out who killed him."

The woman downed the last of the drink in front of her in a single gulp and tapped the glass on the bar to indicate she wanted another one.

"It's not hard to figure out, is it? Just find out which one of them actually committed the crime." Skylar actually looked at her then, seeming surprised that Rileigh refused to take the hint. "If you're helping to investigate the murder, go investigate."

"I need to ask you a couple of questions."

"Why me? I didn't kill him." She bristled then, and the hard look was not flattering. "Though I would have, I could have, I *should* have, if I had known."

Her eyes flashed and her voice hardened. "Can you believe that bitch?" she said with such force that she actually spit. "I saw her running down there and I had no idea why anybody would … and then I figured it out. That whore. That—"

"So you had no idea that your husband was seeing Ruby Cunningham?"

"So you had no idea your husband was seeing Ruby Cunningham?" Skyler mocked. "Of course I had no idea he was seeing Ruby Cunningham — or anybody else. You think I would have put up with that? If I'd known he couldn't keep his pants zipped, I'd have cut it off."

She barked out an inappropriate laugh. "It never crossed my mind that in this little podunk town in the middle of nowhere, there would be somebody for him to hook up with. Never dreamed it in a million years."

Though Rileigh knew the answer to the question, she asked it anyway. "Why didn't you move here with him?"

"Move here? To this place? You've got to be kidding me. Who in their right mind would live in this place?"

She obviously knew that Rileigh was a local and there was no apology, no *oops* before she continued her rant.

"I'm telling you this much. We had a life in Nashville, and it was a good life. Then suddenly he decides he's going to move to this Black Bear Forge, Tennessee. Are you kidding me?"

Skylar stopped and her demeanor changed. Tears filled her eyes and her lower lip began to tremble.

"We did have a good life, Hunt and I. It was a struggle in the beginning. When I married Hunter, he was just starting out. I worked in the make-up department in Macy's while he was out showing houses, before he made his first big sale. It wasn't easy, those early years, but we made it. We had a beautiful home and wonderful friends.

We went to parties and social events..." She stopped, took a breath, and when she said the rest, there wasn't hostility in it. "He was my husband. Mine. Not some other woman's. *Mine.* I loved him. And somebody *killed* him."

"Is there anybody who's on the boat tonight who might have a grudge against your husband?"

Skylar barked out a laugh, the shield back up, the vulnerability gone. "*Any*body? Try *every*body on the whole damn boat. They all have something against my husband. He's going to build something in their precious mountains and destroy their precious trees or birds or squirrels or whatever."

Skylar wasn't drunk, but she was getting there.

Rileigh said, "I was asking if perhaps there was some *other* motive less obvious that we wouldn't think to consider. Perhaps you knew of someone else who had something against your husband that we wouldn't know about."

Skylar gestured over her shoulder toward the room beyond. "You think I *know* any of these people? Seriously? I know the names of maybe three people in the whole county. One of them is the mechanic who fixed my Ferrari, one is that lady in that store on Main Street that sells fudge and funnel cakes, and the third is the pharmacist who replaced the birth control pills I lost."

You could tell it had just occurred to her.

"Holy shit. I hope that woman was using protection because Mitch sure as hell never did. He thought condoms were like putting on a raincoat."

Rileigh didn't really want to go there, so she moved the conversation in a different direction. "Can you tell me if your husband had other business dealings in which he might have made some enemies?"

"My husband made enemies with all his business deal-ings. Like I said, he was trying to build things in these mountains. And every hillbilly out there, all the tree huggers were determined to stop him." Her voice hardened again, had an edge of flint in it. "Find out who did it. Find the son of a bitch and give me three minutes alone with him before you put him behind bars. I'll claw his balls off."

Chapter Twenty-Four

RILEIGH WAS RELATIVELY sure that Mildred Hanover would look after Mama, but because all Mama's friends were in denial, she couldn't count on them to be as watchful as they needed to be. You couldn't let a three-year-old wander around unsupervised, and though her cognitive ability hadn't been severely affected yet, a first grader had greater impulse control and better judgement than Rileigh's mother.

Then there were her delusions. Her friends didn't want to think that Lily was not dragging a full string of fish anymore. They chose to ignore her quirks, as they called them, her idiosyncrasies, her, *just Lily being Lily* moments. Her friend, Millie, was fond of saying: "Lily Bishop still has every marble she came into the world with, and a whole bunch more she's collected along the way." That made Mama sound fun and charming, and certainly she was. But she was also a woman who had forgotten the recipes for all the dishes she'd prepared her whole life — meatloaf might have ham in it, and lemon meringue pie, no sugar. She thought she was dating Rhett Butler. And — this was the hard part — she clung with all her strength to the delusion that her oldest daughter was coming home someday.

Rileigh found Mama where she had left her, at the third of the six slot machines on the starboard wall of the casino. Mama and Millie had parked there when they got on the boat and they'd never left. Rileigh had no idea how many chips her mother might have fed into the machine. Georgia had stopped her earlier and said she'd seen Mama jumping up and down, excited that she'd won six hundred dollars. Rileigh was grateful that she'd won, but she had no intention of buying Mama more chips when she ran out.

As Rileigh walked up to her mother, adorable chubby fairy godmother that she was, and Millie as Mary Poppins, she saw Georgia crossing the room toward them, holding her skirt together.

Georgia's costume made a statement. But it was an inside joke and only a handful of people even understood it. It was a really bad idea for a Halloween costume.

"I'm literally falling apart," Georgia announced, flouncing down on the stool next to Mama in the Princess Bride dress she'd made of duct tape. *Red* duct tape. The inside joke was that long ago Rileigh, had used red duct tape to tape Georgia to a chair so she couldn't go out on a date with a drug dealer. She'd gone anyway, got busted, and came within a hair's-breadth of spending the best years of her life in prison because of it.

Georgia had created the dress by weaving red duct tape stuck to itself into a single piece of "fabric" That she'd then used to make the long skirt of the dress by duct-taping it together at the waist. She'd made the top of the dress by wrapping her upper body in duct tape. That part had been no problem. What had turned into a problem was trying to keep the skirt of the dress from falling down or coming apart.

"I could have told you it wasn't a good idea if you'd asked," Rileigh said, "but you didn't."

Georgia stuck out her tongue.

"Now there's a mature response to constructive feedback."

"Put a sock in it," Georgia said. "And speaking of socks, did Mitch ever find a pair of shoes?"

"Yeah, Gus sacrificed his own for the cause."

Suddenly, the lights on her mother's slot machine began to flash and bells sounded.

"Look, look, I won. I won," Mama squealed, so excited she seized Rileigh in a suffocating bear hug, then hugged Georgia, then Millie, and would have grabbed hold of anybody else who happened to come near.

Mama could go home $150 richer if she cashed out her chips, but she wouldn't, of course, she'd use them to gamble more. Well, it was keeping her occupied and that was all Rileigh could legitimately ask.

Mama scooped up the chips she'd won out of the tray on the machine — a tray intentionally made too small so the chips would overflow out onto the floor — and stuffed them into the big pocket on the front of her fairy godmother costume.

"My turn now," Millie said, using her butt to scoot Mama off the seat where she was sitting. "She's won three different jackpots. I've won zip."

"You're just not lucky, Millie. No sense feeding chips into the machine if you're not lucky."

"I don't think a person is either lucky or unlucky. It's just random chance."

"What about Gus?" Mama asked.

"Gus who?" Millie asked.

"Gus Hazelton. You know who he is, don't you?"

"More or less, he's the county coroner, right? I've heard of him."

"He's the coroner, all right. Yarmouth County has the most well-stocked, efficient, and modern coroner's office in the whole state, and it isn't because taxpayer dollars were used to build it. Gus built it out of his own pocket with money he won on the lottery."

"You serious?"

Mama looked at Rileigh.

"You tell her."

Rileigh told Millie how Gus had stopped at a convenience store to go to the bathroom. And it was one of those picky ones where the owner required that you purchase something or he wouldn't let you pee. So Gus had looked around, pointed to a one-dollar scratch-off lottery ticket, and said, "Fine, I'll take that."

"One ticket, just one ticket never wins," Millie said. "People win who buy hundreds of tickets in blocks. Groups of people pool their money. Nobody wins with just one ticket."

"Well, Gus did," Mama said proudly. "And that's what I mean by Gus is lucky."

"That was certainly a lucky occurrence," Millie admitted. "But that doesn't make the man intrinsically lucky, any more than I'm intrinsically unlucky because I keep losing."

Millie reached into her pocket and pulled out a small handful of chips.

"I'm going for it," she said, and started to feed them into the machine.

"It's not called a one-armed *bandit* for nothing," Georgia warned, then she and Rileigh stepped away from the machine as one old lady fed chips into it and another harangued her about her luck or lack thereof.

"Have you seen Ian?" Rileigh asked. "I need to talk to him."

Georgia opened her mouth, then closed it again. "Wait a minute. You want to talk to him about what?"

"I just want to talk to him. Is that a crime?"

"It is if you want to talk to him about the murder of Hunter Dobson."

Rileigh said nothing and Georgia leapt on it.

"That's it, isn't it? You want to question him because he's a suspect in the murder of Hunter Dobson. Seriously? Listen to yourself."

"What? I didn't say anything."

"Listen to your mind then," Georgia sputtered. "We're talking Ian here. Ian couldn't have killed anybody. Surely you figured that out by now. You suspected him of killing Tina Montgomery, and when that wouldn't fly, you decided he had killed Jillian, and when that–"

Mama heard the name and rose to the bait. She grabbed Georgia's hand. "Did you know she's here tonight?"

Georgia just looked at her.

"Jillian is here tonight," she said.

Georgia cast a look at Rileigh.

"Uh … that's nice."

What else could you say to a woman who believes her murdered daughter is walking around in a Cinderella costume on a gambling boat stranded in the middle of a lake with a dead body behind a curtain in the dining room?

But Mama was on a roll and there was no stopping her. "Oh, she's here, alright. I knew she was here and then I saw her."

Rileigh and Georgia exchanged looks.

"You saw her?" Georgia asked.

Rileigh's heart took up a staccato rhythm even though she willed it to stay calm. She knew it was just her mother's imagination. She knew she was talking to the woman who believed she was dating Rhett Butler. She knew... but it didn't matter what she knew. And even though she was a hundred percent certain that it was nothing but the wild imaginings of her crazy mother, she couldn't help herself. The words clanged in her head, in her heart, and in her soul.

"She's here," Mama looked from Georgia to Rileigh. "I saw her. I told Rileigh to look for her. Did you see her?"

"I really need to go now," Rileigh said, patting her mother's hand. "Have a good time and keep winning."

She walked away with Georgia, saying, "You never did answer my question. Do you know where I can find Ian?"

"And you never did answer my question. Do you want to talk to him to accuse him of murder yet again?"

"I don't want to accuse him of anything. And if he doesn't talk to me, he's going to have to talk to Mitch. The sheriff or me. He gets to pick. Because *somebody's* going to talk to him."

Rileigh sighed when Georgia shook her head. "Come on. He showed up at the zoning board meeting with an orchestrated protest that shut the place down and started a near riot. Nobody knows who the members of the Save Gum Tree Hollow Association are, but everybody knows Ian's in charge of it. When the man who planned to build the development that all those people showed up to protest gets murdered, somebody in law enforcement is going to go knocking on Ian's door. Now who's it gonna be? Me or Mitch?"

"You know he didn't do it."

"Hell yeah, I know he didn't do it. Now, tell me where

to find him so I can start the annoying but necessary process of *proving* he didn't."

"He came on the boat with me, but then he vanished for a while. I don't know where he went. Of course, I'm not going to tell anybody but you that. Truth is, I've only seen him for a few minutes all night. But if anybody else asks, I'll say I haven't left Ian's side from the moment the two of us set foot on this boat."

"Fine by me. Now where is he?"

"There's a spa on the third deck. It's in that little area where the elevators and the stairs are. It's not turned on, but Ian's been on the boat before and he knew that the benches in there are padded and comfortable. After the murder, he wanted somewhere to sit down where it was calm and quiet and nobody was going to be peppering him with questions. You're not going to say I ratted him out and told you where to find him, are you?"

Rileigh lifted an eyebrow. "You think he won't figure it out on his own?"

Georgia sighed. "Yeah, I suppose." She looked down at her dress and grumbled. "Damn. It's come untaped again."

Chapter Twenty-Five

THOUGHTS FLYING through his head like comets streaking across his mind, so fast he could only see the light of them, bright and shining.

No, not comets, water spiders. Water spiders flitting over the surface of a still pond.

Zip!

Zip this way.

Zip that way.

Too fast, *too fast.*

The water-spider thoughts were zipping around so fast he couldn't grab any of them long enough to think it.

He had to slow his thinking down.

Water spiders!

Comets!

Stop it. Calm down, *calm down.*

He had to think. Not these zipping thoughts, but real thoughts.

Zip, zip.

Stop it, stop it.

Dammit, *stop!*

He leaned against the wall, watching people wander past, hearing conversations but not listening to them. Everyone ignoring him like he wasn't there, and that was good. Yes, that was good. No one would remember that he was there, no one noticed him, no one saw.

Zip, zip, the thoughts flew by.

Gotta make them stop, gotta.

Heart pounding, palms sweaty, hands trembling — calm down, calm down, dammit.

He pressed himself against the wall, and as he did, he felt the thing, the *weapon* he'd stolen, stuck down his pants, it poked him hard in the ribs. It hurt. The pain startled him, and his zipping thoughts stumbled. So he jabbed himself harder, concentrating on the pain, thinking about how bad it hurt, willing his mind to do nothing but concentrate on that one little point of pain in his side. No other thoughts at all, no thoughts, no racing, scrambling thoughts.

Just the pain.

That one point of pain.

Think about the *pain.*

He bit his lip in concentration, and the pain of that helped, too, it was another point of pain to think about. Pain was the thing, pain would calm him down. It was almost funny, in a sick way. Pain was what he needed to calm him down so that he could inflict pain. That was rich.

He almost laughed, but held it in, concentrated on the taste of blood on his tongue like he had a mouth full of pennies.

The jabbing pain *hurt.*

Concentrate.

His racing thoughts slowed down. The water spiders

stopped whizzing across the glassy surface of his mind. The comets grew fewer and fewer, until his mind was finally still.

He took one deep breath and let it out, in through his nose, out through his mouth, slowly. His hands stopped shaking, he felt good, normal, centered. More than that. Excited wasn't the right word. Anticipatory, that was the right word, that's what he felt. He was ready now, he could do it.

A small smile creased his lips, and he grimaced from the pain of the place where he had bitten himself. As he stood there calmly, his senses became more and more acute, more aware. That's what he needed. He wanted all five of his senses to record the next few minutes for him, so that he could replay them again and again.

He was going to kill her, oh my yes indeed he was, he was going to kill her and he was going to *enjoy* it. He really hadn't enjoyed his first, at least not to the fullest. But he supposed the first time you did anything, you couldn't fully appreciate the cosmic nature of it. Your mind didn't, your mind was so occupied with the doing that it didn't record the event in the kind of detail you'd like. But this time, this second time, he was not a virgin anymore. This time he would record and savor every second.

For a time tonight, after the first one, he had trembled uncontrollably. Went into the little janitor's closet and closed the door behind him so no one would see. Since then, he had processed, had to shake hands with the fact that he was not the man he had been yesterday, would never be that man again. He had crossed a line into a world of extremes, and it was like being drunk and high and the best sex he ever had. The *power* of taking a human life. The man he had been, what seemed like a year ago, ten years, a century, a geologic epic was so flat and feature-less and pathetic.

Seeing the blood and hearing the bones crack had awakened a hunger in the very depths of his soul. He had to feed that voracious hunger. Would he have to feed that hunger his whole life? Is that what serial killers experienced?

It struck him then, like a bolt of bright light, that in a few minutes, he would be a serial killer too. How very odd a thought. Odd and perfect in a way he couldn't have articulated but understood somewhere deep inside himself. It was remarkable that he had come so far, so fast. But he was at peace with that. More than at peace, he gloried in it. This was who he really was, this man standing here, armed and ready.

Armed, he smiled at that. Yes, he was armed with the perfect weapon, which he had stolen from his victim without her even noticing. How flawless was that? It was the stars aligning just right in the universe, putting their blessing on him and the act of violence he was about to commit.

He was suddenly alert. There she was! He had followed her for a while, looking for a chance, hoping for an opening. And then he lost her in the crowd. He had searched the whole boat, up and down, and could find her nowhere. But there she was.

He leaned against the wall down from the bathrooms with his phone in his hand, looking at the screen as if absolutely absorbed in something when it wasn't even turned on. A crowd of people passed by him, but once he caught sight of her, it was like she was the only person in the room. It was like she glowed. Like he could have followed her light in absolute darkness.

His heart took up a staccato rhythm in his chest. She

was coming this way. He didn't move, didn't raise his head from his phone, just watched her out the corner of his eye as she approached. No one spoke to her. She was a pariah now. No one quite knew what to do with her, and when people don't know what to do, they slink away and pretend not to notice. She was weaving in and out among the people who pretended she wasn't there in the way of a person intent on a destination. And his heart leapt in its throat when he realized her destination was the bathroom right next to where he was standing.

The bathroom had one entrance, and after you walked in, ladies went to the right, gents went to the left. He had been in the men's room and supposed the ladies' room looked the same, except for the absence of urinals. As soon as you rounded the corner from the dual entrance into the men's restroom, there was a lounge area/sitting room with chairs and a settee, lamps, coffee, and end tables. The doorway from there into the bathroom was on the other side. The bathroom was divided in two — one side with a row of sinks on the left and six stalls and six urinals on the right, and a mirror image one on the other side of it where the sinks were on the right wall and the stalls and urinals on the left. He had watched women filing in and out of it for the last half hour as he stood pretending to be interested, oh so interested, in what was on his phone.

She kept coming. And coming.

He watched her pass, felt her presence, smelled her perfume, and fingered the weapon he had taken from her, the murder weapon she was providing to him. And he wanted to laugh again, but he didn't.

A group of women went in right after she did, and his hopes sank. One was the loudmouth teller at the bank, and she could talk for hours. But from their chatter it appeared they only wanted to wash a spot off the loudmouth's dress, then they came right back out. He waited. One beat. Two. She was in there alone. Did he dare? He'd never get a better chance.

He moved like a shadow into the room after her. After his prey.

Chapter Twenty-Six

As RILEIGH WENT to find Ian in the spa, she remembered the first time she'd had a run-in with the Save Gum Tree Hollow Association, though she hadn't known that's what it was at the time. She had been doing the same thing she was doing right now, which was going to look for Ian. Georgia had said that day he was on his way to the old Wheaton Estate outside Gatlinburg, and Rileigh needed to talk to him about the murder she was investigating. She had just found out from Georgia what had happened the night before Jillian's wedding: Jillian had come home and caught her own father molesting Georgia. She had taken Georgia home and told Georgia's older brother Ian that she was going to the police. Ian had gone to Jillian later that night to beg her not to, because Georgia didn't want to have to testify.

Rileigh had had no idea what had happened all those years ago on the night Jillian disappeared. Georgia had never told her. As Rileigh had driven from Black Bear Forge to the Wheaton Estate outside Gatlinburg, she had mulled over all the horrible things she'd just found out and came to the erroneous conclusion that perhaps Ian had killed Jillian. He had gone to her that night to plead with her not to go to the police because his baby sister didn't want to have to testify. When Jillian refused, Rileigh assumed Ian killed her. As she looked back on it now, it was hard for Rileigh to believe that she had ever come up with such an outlandish idea. That day, she'd meant to confront Ian, demand to know the truth.

But before she ever got there, odd things happened. The Wheaton Estate was out in the middle of nowhere off a seldom-traveled road. But there was a car in front of Rileigh before the Wheaton Estate turnoff, and that car had suddenly turned off up an old logging road that Rileigh didn't know anybody ever used. She watched the headlights go up the mountain and then saw taillights come on, meaning the car had stopped up there. That was odd.

She wrote it off until a few moments later, when a car approached from the other direction, passed Rileigh, and damned if it didn't turn off at that logging road, too. She watched its headlights go up the mountainside, saw the brake lights come on, then saw a dome light and someone get out of the car. Rileigh pulled over to the side of the road, turned her own headlights off so they wouldn't see her, and watched as two little flashlight beams went through the woods.

She feared that perhaps she had stumbled upon the big bad drug operation that was whispered about in Yarmouth County, the kind of thing that was probably rural myth, but nobody knew. And because she feared that it might be dangerous, she had sneaked up to the house to peek in the window and see what was going on. Unfortunately, she got caught. Somebody stuck a gun in her back, put a ski mask over her head so she couldn't see, and took her inside.

She was terrified.

Finally, the people she couldn't see left her alone in a room, and she started trying to wiggle out of her restraints when she heard a familiar voice. It was Ian. He yanked the ski mask off her head and took the duct tape off her hands, berating her the whole time.

Why had she sneaked up on the house? Why had she been peeking in the windows? What was wrong with her?

She told him she thought she had stumbled onto drug dealers and demanded to know what the hell those people were doing up in the woods in the middle of the night. Why did somebody stick a gun in her back? Why did they put a mask over her face so she couldn't identify them?

Ian wouldn't tell her, said it was none of her business, that those people were not breaking the law. He paused then and said the word that slid ice down her spine. "They're not doing anything illegal … *yet.*"

It was a long time before Rileigh figured out that the people she had stumbled upon were the unknown members of the Save Gum Tree Hollow Association. When she'd confronted Ian about that, he had told her that one day, she was going to have to pick a side.

At the zoning board meeting Monday night, Ian had called out the troops. People leapt to their feet and held up signs, yelling, until the protest got out of hand and people were arrested.

Now she had questions that Ian was going to have to answer.

She got to the door of the spa and shoved it inward and the light came on. Brightness filled the room. She was surprised to see Ian sitting there in one of the comfortable chairs just inside the spa.

"What were you doing sitting in here in the dark?"

"Thinking. The lights are on a timer and it just went

off. Before I could turn it back on, you came in."

Rileigh sat down in a chair beside him. "You're sitting in here while everybody else is out there. What are you hiding from?"

Ian sighed.

"I knew as soon as somebody killed Hunter Dobson that the coonhounds were going to be on my trail."

"That makes me a coonhound?"

"Well, are you?"

"If by being a coonhound you mean, am I the representative of law enforcement coming to talk to a man who had every reason in the world to kill the guy who just got murdered, then yeah, I'm a coonhound."

"Do you think I did it? Is that it?" Ian got to his feet and began to pace. "You think I killed Hunter Dobson?"

"Ian, you are in the unfortunate position of having to prove you're innocent. You're the guy with the target on his back. Everybody knows you're the head of the Save Gum Tree Hollow Association and that association wanted to get rid of Hunter Dobson."

"What do you want me to say, Rileigh? You want me to tell you that I didn't do it? Okay, I didn't do it. You want me to prove that I didn't? How can I prove a negative?"

"I came to talk to you because I'm what's standing between you and Mitch. If you'll talk to me, you won't have to talk to him. But if you won't …"

"Fine, I'll talk to you. What do you want to know?"

"Where were you when Dobson was murdered?"

"I was standing in the back of the room. The curtains opened and there he was on the stage, dead."

"Did anybody see you standing back there? Georgia said that you vanished after the two of you came on the boat and she didn't see you again. You ditched her, didn't you?"

"Why would I do a thing like that?"

"So that you could hang out with your Save Gum Tree Hollow Association buddies without her knowing who they were."

Ian said nothing. So Rileigh continued. "Why did you come here tonight, Ian?"

He looked uncomfortable and didn't answer.

"Come on, tell me. Everybody who was opposed to that project called tonight's cruise a bribe. I'd think you wouldn't want to be here. So why did you come?"

"I can't answer that."

"You mean won't answer."

"All right, won't answer."

"Fine. Don't answer me. But Mitch is going to ask the same question and he's not going to take *I don't want to talk about it.*"

Ian sighed, plopped back down on the chair, and looked Rileigh in the eye.

"I was worried about what might happen tonight, okay? That's why I came."

"You thought somebody was going to kill –"

"Hell no, I didn't think somebody was going to kill him, but …" He looked uncomfortable, then finally finished the sentence. "But there is one loose cannon, shall we say, in the group. One of the members is more inclined to take the law into his own hands than we'd like."

"You're saying one of your group damaged that construction equipment?"

"I don't know whether he did or not. I just know I was worried about him. He's a hothead. I didn't want him to get into a fistfight with Hunter Dobson, so I came to make sure that didn't happen."

"Where was this loose cannon when Hunter Dobson was murdered?"

Ian looked at the floor between his feet. "I don't know. That's why I was standing in the back of the room. I was scanning the crowd, trying to find him. I'd been talking to him, trying to talk him off the ledge, and he got mad and stormed off. After that, I couldn't find him. Then the lights went off, the curtains opened, the lights came on, and there sat Hunter Dobson, dead."

"Do you think this loose cannon killed him?"

"No, I don't think so." He sighed. "I don't *want* to think so. I just don't know."

"Who is this guy?"

"You think I'm going to tell you that?"

"You're going to tell me or you're going to tell Mitch."

"I'm not going to tell anybody. I'll handle this."

"Like the spectacular job you've done handling it so far?"

"Damn it, Rileigh. Just trust me on this, okay? I know the guy. I'll find out where he was."

"You think he'll tell you the truth?"

"I'll know if he's lying."

There wasn't anything else Rileigh could do. She had no way to force Ian to give her the name.

"I'll find him," Ian continued. "I'll talk to him. And if I'm suspicious, I'll tell you. Fair enough?"

"No, it's not fair at all, but you're holding all the cards."

Rileigh stood up and started for the door.

"Rileigh, girl, you remember what I said."

She turned back around to face Ian.

"Don't be on the wrong side of this," he said. "You're a homie. These are our mountains. Those people are destroying them. I told you that one of these days you were going to have to pick a side. Well, that day has come. Whose side are you on, Rileigh?"

Chapter Twenty-Seven

THE KILLER STEPPED QUICKLY into the alcove where the bathrooms divided, moved through the doorway on the women's side, and crossed the lounge area into the bathroom beyond. These stalls had a red tag that flipped up when they were occupied, and all of these were empty. He went without making a sound. He went to the second set of sinks and stalls. None of them had a red flag except the one at the end, the big one, the handicapped stall. That's where Ruby Cunningham was.

He went down the row of stalls and stepped into the one next to Ruby. He knew she could see his feet from where she was seated and would be able to tell that they were men's shoes. Still, this was a costume party — women could be wearing anything. And besides, he could hear the sniffling. He doubted that she was firing on enough cylinders to even notice. The deathly pale woman who had crossed the lounge toward him looked like she'd aged ten years, and seemed to be oblivious to her surroundings.

He stood waiting, listening, growing more and more

tense by the second. They were alone in here right now, but that wouldn't last. *Come on*, he thought. Do your business and leave.

He realized then that there was no sound coming from her stall, not the sound of pee hitting water, nothing. She was probably just sitting in there, wanted somewhere to get away from the crowd and cry.

Shit. If she was just sitting, she might stay for an hour, and he didn't have that long.

He stepped out of the stall next to hers and in front of the door so she couldn't see any part of him through the crack. Then he knocked on it and whispered, "You're in the handicapped stall, honey, and I need it."

Ruby mumbled something about being sorry, and he heard her get to her feet. She didn't flush the toilet, so obviously she hadn't been using it. The door opened inward. The instant she put her hand on the latch, he threw all his weight against the door, slamming it into her, knocking her backward. The toilet caught her in the back of the knee and tripped her, and she sat back down.

He followed the door into the stall and all his movements snapped into fast forward, his actions too fast to follow. At the same time, the world shifted down into slow motion and he was merely a spectator, enjoying the show.

He watched himself slam her head backward into the wall.

He watched himself lift the knitting needle he'd stolen from her basket up like a stiletto.

He watched her face, saw recognition dawn there. She didn't fight back.

He returned to his body to *feel* the knitting needle puncture her left eyeball and slide through it into her brain.

Ruby tensed and began to jerk and wiggle and squirm. He didn't know if it was voluntary and she was trying to get away, or if it was simply the reaction to having a knitting needle jabbed into her brain. The movements didn't last long. Then she slumped, collapsed like all the air had been let out of her, and sat there on the toilet with her head against the wall, a knitting needle stuck in her left eye, blood surging down her face and dripping off her jaw.

Everything was still in slow motion. He so wanted to savor every second that he just stood there and looked at her, his heart pounding, a feeling of exhilaration like nothing he'd ever experienced in his life. Well, until he'd killed Hunter Dobson. But this was especially sweet because this time he had made himself record the experience. His senses were heightened, and he was sure that every second was recorded in minute detail, the feeling of her legs kicking out at him, the smell of the blood that pooled out of her eye, the look on her face. He would be able to replay it again and again and again.

The rubber band of time had been pulled too tight and snapped back. He was fully present here and now. He turned to go, but then he couldn't. Just one more, he thought, just one more. He reached down and grabbed the other knitting needle out of the bag at her side. It was sticking up as the first one had been when he'd passed her earlier in the evening and snatched it without her noticing. He pulled this one out of the ball of yarn and put it up to her other eyeball, her right eyeball, and shoved it slowly this time, deliciously slowly, gloriously slowly, feeling every inch of it as it popped through her eyeball and into her brain. He didn't stop shoving until the end of the needle hit the back of her skull.

He took one breath, two. Held his breath and felt the thrill in every nerve in his body.

Now he had to go. He reached into his pocket, pulled out the piece of cardboard and set it in her lap, then went out the door and closed it behind him. But it wasn't locked from the inside, so there was no red tag. Soon somebody would open that door, expecting that the stall was empty. How he wished he could watch their face.

He rushed past the other stalls and through the lounge area to the alcove that led to the men's/women's room opening and hurried across it into the men's room. It was empty too and he ran to the last stall, opened it and went inside and sat, his breathing ragged.

A man came in and went to the urinal. He waited until the man left, then left the stall, washed his hands in the sink, and passed a woman going into the ladies' room as he walked out the men's room door. She paid him no mind. He kept walking, back to the spot on the lounge wall down from the bathrooms where he'd been standing before, leaned against it and took out his phone.

His hands were shaking.

He looked at his watch. The whole thing, start to finish, had taken less than three minutes. Three of the longest, best minutes of his entire life. He would bet his life … actually, he *was* betting his life … that nobody had missed him. Most of the people in the crowd milling around the lounge had never noticed him, but those who had would swear he was leaning against that wall all evening, had never left that spot.

He waited. Watched two men go in the door, then come out. A woman who still wore her Dorothy from the Wizard of Oz costume went in and came back out. Two more women went in … and then he heard it, the shriek-ing, the screaming. It took a huge effort not to smile. He kept his face neutral, looking surprised like everyone else as the woman dressed as Peter Pan came running out of the bathroom wailing. It was one of the high points of his entire life.

As her shrieking ignited an explosion of response, he thought to himself, *that's two.*

There was only one left — Rileigh Bishop.

Chapter Twenty-Eight

MITCH FOUND Steve Cunningham by himself in a corner table in the bar. He was sitting in the only chair at the table, and Mitch suspected that he'd moved the other chair away so no one could come and sit with him.

Mitch walked to the table, pulled up a chair from the table next to it, and sat down.

"You're probably not looking for any company, are you?"

"Nope."

"I have a few questions I need to ask you, Mr. Cunningham, then I'll leave you alone."

Cunningham had taken off the top part of his piglet costume. It had a full head mask with a face cut out, and he could have pulled it down off the top of his head and left it dangling like the hood on a sweatshirt. Instead, he had taken off the whole top part of the costume, which left him in nothing but a wrinkled white t-shirt. Mitch was grateful then that he'd left his uniform on under his own costume. It was bad enough to be the barefoot sheriff. It would have been infinitely worse to be a barefoot sheriff in a t-shirt. Cunningham was wearing the bottom portion of the costume, the pig legs with a squiggly pig tail sticking out behind. Mitch was sure he had only left that much on because he had not worn any pants underneath and would have been left walking around in a t-shirt and his tighty-whities.

Mitch had never met Steve Cunningham. He looked to be a good deal older than his wife, Ruby, but perhaps he wasn't, perhaps he was just one of those men who didn't age very well. He was losing his hair on top, though it wasn't all gone. And Mitch usually found that to be a curse. In his experience, men who lost all their hair accepted it and moved on with life. Men who lost part of their hair bemoaned what they no longer had. They usually managed to convince themselves that what little hair they had left was sufficient to cover the tops of their heads and nobody would notice. This was seldom true.

Steve Cunningham appeared to have made that unfortunate decision. He likely didn't comb his hair this morning so much as place his hair where it would cover the most of his bare pink scalp. That was before he had taken off the piglet mask that sat on top of his head for hours. What little hair he had was in disarray like bedhead. And it was obvious that Steve Cunningham couldn't care less.

"If it was so clear to you I didn't want company, why did you sit down?"

"I just need to ask you a couple of questions, sir, and then I'll be on my way."

"Questions about what? You think *I* killed him?" There was such a note of incredulity in his voice that if Mitch had ever believed he was the killer, he'd have marked the man's name off the list now. Mitch had never really suspected him anyway. He just had to do the do, dot all the i's, cross all the t's.

Steve Cunningham took a big swig of the drink in front of him, looked around and held his glass in that "give me another one" gesture bar patrons have, and the steward came to take his order. "More of the same," he told the steward. "Bourbon on the rocks."

If he'd been knocking back double shots of bourbon ever since he sat down at this table, he had a remarkable tolerance for alcohol. Because his speech was not slurred, and he seemed cold sober.

"So I'm a murder suspect, am I?"

"I didn't say that."

"Well, why the hell else would you want to talk to me?"

The steward arrived then, gave him another drink, which, thanks to Dimitri Mikhailov was only half price. Yep, that's exactly what Mitch needed, a boat full of drunks.

"Where was I? Oh yes. Let me set your mind at ease, Sheriff Webster. I didn't kill Hunter Dobson. I didn't have any reason to. At least I didn't know I had a reason to until tonight." He barked out a sardonic laugh. "Maybe I would have killed the son of a bitch if I'd known."

He took another swig of his drink, and his demeanor changed. The hostility vanished, and he looked into Mitch's eyes with such pain in his own that Mitch felt sorry for him.

"But you see, I *didn't* know — not until tonight."

"You never even suspected."

He mulled that question over. "I suspected *something* was going on with Ruby." He barked out another harsh laugh. "But I sure as hell didn't think she was having an affair. That never occurred to me. Isn't that astonishing? It never even crossed my mind." He shook his head in sad disbelief.

"A few months ago, I can't remember when it was now, I would get home from work, and Ruby would be gone. There'd be a note on the table telling me she was going to some meeting or another, or to some girlfriend's house or another, or to a movie with a friend."

"Did you ask her about her evening when she got home?"

Cunningham snorted.

"I was in bed sound asleep by the time she got in." He smiled ruefully. "I'm that guy, the one who wakes up every morning at five o'clock, eyes pop open like you'd let go of one of those roll-down shades. My whole life, I've never been able to sleep in. I should have been a dairy farmer. And if you're a guy who wakes up every day at five o'clock and you're my age, you're in bed asleep by nine o'clock at night. I don't know what time Ruby got home. Midnight maybe."

He was sipping his drink now.

"After a while, I began to wonder what was going on. You want to know what an idiot I am? Let me tell you how blind I was. The only possible explanation I could come up with for Ruby being gone night after night was that she was doing something about the house. Ruby loved to decorate. The curtains, the wallpaper, everything was so spectacular people would ask for the name of our decorator. But she didn't just go out and buy curtains to match the wallpaper. She went out and bought fabric and *made* curtains to match the wallpaper. She didn't find a vase to put on the table that complemented the color of the fabric and the couch and the chair. She *made* a vase, went to ceramics class and learned how. She decided she wanted a parquet floor in the den. And when I told her we couldn't afford it, she showed up two weeks later with boxes of parquet flooring and proceeded to lay the floor herself."

"How'd she know how to do a thing like that?"

"YouTube videos."

When he said that last part, he slurred the word "tube" and Mitch could see the liquor getting to him.

"I figured she decided she was going to do something whiz-bang special. Maybe she was out, oh I don't know, taking lessons in how to weave so she could put hand-woven afghans on the couches. Or maybe she was learning how to make stained glass to replace the glass in the door. I even thought…"

He stopped then and swallowed hard. "I even thought maybe it was something about *me.*" He barked out another sad laugh. "You know, like maybe she decided to learn how to sew so she could make me a shirt."

He lost his composure a little bit then.

"Hell, I don't know. I was such an idiot. I never saw anything. I never saw it coming. And then suddenly…" He stopped himself then, grabbed hold of his emotions, took another drink, and set the glass down carefully on the table in front of him. "Full disclosure? I always wondered why she married me, and after she did, I always wondered why she stayed. A woman like that, a woman like Ruby. Oh, I get it — I was 'escape.' Her home life was dysfunctional on steroids, all those brothers and sisters and she was the oldest, taking care of all of them. That's why she didn't want any children. She'd already raised a house full. And I was a ticket out of there. I knew that at the time … but why *me?* Of course, Ruby was a bit of a late bloomer. She just got prettier the older she got." He looked down at his rumpled tee shirt. "And I just got fatter."

He held up his empty glass and communicated with hand gestures that he wanted more of the same.

"You want to know something really funny? I've been saving my mileage checks. I travel all the time. The company pays for the gas and then I get paid by the mile if I take my own car. I just about had enough socked away to surprise her. She always said she wanted to go to Europe, wanted to see Paris. I almost had enough."

He sat quiet then, looking into the bottom of his empty glass as if the answers to all the mysteries of life were written there in the last drops of bourbon. Would he divorce her? Try to put their lives and their marriage back together? Mitch couldn't imagine that would work. When you've held your wife in your arms as she sobs in devastation over another man, there probably wasn't any going back.

"Thank you for your time, Mr. Cunningham." Mitch started to get to his feet, scooted his chair back.

The man looked up at him with eyes that were suddenly wet. "What do I do now?" he said softly. "What's my life about now?"

Mitch had no answer for him, just said softly, "I don't know. I'm sorry."

He turned but hadn't even taken a step away from the table when the room exploded with an ear-piercing scream. He looked in the direction of the sound and a woman came running out of the lady's restroom, screaming, shrieking.

Mitch's stomach fell into his shoes. *No, please not again.*

Chapter Twenty-Nine

THE SHRIEK that sliced through the room cut deep into Mitchell Webster's soul, because he recognized the sound. He'd heard it before. It was the kind of deep-gut scream that had to be ripped out of a person by some unthinkable horror. He felt the blood rush out of his face. The sick feeling in his stomach was drawing all kinds of pictures in his mind, horror pictures, nightmare pictures, and he felt a genuine fear that even those images wouldn't be as bad as what he was about to see when he went into that bathroom.

He was up and moving before he even thought to leave. He was only a short distance from the bathroom and whatever was inside that had made the woman dressed as Peter Pan scream, but he didn't rush into the room with no thought. He had the presence of mind to look around. As far as he knew, there was only this one door in and out of the bathroom. So whoever had done whatever had happened in that bathroom had come out in the last few minutes *through these doors*. He looked around, trying to memorize who was nearby, trying to take a mental picture of the crowd as it stood.

The woman didn't stop screaming when she flew out of the room. She didn't stop running either. She barreled through the lounge, shrieking hysterically, ran up the stairs toward the casino and disappeared, trailing her scream in the air behind her like the tail on a kite.

After taking his mental snapshot, Mitch went slowly to the door of the bathroom and called out, "Is anybody in there?" There was only silence.

"I'm coming in," he called. More silence.

He didn't draw his sidearm because he really didn't think he was going to meet an adversary. He knew in his gut that he was going to come upon a scene in which the violence had already happened.

He went through the lounge area into the first bathroom. There was a set of stalls along one wall and sinks along the other. No one was in any of the stalls. He went around to the second side where the sinks were backed up against the other sinks and the wall, the far wall was occupied by bathroom stalls. He leaned over and could see that someone was in the last stall, the biggest one, the one for handicapped people. And that's not all he saw when he leaned over. He saw blood on the floor.

Somehow McCreary, materialized right behind him. Mitch hadn't seen him anywhere and how he'd got there so fast, he didn't know.

"What's going on?" McCreary asked.

"We're about to find out."

Mitch walked slowly to the last stall and used his elbow to open the door. It would be a useless endeavor to try to get prints off the door, given how many people had come and gone there, but the habit of leaving a crime scene pristine was well-ingrained.

What greeted him when the door swung open was a sight that would send any normal human being screaming out the door. A woman was sprawled on the toilet seat, her head thrown back against the wall. It was Ruby Cunningham. He'd been talking to her husband only moments before, knew that Steve had likely joined the crowd outside the bathroom to see what all the screaming was all about. Mitch had to keep him out of here. He'd tell the man his wife was dead, that'd be bad enough, but the man absolutely couldn't see this.

She was dressed in a Mother Goose costume with a basket on her side that contained yarn and knitting needles. He remembered it from watching it bounce against her leg as she ran screaming toward the stage where Hunter Dobson sat in an overstuffed chair with his skull caved in and his belly slashed open.

She had been murdered, savagely murdered. Only minutes ago. Mitch had been fifty feet away and hadn't known it. Apparently, she had died without making a sound. The murderer was out there somewhere in that crowd *right now.* Might have been standing just outside the door when Mitch went in.

How could death happen so fast, so close, and he could do absolutely nothing about it? Helplessness like a balled-up fist punched him in the gut.

McCreary stood just behind him and could see what he saw, and he heard the man suck in a gasp and make some kind of groaning sound. At that moment, he felt sorry for the head of security. He didn't know what McCreary's profession might have been in some other life, but being on the security team for a riverboat casino wasn't the kind of job where you encountered a lot of dead bodies, and certainly not brutally-murdered ones. Two of them in one night. The guy was holding it together pretty well, considering.

"What in the hell —?"

That's as much as McCreary got out, but he didn't have enough air to finish it.

Forcing his mind away from shock and horror into analytical mode, Mitch studied the scene, trying to take in every detail of what he saw. Applying the first touches of analysis to it as his eyes roamed over the woman's dead body.

Either she'd put up no fight or the struggle had been brief and she'd been overpowered quickly. Why hadn't she cried out? There was a crowd of people, people who could have come to her rescue, but if she'd made a sound, nobody had heard it.

There was very little blood. It was possible the killer had come out without a trace of it on him. Whoever had killed Hunter Dobson had to have been splattered with his blood, but maybe cut him open from behind to avoid the worst of it. Splatters from the head wound, though, would have been unavoidable. Mitch had been looking for those. He'd examined everyone he saw, looking for red splotches. But the killer could have washed the blood off, or could have changed clothes, or been wearing a costume where splotches wouldn't show up.

His first thought was that whoever killed Ruby Cunningham was enjoying himself. This was a passion killing. The first knitting needle jabbed into her eye killed her. So why the second? What was the point of sticking another knitting needle in her other eye?

He tried to put himself into the mind of the killer. He'd just killed a woman, in a crowded place where he could be discovered at any time. He'd taken an incredible chance to be so public about it, but he'd gotten away with it. Now was the time to run, to make his get-away as clean as the killing had been. But the killer hadn't run away. He had taken another knitting needle from the basket at Ruby Cunningham's side and stabbed it into her other eye. Why?

They were dealing with one sick bastard, or someone motivated by an emotion Mitch had never felt and never would.

The murder of Hunter Dobson, the savage blows to the head and then the evisceration, spoke of such a violent emotion it was hard to fathom.

"Oh shit," McCreary said, and Mitch followed his gaze. There was a piece of cardboard lying in Ruby's lap. It had probably been set up so that whoever found the body would see it immediately. But it had fallen over, was lying face down in her lap, and Mitch hadn't noticed it right away. It was made from the same material as the piece of cardboard they found in Hunter Dobson's lap. Only this one didn't have the number one on it.

This one had the number two.

Chapter Thirty

RILEIGH PUSHED her way through the crowd jammed in front of the bathroom door. It was so tight she could barely wedge herself between bodies. She wanted to scream in anxious discomfort, but she wanted way more to get into that bathroom and see if, please God, tell me no, the rumor that had blown through the crowd like wind through wheat was true.

The jam-packed crush of people blocking the door refused to move when she tried to push through. She finally elbowed Howard Tanker and snarled in his ear, "Get out of my way, I want through."

The man looked at her and babbled, "They say she's dead. Did you hear? They say she's dead. Somebody stabbed her or cut her throat, maybe strangled her. They say she's dead."

"I need for you to get out of my way." Rileigh spaced the words out slowly and with emphasis. "The sheriff needs my help. In there."

Howard looked at her, then actually *looked* at her and saw who she was. He stepped back out of her way, using his long arms to drag the people around him away so Rileigh could squeeze through.

The man dressed as the dwarf, Doc, one of the security team members, stood as the final barricade in front of the door. He recognized Rileigh and let her in.

She stepped into the empty lounge area of the bathroom and walked through it slowly toward a sight she didn't want to see but knew was there, glancing into the first set of toilet stalls and sinks. She saw no one.

The door to the second set was blocked by a dwarf whose orange hat identified him as Bashful. She'd seen them all now, except for Dopey, who was bound to be around somewhere. Bashful wasn't there to keep people away, was not the final line of defense against the crowds pouring into the bathroom or anything like that. He was standing there mostly slack-jawed, like he'd wandered in off the street and didn't quite know where he was.

She pushed gently past him, into the room. The small room. The small *windowless* room with walls that were already beginning to feel closer.

Whatever there was to see was in the stall at the very end of the room, where Mitch and Gus stood. Rileigh resolutely forced herself to walk to them without hesitation. Gus was leaning over the body of a woman who was seated on the toilet. Her head was leaned back against the wall behind the toilet and knitting needles protruded from both of her gouged-out eye sockets. Rileigh was horrified, could say nothing. *It was Ruby Cunningham.*

Ruby, who had bared her soul to Rileigh earlier that evening, admitting that she had loved the man she was having an affair with and that they were going to run off together. Of course, that would never happen. The man was dead. And now so was Ruby.

Rileigh was so staggered by the sight that it was all she

could do not to step back from it, not to gasp, not to cry out, not to react in some way. But she managed to hold onto it, gritted her teeth, balled her hands into fists, and asked Mitch quietly, "Tell me about it."

"Nothing to tell. I was talking to Steve Cunningham." He looked at her then, made eye contact. "I was talking to this woman's husband while she was being murdered."

The wrecking ball of his words slammed full into Rileigh and almost knocked her off her feet.

"Yeah, right pal," Gus said, "So that makes it all your fault."

Mitch shot Gus a look so hostile Rileigh thought he might hit him. Then Mitch moved his neck as though he was trying to pop it, visibly relaxed, and stepped back.

Gus answered Rileigh's question, "You know almost as much as we do. Mitch was talking to Steve Cunningham. I was on that settee in the lounge, was sitting on half of it and had my feet under the cushion of the other half. Then suddenly I heard this woman shrieking."

"It's just ... what? I don't even know the word. Stunning? Staggering. Something more than that to believe that it could have happened this fast in this small space with this jammed-together group of people. Somebody could commit a murder and get away with it." Gus stopped. "Well, they committed a murder. We'll see if they get away with it."

"Excuse me for a minute," Mitch said and stepped aside, pulled out his telephone, and began to talk into the notes app. A string of names, one after another, at least a dozen, maybe more. He stopped, thought, then added another. And another.

Rileigh stood and listened, unable to drag her eyes away from the woman who lay there dead. So recently dead that her cheeks were still pink.

When Mitch stepped back to the other two, he said, "I wanted to get that down while I could still remember it. Before I came into the bathroom, I looked around and tried to memorize everyone who was standing in close proximity to these doors. That's the list of those people whose names I know. I'll remember the others' faces, point them out to you when I see them, and you can add them to the list. Whoever killed her couldn't have gone far."

"Almost bloodless way to commit murder," Gus said, nodding toward Ruby's face. "It's hard to imagine how this guy killed Dobson and didn't get splattered with blood, but there wouldn't have been much trace here."

"Why?" Rileigh said the word quietly, and it wasn't even a question.

"Why wasn't there much blood? Because the eyeball—"

"No, why Hunter Dobson and then Ruby Cunningham?"

"And why 'number two'?" Mitch nodded toward what Rileigh had not yet noticed: the piece of cardboard in Ruby Cunningham's lap with the number two on it.

"Holy shit."

"I'll see that holy shit and raise you one," Gus said.

"What is going on here?"

"Whatever it is, it's not random," Mitch said. "Somebody thought this out, planned and organized it. And it all means something. We don't know what right now, but it all means something."

"Where were you?" Mitch looked at Rileigh. "When—"

"When we heard the commotion, I was in the spa talking to Ian McGinnis."

"Well, I guess that lets him off the hook," Gus said.

"He never was on the hook," Rileigh snapped. She shook her head slightly to herself then reached out and lightly touched Gus's arm. "I'm sorry. I didn't mean to bite your head off."

Mitch carefully stepped out from where he had been standing on the right side of Ruby's body, and Gus did the same on the left. Both men backed out of the toilet stall, and with Mitch no longer leaning against it, the door slowly closed behind them, hiding the gruesome sight of Ruby's corpse.

"Now we have to protect the integrity of two crime scenes," Gus said.

Mitch looked at the young security guard who was standing in the doorway of the bathroom, the one who looked like he'd been washed up on the shore by a big wave.

"No one is to get past you into this bathroom," Mitch told him. "No one."

The young man looked startled and then said, "Yes sir. I mean, no sir, nobody will get past me."

"That means *nobody*. Not her husband, not the mayor or the governor or the president of the United States. Nobody comes into this bathroom. Are we clear?"

"We're clear, sir." Mitch turned toward Rileigh and Gus and sighed. "I have to go talk to Steve Cunningham."

The room was instantly silent and still. Rileigh was glad that wasn't her job, and she was sure Gus felt the same.

"Afterward, it'll be time for a rerun of the Mitch show." Gus crinkled his brow, but Rileigh knew what he meant.

"Do you really think it's necessary? Everybody already knows."

"Everybody thinks they know. Nobody knows the whole thing. All of these people are entitled to that information. And it's my job to give it to them."

"At least this time you'll have shoes on," Gus said.

Chapter Thirty-One

SHERIFF MITCH WEBSTER stepped back up in front of a microphone for the second time in only a handful of hours, but this time he wasn't about to deliver new information.

But what he was about to say now would be new information to nobody.

The crowd was restless and grumbling and scared. You could see it in their eyes, and why wouldn't they be? They were stuck, they were captives here on this boat where a murderer was prowling around, and for all they knew, killing people at random. The folks on the zoning board looked like terrified rabbits and Mitch didn't blame them.

"May I have your attention, please?" he said into the microphone, but the crowd didn't immediately quiet as they had before. The grumbling and rumbling were venting emotions, and at this point, they weren't in a frame of mind to take orders from anybody.

Mitch spoke louder and more authoritatively. "I need your attention, please."

That quieted the crowd, so Mitch went about telling a couple hundred scared people what they already knew.

"I know this isn't news to anybody, but there has been a second murder."

The crowd went off again, became a rumbling, grumbling, unruly mob. There were cries from among them, not surprise, but disbelief. Mitch tried to put himself in their shoes and he knew that he'd have been as scared and disoriented and probably as uncooperative as they were being.

"As I'm sure you've all heard, Ruby Cunningham was murdered a short time ago in the ladies' room off the lounge."

"I was in there right before she was," cried a voice. "You think the murderer was hiding when I went in there to pee?"

"That killer was in there when I was in there. I'm just sure he was I could just … sense something … evil."

"How could this happen right under…?"

Mitch called out a couple of times for quiet before the rumble of the crowd silenced enough that he could speak.

"They're working as hard as they can to get the fire under the boiler hot enough to produce steam so we can get back to the dock. But the last time I checked, the engineer said it would be several more hours, and that's as good an estimate as he could give me."

"Several more hours?" somebody cried. "We're gonna be stuck here all night!"

"Can't somebody come and get us off this boat?" someone else said.

"There's a murderer here in this room," somebody else cried. "Right here, right now!"

The emotion level was rising with every exclamation. Mitch grabbed hold as best he could and called for order.

"From now on, every person in this room is to stay here on the main deck. I don't want anybody wandering around outside or on one of the other decks. Stay in the Grand Salon, the casino, or the lounge on the bow of the boat."

"There's a dead body in the … in the *bathroom*," a woman said. "Where are we supposed to …? How are—?"

"There are two other ladies' restrooms on this deck. One on the far corner over there," and he pointed toward the starboard side of the boat, "and another two in the dining room."

"Yeah, in the dining room where there's a dead body on the stage."

The rumble that came after that was hard to silence. But when Mitch could finally speak again, his voice was quiet.

"I don't blame you for being scared. I wish there was more we could do to help you. We're all stuck here until that boiler has enough steam to run the paddlewheel."

"How did she die?" Someone called out.

"Somebody said her throat was cut."

"She was stabbed."

"Somebody strangled her."

"We need to get off this boat," cried Estrella Alvarez. She was dressed as Peter Pan and her husband, Mateo — dressed as Captain Hook — was a member of the zoning board. "Aren't there any lifeboats? Couldn't we just get lifeboats and row to shore?"

"In that ice storm out there, visibility is about 10 feet. You can't really believe it's a good idea to go get in a boat in the freezing rain and try to row three miles to a shore you can't see."

"What's going on here, Sheriff?" Adrian Onassis, dressed as Charlie Brown to his wife's Lucy, was another member of the zoning board. "None of this makes any sense. Why did somebody disable the engine? Why does somebody want us stuck out here?"

Mitch just shook his head. "I don't have any answers for your questions. I wish I did. I don't have any way to get you off this boat. I wish I did."

He paused, then let his eyes trail over the crowd, from one person to the next, for several seconds before he continued.

"Someone among us is a killer." There was a single squeak cry, but no one else reacted. "I said it before and I will say it again. Our only safety is in numbers. Do not, I repeat, do *not* go *anywhere* by yourself. The two victims of this killer were only alone for a few minutes and that was all it took. So, stick together."

Mitch didn't have anything else to tell them. He wished he did. He felt so damned helpless. "Thank you for your time. I will keep you posted on the progress in the engine room."

Then he turned and stepped away from the microphone. He was as certain as he was of sunrise on Easter Sunday morning that it was going to get ugly in this crowd pretty soon. The tension, the fear, the uncertainty, and the damned alcohol that the first mate had made half price were a volatile cocktail that he was sure was going to explode eventually.

Hunter Dobson carried on him the same stamp of disapproval that Mitch did. He was not local. He was from Away From Here, and though Dobson's death certainly dismayed, distressed, and terrified the people on the boat, it wasn't like any of them were his relatives or best friends. The same could *not* be said of Ruby. Her husband was here. When Mitch had told him about his wife, he had broken down and sobbed. Steve's brother, Mike, and his wife were in the crowd.

As a doctor, Gus had requisitioned some medical supplies from the paramedics and gave Steve an injection. Not enough to knock him out, but enough to fuzzy the world so his gut-wrenching grief would not rip him apart. There were several supply rooms on this deck, and Mitch had asked the captain to get crew members to empty them of whatever was in them. The empty rooms were small, but they were private. The crew dragged in some furniture, a couch and some chairs, and Gus made Steve Cunningham as comfortable as he could in one of the rooms.

Skylar had refused everybody's help, demanded to be left alone, sat at the bar knocking back drinks until she was so drunk she was unaware of her own grief. Gus had made her comfortable on a settee with some pillows and blankets in the dining room, in a corner away from the crowds.

It was all they could do, and it wasn't enough.

Mitch looked up and saw Mayor Rutherford, and he knew at that moment what a rabbit felt like when it saw an eagle with talons bared swooping down on it.

If Rutherford had been a cartoon, a real cartoon instead of a pretend one, he would have had steam coming out of his ears. He had removed the long Pinocchio nose, but still wore the little puppet's clothes — shirt, shorts, suspenders, a big blue bowtie, and a hat with a red feather in the band. He stormed up to Mitch and stood too close, as if to intimidate him. Mitch didn't budge, and the mayor stepped back and said harshly, "We need to talk."

"What would you like to talk about, Mayor Rutherford?"

"Not here."

"I just told all these people to stay in one room, to stay together. I'm not leaving them."

"Over here then," the mayor said, and reached up to

take Mitch by the arm and drag him over into the corner. But he saw the look in Mitch's eye before he touched him and dropped his hand. He stomped over to a corner away from most of the other people in the room. Mitch walked up and stood in front of him in a stance the military called parade rest. Feet apart, hands clasped behind him.

"What would you like to talk to me about, sir?"

"As if you don't know — what the hell is going on here?"

"Mayor Rutherford, I wish I knew."

"It's your *job* to know. Why the hell don't you? That woman was murdered within fifty feet of where you were sitting and you didn't do a damn thing!"

Mitch almost lost it, but didn't. He did grind his feet, and the mayor saw the gesture.

"Do you think I'd have sat there and done nothing if I had known what was happening? If I'd known some batshit-crazy lunatic was stabbing knitting needles into Ruby Cunningham's eyes? Are you insane?"

The mayor backed off a bit then, but he was under too full a head of steam to be intimidated for long by the bigger, stronger, younger sheriff of Yarmouth County.

"You have to … this has got to stop, Sheriff. These people are my responsibility and–"

"They're *my* responsibility too."

"And two of them have been murdered while they were in your care!" The mayor regrouped, said the next words carefully and quietly. "Listen to me, Sheriff Webster because I'm not going to say it but once."

Mitch knew what he was going to say. He was going to tell Mitch that if he didn't do fill-in-the-blank, the mayor was going to fire him. Mitch had heard this speech before.

"If anybody else among these people is harmed in any way, and I mean if one of them falls down and stubs their toe, you are fired. You got that? And Melissa Mendoza from WATE News won't be able to save your ass this time."

Mitch looked at him coldly, considered punching him out, and discarded the notion immediately. But he was damn well not going to take a dressing down about this.

"And you listen to me, Mayor Rutherford. I have done everything humanly possible to ensure the safety of the people in this boat, and I will continue to do so. Do you really think threatening to fire me will make me ... what? *Try harder*?"

Mitch could tell that the mayor was disappointed that his threat had not put the fear of God in Mitch's soul. And that pissed Mitch off worse than anything the mayor had said. Mitch drew in a slow breath as the mayor stood fuming and fumbling, trying to come up with an impressive retort and not finding it anywhere inside him.

Mitch watched the mayor try to puff himself back up into his previous state of moral superiority, outrage, and self-righteous indignation, but he flat out did not have the air to do it.

He cast a final scowl at Mitch and started to storm off. Mitch couldn't let it go. Not this time. He grabbed the mayor by the upper arm and without even turning to face him, leaned in and said,

"Go ahead! Fire me. *Make my day.*"

The mayor's ears turned bright red, probably the rest of his face did, too, but Mitch couldn't see it. It would have been comical, and god knows Mitch needed something to lighten his mood right now.

Then the mayor wrapped his tattered dignity around him and stormed away.

Chapter Thirty-Two

"PLEASE TELL me you've come to kidnap me and take me to a remote cabin somewhere in the woods and ravish me."

That's what Yarmouth County Fire Chief Pete Brady had said to Rileigh the last time she'd seen him — last summer, when the Good GI's, Gatlinburg Investigations, had hired her to investigate some suspicious insurance claims for fires that'd been classified as arson.

When she'd declined his offer, Pete had countered.

"What do you say we skip the kidnapping part and I come along voluntarily?"

Pete Brady was a big bear of a man who'd gone to high school with Rileigh and had had a crush on her for years. The reason that conversation had come to mind now, as Rileigh stood in the lounge of the Queen of the Smokies paddlewheel boat investigating *two* murders, was the interaction between Pete and Ian McGinnis on the other side of the room.

Maybe it meant absolutely nothing at all, but then again...

Rileigh had been watching Ian whenever she got a

chance, seeing who he spoke to. Pete was dressed as Santa Claus, which wasn't exactly a storybook character, but he already had the suit. In fact, it was probably getting worn out by now. He had worn it in every Christmas parade in Black Bear Forge for the last five years.

What interested her about the conversation between Ian McGinnis and Pete Brady now was that it looked like, at least from afar, an argument.

Pete Brady was about as genial a man as you would find anywhere, and it was almost difficult to imagine him angry. But he was angry now. You could tell it even in a Santa Claus suit, though he had taken off the beard, the long hair, and the red hat with the fur-ball.

Earlier, Ian had said that the members of the Gum Tree Hollow Association were righteous citizens who would never even think of jaywalking … well, except for maybe one loose cannon.

It was as hard to imagine Pete Brady a loose cannon as it was to imagine him angry. He was such a kind and gentle man. But he was a man who deeply loved the Smoky Mountains, had become the fire chief after a stint as a forest ranger in the Great Smoky Mountains National Park. For him, and for the rest of Yarmouth County, the emotions ran bone deep and raw when they'd learned that the last pristine hollow in the whole county was in danger. That it was about to be destroyed by commercialization. It had been pure D bullshit, and the people at the zoning board could smell the stink when Hunter Dobson said his development in Gum Tree Hollow was "for people to come and raise families."

If the people who'd be living in the outrageously expensive homes that man was going to build were raising families, they weren't doing it in Yarmouth County. Their children wouldn't go to Yarmouth County schools with other county children. Gum Tree Hollow was about to be raped and pillaged, trees cut down, land bulldozed to make way for houses for *rich* people — from Nashville, Knoxville, Atlanta, Chattanooga — people who had no interest in these mountains except as a good place to build an expensive vacation home where they could spend a couple of weeks every summer.

Yarmouth County was fed up with being trampled by fast-talking hucksters. They had drawn a line in the sand in front of Gum Tree Hollow and said, *no more! This is the hill we're all willing to die on.*

It was possible a man like Pete Brady had got caught up in all that and had become Ian's loose cannon. Maybe he'd gotten so riled up he'd gone over the edge for the cause.

It was absolutely inconceivable that Pete Brady had committed murder. In truth, it was unfathomable that anybody in that room had done it. But somebody had. Twice.

She made her way, as surreptitiously as it was possible to do in a crowd of people, to where Ian and Pete were now almost shouting at each other. She could hear their raised voices the closer she got, but she couldn't catch what they were saying. Suddenly, she felt fingers grip her upper arm and squeeze, and she turned to find ...

"Mama?"

"It's Cinderella!" her mother cried, as excited as Rileigh had ever seen her. "I saw her. Jillian's here, she came to the party tonight dressed as Cinderella."

As if that statement weren't shocking enough, suddenly all the lights in the room went out.

A communal gasp rose from the crowd at the sudden darkness. There were cries of alarm. You could feel the surprise and fear. And then a voice rose above the others that she recognized as the ship's captain.

"This is Captain Rowe," he called out. "Please remain calm. The emergency generators will kick in in just a minute or two. That ice storm out there is wreaking havoc on our electrical systems."

As promised, shortly after he stopped speaking, the lights blinked back on, off again, then back on and stayed. The lights had a kind of golden glow to them rather than the crisp white of earlier, and she suspected that that was possibly due to lesser voltage going through the lines. But the lights were on. Definitely on.

Rileigh looked where Ian had been talking to Pete Brady. Ian was still standing there. Pete was gone. Then she turned back to her mother beside her, who had only moments before grabbed her arm. Mama was gone too.

Where could they both have gone in only a few moments of darkness?

Rileigh stood up on tiptoes, trying to see through the crowd of people to locate her little fairy godmother mother who'd been standing by her side, babbling something about ... For the first time, Rileigh connected to what her mother had been saying. She'd said that she'd seen Jillian dressed as Cinderella.

Rileigh shook it off — Mama's delusion. Still, she couldn't help searching the crowd for Cinderella as she tried to locate her mother and Pete.

A big man in a red Santa suit ought to be hard to miss, but she couldn't find him. The room was crowded with people milling around, and Rileigh was forced to stay on the move to keep out of big clots of people pressing in on her.

She had to admit she was proud of herself for coping as

well as she was. She absolutely had NOT wanted to come to a crowded party where she could get crushed in among the people. But she'd done it because she had to. She could either roll over and play dead, never go anywhere, watch her world shrink as the terror of claustrophobia took over her life. Or she could fight it. Rileigh had picked Plan B. That's why she'd come tonight, knowing she would be gritting her teeth and suffering waves of crippling anxiety.

But to her delight, the level of her anxiety, rather than getting worse as the evening wore on, was getting better. Unfortunately, she could lay much of the credit for her recovery at the feet of two dead people. She'd been forced to forget about herself and her personal emotional needs as soon as the curtains opened on the stage ... what? Three, four hours ago? — and Dobson sat there dead in a chair. And Ruby ... the sight of her with knitting needles in her eyes was so occupying her mind that she'd gone on something like autopilot, performing as a normal, rational human being would, not someone debilitated by a raging, irrational fear.

At the same time, she understood how fragile her rationality was. The monster was still hanging around in the wings, waiting for a chance to take center stage again.

Chapter Thirty-Three

FINALLY, Rileigh gave up and stepped up on a chair to get a better view of the crowd, trying to spot her mother's white hair in a bun or Pete's red Santa suit.

But even with an elevated view, she could see neither one of them. Someone tugged on her skirt. Georgia.

"Lost something?" Georgia asked.

"Someone."

"Let me guess. Lily's missing."

"Give that girl a Kewpie Doll." Rileigh climbed down off the chair. "I don't know how she got away from Millie. All I know is I was standing here, and she came running up to tell me she'd spotted Jillian dressed up as Cinderella. Then the lights went off, and when they came back up, she was gone."

"Knowing your mother, she's not likely to obey the rules and stay here in this room like the sheriff told everybody to do." Georgia set her jaw. "Okay, let's divide and conquer."

"You take this side of the room." Rileigh pointed to the starboard side of the lounge area. "And I'll take the other.

If we can't find her on this deck, we'll just have to break the rule–"

"And be the idiot in the slasher movie who goes off by themselves and–" Georgia started to make a slicing motion across her neck but stopped.

"That's not funny, is it?" she said softly, her face bleak.

"Oh, Mama's up here on this deck somewhere," Rileigh said, not at all convinced she was right. "We won't have to break the rule."

Georgia nodded and saluted.

"Be careful!" Rileigh called after her as Georgia marched off into the crowd, holding on to the recalcitrant red skirt made of duct tape that was losing its stickiness.

Rileigh searched among the clots of people standing and sitting together, talking in subdued tones. All of them were way past being in a party mood, most of them having taken off whatever part of their costume they could remove. Being dressed up as Mary Poppins didn't feel quite right anymore.

To add a pinch of spice to the evening, the lights continued to blink on and off periodically. When they were off, everyone hauled out their cell phones and tapped their flashlight apps. It felt a little like being in the audience at a rock concert.

She made two circuits of her area, then caught sight of Georgia on the other side of the room, who gave her a shrug indicating she hadn't found Mama either. So at the end of the third circuit, she left the room, and went up the steps to search the deck above. The buffet restaurant on Deck 3 was deserted, not surprising, since everybody had been ordered to stay together on the main deck.

Why had Mama gone wandering off?

For the same reason she thought she was dating Rhett Butler.

Rileigh went through the library and stuck her head in the empty video game room. Half an hour later, she was wandering around in the maze of passageways connecting the staterooms that had been closed up since Labor Day. She was hopelessly lost.

She shivered and hurried down the passageway. It was way too narrow, way, way too narrow, with nothing but doors opening off it one after another. It felt like being in an empty hotel.

Like the Overlook.

Now there was a grim comparison — this boat to the haunted hotel in Stephen King's *The Shining*, where the little boy kept reading **REDRUM** in the mirror without realizing it was **MURDER** spelled backwards.

No, couldn't think of that.

She saw an intersection up ahead and almost burst into a run to get to it, but when she arrived, there was no relief. Down all four points of the compass were more hallways. She felt her heart rate begin to gallop, felt that horrifying sensation of her gut tightening as the walls around her began to close in. Of the four offered alternatives, she picked going straight ahead. Seemed like a better plan than maybe going around in circles. She'd get to somewhere at the end of this passageway. She was sure of it. She managed not to run.

Until the lights went out.

The hallway went from brightly-lit — with white walls and doors, dozens of doors — to pitch darkness. It was like being inside a lump of coal. She staggered to the nearest wall, putting out her hand, leaning up against it, her heart, hammering, her breathing coming in horrified gasps.

Dark, dark and closed up. Have to get out of here. *Have to get out of here.* She couldn't help running then, couldn't stop herself. The farther she ran, the more terrified she got

— running blindly in the dark, like running *inside a coffin*. Her terror fed upon itself with every step. She heard herself making little squeaking sounds, not crying exactly, more like the sound a baby rabbit would make.

The lights flickered back on in the passageway.

Thank G—!

Her gasp of relief died in her throat when the light revealed the shadow of someone behind her.

Then the lights went out again.

She didn't scream, grabbed hold of reason and rationality, or maybe just reverted to training. A voice in her head commanded, "Down, soldier!" and Rileigh immediately dropped to her knees.

When she did, the person coming up from behind stumbled over her, tripped and fell on top of her.

Nightmare fighting in the dark.

Grabbing, grunting, clawing to find purchase, arms and legs going every which way.

Unable to get a hold on anything.

Unable to land a blow on anything.

She punched out wildly with her fist, connected with bone. A jaw. A knee.

She bared her fingernails like a cat and struck out to claw, racked them across … something.

A big fist caught her in the shoulder. A blow landed on her hip.

As she'd been taught in combat training, she used her elbows as weapons, sharp and hard. Jabbing into the void. She connected with something hard and lightning bolts of pain shot up her arm.

She kicked, hit something.

Lurching upward, she tried to throw the weight off her.

Then it was gone and she was fighting nothing at all. She heard running footsteps.

She rolled over onto her knees, didn't dare stand, crawled frantically forward in the opposite direction. She bounced off the wall, kept crawling …

The lights blinked back on. She turned toward where the attacker had run, crouched to launch herself at …

There was no one there, no one in front of her, no one behind. She leapt to her feet and took off in a dead run for the end of the passageway. She went through the door there into another equally-unadorned hallway and ran down it to the end. When she opened the door there, she came out into the open area in front of the library she had searched earlier.

How had she gotten turned around?

She stood panting, gasping for breath, trying to get in enough air. Even this bigger, more open space was not enough. She had to get out! Outside!

Racing down the corridor, she slammed through the door outside to the deck.

Stepping from the warmth of the boat into the blast of freezing cold outside was like being shocked back to life with paddles.

The cold smacked her in the face. Ice crystals the size of BBs attacked every piece of exposed flesh. She took another step, and her feet flew out from under her on the sheet of ice that'd formed on the deck. She crashed down hard on her butt and slid all the way to the railing. She lay there on her back, squinting up into the floodlights on the upper deck, gasping and crying. Her heart tried to hammer its way out of her chest.

The cold shocked all her senses, but the open space released the grip of panic in her gut. She lay where she was, her clothing beginning to stick to the sheet of ice beneath her.

When she got her breath, she was afraid to stand, but

crawled back to the door and pulled herself to her feet with the handle, opened it and fell inside the boat shivering.

She took a couple of steps and leaned against the wall, breathing the warm air, clutching the heavy fabric of her Red Riding Hood cape around—

Her fingers touched ragged cloth. When she held out the cape, she saw the hood and the back of the cape had been sliced apart.

The person in the hallway had had a knife. And if the blade hadn't snagged on that bulky hood and cape, she'd be lying there on the passageway floor with the knife stuck in her back.

Chapter Thirty-Four

As soon as Mitch could reasonably extract himself from conversations, he stepped away, wanting just a few minutes to himself to collect his thoughts, organize them, make sense of them.

His rage at the mealy-mouthed mayor's pathetic threat to fire him was like a flashfire. It had burned incredibly hot — maybe he should have decked the stupid son of a bitch — but it burned itself out fast, and when it was over, there wasn't even a pile of gray ash left behind to mark where it had been.

But the words the two of them exchanged still rang in Mitch's head like a gong, loud and insistent.

"These people are my responsibility," Mitch had told the mayor.

"And two of them have been murdered while they were in your care!" the mayor had retorted.

. . .

Maybe one of Mitch Webster's worst faults as a law enforcement officer was his propensity to get too involved in the cases he was working on, and this one was the hardest of his career. How do you get your mind around a murderer who strikes within, seventy-five yards of where you're sitting, not once but twice, and you can't do a thing but clean up after?

Mitch would have protested in very eloquent terms that what'd happened was not his fault. He wasn't responsible for the behavior of the killer. There was nothing he could have done. To think otherwise was absurd.

That's what he would say if you asked him. But if you didn't ask him, if you just listened to the voices in his soul whispering to each other, it would be a very different story. He'd warned them, suggested they stick together in groups, but he'd been trying to balance that warning with reassurance to keep them from panicking. If he'd been more vehement, insisted on a buddy system, would Ruby Cunningham still be alive?

The truth, hot and stinking on the stage with a spotlight on it, was that never in a million years did he imagine there would be *two* murders. The fact that there had been even one was stretching the bounds of probability. But two? Two on the same boat, over the space of three hours, it was insane. No one could have expected him to prepare for something like that.

But he should have.

He'd been talking to Ruby's husband while she was being murdered less than fifty yards away. You could slice and dice that any way you wanted, but that hurt. Of course, hindsight was always 20-20. Still, he should have done something specifically about the members of the zoning board. After Hunter Dobson's murder, it should have occurred to him that perhaps, just perhaps, one of the wacko looney tunes in the Save Gum Three Hollow Association was out for blood, intent on stopping development there no matter what the cost. If he had followed that reasonable line of logic, it would have directed him to the members of the zoning board. It would have suggested, at the very least, that maybe they were targets, too. That maybe he ought to do something to protect them. Dammit, if he'd done nothing more than what he'd just done — ordered all the passengers on the boat into a contained space and made them stay there — Ruby Cunningham would still be alive.

But he hadn't done that. He hadn't followed his gut. And Ruby Cunningham was dead.

He had met Ruby when he first came to town, when Sheriff Mumford, the man he was temporarily replacing, had taken him on a howdy-and-shake tour of the "important people" in the county before he left to have his knees replaced. Mitch scratched around in his mind for some memory of that time, something she had said, her smile maybe — anything to replace the image of her running toward the dead body of her lover on the stage, her face a rictus of profound grief.

Anything to replace the image of her face as she had died, her head tilted back and two knitting needles stabbed into her brain through her eyeballs. He didn't want to remember her like that, but he knew he would. He knew he would never be able to replace that image with the image of the woman Ruby had been before she became the second victim of a crazy killer.

Wandering near the windows on the side wall of the boat, he stared out into the nothing of sleet, fog, and freezing rain, a gray emptiness that lay around this summertime boat like a shroud.

But then he did see something. Some*one*. Two someones. There were two men standing on the deck right outside the window. One of them was the head of security, Donovan McCreary. He was arguing heatedly with a man, a crewman, it looked like, that Mitch had never seen. Mitch decided to go out there and see if he could cool down the conversation.

When he stepped through the door from the warm boat to the frigid outdoors, he longed for his Big Bad Wolf costume. It was freezing out here. Ice was on every surface, and he had to grab hold of the railing to keep his feet from slipping. Gus Hazelton's borrowed shoes fit pretty well, but they were dress shoes, as would befit the Headless Horseman, and the bottoms of them were slick, no tread at all. Mitch made his way carefully along the railing, and as soon as he rounded the corner, he saw that Donovan McCreary and the other man were doing more than arguing now. They were fighting.

Mitch tried to rush to Donovan's aid, but you could barely walk on this slick deck, let alone run. He grabbed the railing to keep his feet under him and pulled himself along it as fast as he could. The unknown crew member was a big man, bigger than McCreary, and in the few seconds it had taken Mitch to draw near on the railing, the man had grabbed hold of the sleeve of McCreary's Grumpy-the-Dwarf costume, knocked off his floppy red hat, and was yanking him around. McCreary looked up then and saw Mitch.

He might have been about to call out to him, but the other crewman shoved him against the railing and cut off his words.

Mitch took one more step and McCreary cried, "No, don't!" But Mitch didn't heed the warning, now only a couple of steps away, he reached out to grab the arm of the man fighting with McCreary and —

Something slammed into the back of Mitch's head, and the entire world went completely black.

Chapter Thirty-Five

SOMEBODY HAD TRIED to kill her.

Would have succeeded, too, if Mama hadn't insisted on making her Red Riding Hood cape out of the fabric from those heavy drapes.

Tried to *kill* her.

Rileigh couldn't manage to jam that thought all the way into her head without pieces of it dangling out her ears.

Why would somebody want her dead? Not *somebody*, moron — the killer who'd already claimed two victims. Why did the guy want to kill her? And it was a man, although not a very big one.

She might have scratched him, she wasn't sure, but maybe she'd got him somewhere you could see the scratches. Might be other marks on him, too. She'd landed a shot with her fist, her elbow had connected too, and she'd hit something when she kicked. Maybe she'd gotten lucky and given the guy a shiner.

There were definitely marks on her. Her shoulder was throbbing, would have a fist-sized bruise on it, and there'd be another one equally as big on her hip. But she'd gotten off light. The man had a knife. If he'd been stabbing with it in the dark, it was a miracle he hadn't cut her. Must have gotten it tangled up in her cape and hood.

Rileigh had not quite gotten her breathing under control, was still panting and gasping — the after-effect of the adrenaline rush of fighting for her life, so she pulled out a chair at a nearby table and sat, leaning over and put her head between her knees to clear her lightheadedness.

When someone tapped her on the shoulder, she jerked away reflexively.

"Woah, there — kinda jumpy, aren't you?" said Georgia, who had leapt back from Rileigh's reaction.

"Had a rough few minutes," Rileigh said, thought about explaining further, but didn't bother. "Did you find Mama?"

"Yeah, I found her."

Rileigh looked around. "Where the hell is she?"

"I deposited her back with Millie in the casino. They're shoving chips into a slot machine. A different one than they were using before. Seems this machine is hot, or so they told me. They're expecting to 'hit' any time now. Maybe even 'break the house.' They've picked up some gambling jargon, and now they sound like a couple of little-old-lady hustlers."

"Where did you find her?" Rileigh asked.

"I saw you go up to the third deck so I figured I'd go down to see if I could find her in the hold."

"You found her in the hold?"

"No, but I wandered around down there, stopped at Gerbil Village for some pleasant memories of the day we were there."

"*Pleasant* memories?"

"That was the day my precious baby girl was born.

And the day you give birth to your long-awaited daughter after four rowdy little boys is a hallmark day no matter what else happened. It's a day that shines in your memories. A day that—"

"*Sucked* and you know it. Three little boys lost in a maze does not a pleasant memory make."

Rileigh had never bothered to point out to Georgia that it had been a spectacularly stupid thing to do to send Liam and Eli into those tunnels to find Conner. Georgia adored her kids, would lay down her life for them, but when it came to *parenting* them ... she lacked certain skills in that area.

That was water under the bridge now, though.

"Okay, so you stopped by to pay homage to the maze that gobbled up three of your children. That still doesn't answer my question. Where did you find Mama?"

"I was coming back from having searched the hold when your mother came rushing down the passageway—"

"Let me guess. She'd just talked to Jillian."

"Close, but no cigar."

"How close?"

"She caught sight of Jillian at a distance, she said, and followed her — that's why she went down into the hold."

"So she chased Cinderella—"

"Jillian wasn't dressed as Cinderella. She was dressed as Goldilocks."

"You're telling me Jillian brought along a trunk of clothes to the party, so that when she got bored with one costume she could swap out and be somebody else? Makes perfect sense."

"But she didn't want to talk about Jillian."

"I find that hard to believe."

"She wanted to talk about all kinds of other crazy shit."

214

"How can you get crazier than chasing the ghost of your dead daughter, who's really Cinderella, except she's Goldilocks, unless she decides to be Princess Leia."

"That's not a storybook character."

"You think Jillian cares? She's probably wandering around the boat dressed up as Chewbacca. No, wait — Jar Jar Binks, now there's a good look."

"Apparently, your mother opened every door that wasn't locked and searched the rooms." Rileigh rolled her eyes, but let Georgia continue. "She either ran into some real crew members down there or imagined she did. She said some guy came running past her, literally knocked her down, and it smelled like he'd crapped his pants."

"If she got in his way, he probably did."

"What?"

"Never mind."

"Another crewman was standing in the passageway taking to Rhett Butler ... and she didn't even know Rhett had come to the party."

"Least he didn't have to rent a costume."

"In one room, she found people who'd been ... she said frozen into statues."

"The mannequins. Mitch told me about them."

"She saw a guy down on his knees, cutting a hole in a wall."

"Did he look like Elvis? I hear he's on the boat tonight."

"And she could hear her sisters singing."

"The whole bouquet, or just selected flowers?"

"She said they all were there, except for Delphinium, and she never could carry a tune."

Rileigh shook her head. "I swear, Mama's getting worse. She can't possibly have very many marbles left to lose."

"She was hung up on the guy who knocked her down, the one who smelled like shit, kept going back to that story."

"Maybe because it's the only one where the main character is real."

"To hear your mother tell it, half the crew of this boat has got the bloody squirts."

"Maybe they do. It's possible somebody tried to incapacitate the crew."

Georgia perked up. "Oh, really? You haven't told me that part."

"The current theory is that somebody put something in the crew's dinner tonight to make them all sick so that they would leave their posts, at least long enough for somebody to destroy the radio and disable the engine."

"Your mama said she smelled chili."

"My mother was a bloodhound in a previous life. Thanks for finding her."

"No problem, but it's my last quest. I have to go park my ass somewhere and just sit." She sighed. "That tape you used to tape me to the chair had the tensile strength of titanium. But this …" She gestured down at her costume. "The whole damn thing is coming apart."

Rileigh glanced over Georgia's shoulder and saw a flash of red.

Pete Brady.

Chapter Thirty-Six

RILEIGH WEAVED her way through groups of people, trying to keep the splotch of red in sight. When she finally got close enough to him to call out, "Hey Pete," he stopped and turned her way. She was rushing toward him so fast trying to catch up that she almost crashed into him, and he held his hands out to catch her.

"Hey there, be careful. I'm a wee fragile little thing and I bruise easily."

"Can I talk to you for a few minutes?"

"Rileigh, sweetheart, you can talk to me for a few minutes or a few hours or for the rest of our natural lives after we pledge our vows in holy matrimony."

"I'm not looking for a husband. I'm looking for a murderer. This is serious."

Pete's face shifted. The geniality drained out of it. "I'm real tired of difficult conversations right now."

"Mine isn't the first one you've had this evening, then?"

He didn't reply as Rileigh grabbed his arm and dragged him toward an empty table, sat down and gestured for him to sit across from her.

"So, what's the topic of *your* difficult conversation?"

"First, tell me the topic of the last difficult conversation you just had."

"Love you to death, Rileigh girl, but that's not any of your business."

"Because it has something to do with the Save Gum Tree Hollow Association and that's all private stuff, right?"

Pete raised his eyebrows as if he was a little surprised that she knew that much.

Rileigh decided to bluff.

"I know you're a member. I know the names of just about everybody else who's a member, too, so how about we cut the bullshit." She saw his skepticism. "Do you think I'm stupid? Do you think the sheriff is? Secret societies are real hard to maintain in a little town where there aren't any secrets."

Pete might have bought the bluff and he might not, but either way he blew her off and sat back in the chair.

"Fine. I'm a member of the Save Gum Tree Hollow Association." He held out his hands. "Put the cuffs on me."

"This isn't funny, Pete."

"You see me laughing? There ain't nothing funny about some asshole gonna come in here and destroy what's ours."

Then Pete cocked his head to one side. "And I'm not getting this at all, Rileigh girl. How come you're not on *our* side? You're local. These here's your mountains just the same as they're mine. You ought to be damn pissed that somebody's gonna come tear 'em up. Why aren't you?"

"I'm not here to talk about the Gum Tree Hollow development, which is probably dead in its tracks, if you'll forgive my pun."

"Oh, I hope it's dead all right."

"Doesn't sound like that makes you sad."

"Hell no, it doesn't make me sad. It doesn't make any of us sad. Why would it? If you're talking about Hunter Dobson being dead, don't come looking to any of us for sympathy. I ain't sending any flowers to the funeral."

"Not interested in who's sending flowers. I'm interested in who buried the hammer in the back of his head."

Pete looked startled. Then it dawned on him what she was saying.

"Are you kidding me? Are you gonna sit there and accuse me of killing—"

"I'm not accusing you of anything." If the person who'd attacked her in the passageway was the same person who'd murdered the first two victims, it couldn't have been Pete. Pete was huge. If he'd tripped and fallen on top of her, she'd never have gotten up. "I'm just asking—"

"Asking what? Did I kill him?"

"No. Asking if you know who did. Do you?"

"If I did, I wouldn't tell you."

This time Rileigh sat back. "Can you say obstruction of justice?"

"Look, I ain't got no idea who killed Hunter Dobson, but when you find out who it is, you let me know, because I want to pin a medal on the man's chest. He did every human being in Yarmouth County a terrific favor, and we're grateful."

"Grateful to a murderer?"

"Grateful to anybody who cut that son of a bitch down to size."

"Ian told me there was one of your group who was a loose cannon. Who is it?"

"Loose cannon?"

"A hothead."

"Oh, that's probably—" Pete stopped himself before he finished.

"Go on. What were you going to say?"

"I wasn't going to say nothing. I don't know nothing. I'm just a good ol' boy who come to the party as Santa Claus and–"

"Why do you figure somebody killed Ruby Cunningham?"

Pete did show emotion then.

"She was a right nice lady. I liked her a lot. In the summertime, she volunteered in the concession stand at Little League baseball games when I coached the Cubs. She bought ice cream cones for the boys after every game — not for the winning team, but for the losers, so my boys and I ate a lot of ice cream. I can't imagine what anybody'd have against her. It musta had something to do with Dobson."

"I figure it did ... but you don't know anything about that, right?"

Pete placed his hands on the table with his fingers spread wide apart. "Listen up now, 'cause I ain't gonna say this twice. I don't know jack shit about who buried a hammer in the top of Hunter Dobson's head. Nothing. I'm glad he did it, but I don't know who he is." He let out a breath. "I do love hangin' out with you, darlin', I truly do. But if you're done asking questions ..."

His eyes strayed from her face to look at somebody behind her. She turned to see Ian striding toward them. Good. Now she could get the two of them together and compare stories. Maybe find out what it was Ian and Pete had been fighting about. If Pete wasn't the loose cannon, then who was it? Now she could ask them both. If she watched their faces, she might be able to tell who was bluffing and who wasn't.

Ian stopped in front of Rileigh. Before he could say

anything she said, "I've been talking to your friend Pete here. You know, you're the loose cannon?"

She watched his face for a reaction, but he didn't react at all. In fact, he didn't even seem to have heard her.

"Rileigh, you need to come with me," he said.

"Come with you where?"

"Mitch has been hurt."

Rileigh felt the bottom of her belly fall to the floor. For a moment or two she couldn't process the words, but managed to keep herself from saying, *What do you mean, hurt?* Because how many things can *hurt* mean?

"What are you talking about?"

"Gus sent me to find you," Ian said. "He's taking care of Mitch."

"What happened?"

Ian literally took Rileigh by the arm and lifted her up out of the chair.

"I'll tell you everything I know, but let's talk while we walk."

When they had passed through the lounge full of people, Rileigh shook out of Ian's grip and stopped him, turned him around to face her. "Tell me what's going on."

"Somebody found Mitch lying outside on the deck, unconscious. They took him to somebody named Hastings, who apparently is a paramedic. The captain knew that Gus is a doctor, so they got him to take care of Mitch."

"Is he going to be all right?" She didn't like the way her voice sounded so frail and pitiful, almost pathetic, but she couldn't help it.

Ian just looked at her, but then that was Ian. Ian never said three words that he didn't absolutely have to say, and you usually had to pull two of them out of him.

"Just come with me. Gus will tell you everything he knows."

Chapter Thirty-Seven

AFTER RILEIGH and Mitch had accompanied Captain Rowe to the engine room earlier, the captain had taken the injured engineer to see Hastings to treat his head wound. Rowe had said then that the boat didn't have a real infirmary, but they never sailed without one of the two certified paramedics — both of whom had other jobs on the boat, but who could be pressed into service if someone got hurt.

Ian led Rileigh to the infirmary, a small room with an exam table somewhere in the bowels of the boat. She had gotten lost at the first turning of the passageways, and had to trust that Ian was taking her where he said he was.

When they turned the corner in the final passageway, Rileigh saw Captain Rowe standing outside a door about halfway down the corridor. He looked up, but he didn't smile.

"There's not a whole lot of room in there, I didn't want to crowd in," the captain told Rileigh. "Gus said he wants to talk to you."

Rileigh stepped into the small, brightly-lit room. Mitch

was stretched out on the exam table in the middle of the room, unconscious.

He was covered up with a sheet all the way to his chin, and even that looked ominous. As she approached, she saw the shirt of his uniform hanging over the back of a chair.

"Gus, what's going on?"

"Somebody knocked Mitch out, and a crewman found him lying on the deck outside. It's a damn good thing he found him when he did. Mitch could have died of hypothermia out there."

"What was he doing out on the deck?"

"Hell if I know."

"Is it serious?"

"Not gonna lie to you, sweetheart. It's bad."

Rileigh fought back and won against the sob that rose in her throat.

"Mitch certainly has a concussion, but he may also have what's called a closed head injury," Gus began, but Rileigh held up her hand.

"You don't have to define it for me. I know what a closed head injury is."

And indeed she did.

THE SOLDIER'S name is Possum. It's the only name Rileigh knows. He's in her platoon but not her squad. She and another soldier have just dragged him out of a small hut where somebody set off an IED.

She can't find any obvious wounds, turns him over to see if he has shrapnel in his back, maybe, or if he's been shot. She doesn't see any blood.

When the corpsman rushes to her side, she tells him in a relieved voice, "I think he's okay. He's just unconscious."

The corpsman looks at her and shakes his head. "Just unconscious."

"There's not a mark on him," Rileigh says.

"Not one you can see, and sometimes those are the most deadly."

Then the corpsman tells her about closed head injuries. He explains how the brain responds when there is trauma, how it swells. That's a problem because it is encased within the skull, and there's nowhere to swell. The swelling itself, the corpsman says, is often far more damaging than the original injury to the brain.

The medics haul Possum away to a chopper. Head wounds require immediate attention. The next day Rileigh goes to inquire about him. When she asks, the corpsman shakes his head.

"He died last night."

Rileigh nods and walks resolutely away. Possum isn't the first of her comrades to be killed in action. Some of the dead had been her friends. It's just … she can't get it out of her head that he didn't have a mark on him. Shontal Howard had her leg blown off, would have bled out in minutes if the corpsman hadn't gotten to her, and she survived. Possum had no wound you could see, and he died.

And from that point forward, Rileigh lives in sickening dread of the monster called Closed Head Injury. Somehow it seems worse to her than any of the other ways war can rip into your body and tear you apart. You can die here, she realizes, without a mark on you.

GUS WAS TALKING and Rileigh had missed part of it.

"Excuse me, what did you say?"

"I said Mitch needs to be in a trauma center *right now*," Gus said. "He needs to be somewhere they can assess and treat a head wound like this. I can't do a damn thing here."

Gus had been standing on the far side of the examining table when Rileigh came into the room. She stepped to Mitch, wanted to take his hand or something, but he was completely covered up with that sheet.

Gus saw her eyes flit from the sheet to the shirt on the chair and he said, "His uniform was literally frozen to the ice on the deck. The shirt tore when they picked him up, so I took it off him."

Rileigh glanced down to the end of the exam table where Mitch's feet were sticking out under the sheet, still clad in Gus's shoes. He followed her gaze, perhaps wondered if she thought he was going to take the shoes back since—

"Like I said before, he needs them more than I do," Gus said.

"You're really worried about him, aren't you, Gus?" She didn't want to hear the answer to that question, absolutely one hundred percent did not want to hear, but she had to ask.

"Yeah, I am," Gus said. "This could be nothing. He could wake up in a few minutes, tell me I'm holding up three fingers when I'm only holding up two and ..." Gus looked at her and tried to smile but couldn't quite pull it off. "... and we duct tape him to the bed to make him rest for two weeks before he's allowed to get into any bar fights with drunks." He stopped and returned his gaze to the man laying too still under the white sheet on the exam table. "It could be something a lot more serious. And if it is ... the longer treatment is delayed, the worse it is. There's just no way to tell without the kinds of tests I can't run here."

There was nothing Rileigh could say, nothing she could do but stand there and look down at him like he was asleep. She reached over and pushed the sheet back and took his hand, squeezed it, hoping maybe he'd squeeze back. He didn't.

"I suppose you know ..." Gus began. "Or maybe you don't, but when I took his shirt off, I saw—"

"I know what you saw. The scars on his back."

"What the hell happened to him?"

"I don't know. I saw them for the first time a couple of days after I met him. We were working on a murder case, the death of Tina Montgomery. We split up to search for clues. I found Tina's body half covered in a pile of leaves and her tongue cut out."

She didn't have to explain further. Gus knew all about the missing sister that Rileigh's mother believed was still alive.

Rileigh was reluctant to admit the next part — it had just been a knee-jerk response to the shock. Still, it had been a totally unprofessional thing to do.

"I screamed and Mitch came running — without his shirt on. He'd fallen in mud and had taken it off to clean it."

It had been an odd, awkward moment, she remembered, when Mitch asked her to please go back into the woods to get his shirt for him. He said he couldn't leave the body, and she got that, but it had still felt a lot like the "make a pot of coffee" requests women in the workforce often got from male coworkers. When she brought his shirt back to him, she saw the scars on his back.

"I never asked him what had happened to him. I didn't want to pry and–"

"I can tell you what happened to him," Gus said. "Somebody whipped him with a bullwhip. Looks like he was whipped to within an inch of his life." He paused. "I've seen scars like that before."

Rileigh almost asked Gus where he had seen scars on somebody who had been beaten with a bullwhip, but it didn't matter right now.

Her mind was spinning. The two of them stood there in silence, then, one on each side of the exam table.

Gus ground his teeth. "This man does not need to lie here for another four or five hours while we wait for the damn boiler to build up enough pressure to drive this boat! He needs help now."

Rileigh was thinking and didn't even realize she was speaking her thoughts aloud until she heard her own voice.

"The person who disabled that engine and destroyed the radio — had to be the same person who stole all the ship-to-shore handheld radios so there'd be no way to communicate with the shore."

"Yeah, sure. So?"

"Maybe they stole each one, went immediately to the railing and chucked it into the lake. I guess that's possible, maybe even likely. But I'd think you wouldn't want some-body to see you throwing a radio overboard. It seems reasonable to me that they were in a hurry, snatched the radios whenever they got a chance and just stuck them somewhere, you know, shoved them under a bed or some-thing. They knew we'd soon have bigger fish to fry than looking in every sock drawer for radios."

"You think they're still on the boat somewhere?" Gus asked.

"It's possible. And if there's even one–"

"Maybe we could *find* one of those radios and use it to summon help, but chances are they've smashed them, just like they did with Patel's, in case someone did happen to find one."

"The killer might've kept one someplace safe—"

"But right now, the score stands at killer two, good guys zero." Gus stopped, then continued slowly. "Actually, it might be killer *three.*"

"Three?"

"The captain says someone else has gone missing."

Rileigh was reluctant to leave Mitch, and Gus could tell. He reached over and patted her on the shoulder. "I'll be right here. I'm not leaving his side."

She felt tears stinging her eyes, so suddenly that there was nothing she could do about them overflowing and running down her face. She turned away quickly, wiped them, and went out into the hall to find out who the hell else had been murdered.

Chapter Thirty-Eight

Captain Rowe was still outside the exam room in the passageway.

"Gus said somebody else died. Tell me about it."

She knew she was probably being rude and demanding. She didn't care.

"We... *I* suspect, there's no way to know, but I suspect that Donovan McCreary is dead."

Rileigh felt like someone had dropped a piano on her head.

"You said you don't know that he's dead?"

"It's just the assumption that we made when we found Mitch."

"Take me there. I want to see."

Rowe didn't protest being ordered around like a three-year-old. He merely turned and said, "This way."

When Rileigh stepped out of the boat onto the deck, a cold wind slapped her in the face, and she imagined she could feel the streaks of moisture on her cheeks freezing.

"Watch your step," the captain said. "Hold on to the railing. This deck is solid ice."

Rileigh pulled her cloak around her as tight as she could, reached out and grabbed the railing. It was a piece of ice that burned her fingers, but she held on and followed the captain all the way around the boat to a spot where the windows of the lounge looked out on the deck. Then he indicated a place on the ice a few feet away.

"This is where the deckhand found Mitch, lying there on his back. Don't know how long he'd been there. "

Rileigh knelt down at the spot and studied it. The ice wasn't smooth and slick and glassy like it was in other places. Feet had stomped and scratched here. A few feet from the spot where the captain said Mitch's body had been lying was a red stain that could be nothing else but frozen blood. A lot of it.

As her eye traced a path from where the blood had splattered up onto the railing, she saw it. There on the wall of the hull, someone had used the blood to write something on the metal. It was smeared, but it was still clear what it was. She looked at it, looked up at the captain, then looked back again. Somebody had scrawled the number three in blood on the metal there, but it couldn't have been referring to Mitch, because he wasn't dead. So who ...?

"We found McCreary's floppy red Grumpy hat and his walkie-talkie. It had been stomped." He reached into his pocket and pulled out an ID case. It was like those flip-wallet cases plain clothes police officers used to carry their badges. "This was over there under the steps," he said, said, indicating the nearby ladder that led to the roof. "Maybe fell out of his pocket when he was fighting with somebody and slid across the ice."

She flipped the case open. There was an ID card like a driver's license with height, weight, date of birth, and an ugly picture that made McCreary look demented — like everybody else looked in their ID pictures. She frowned.

This ID listed McCreary's birthday as a May date, but hadn't he complained that he was missing his birthday celebration tonight?

It was possible she could have misunderstood, but she didn't think so.

She studied the card for a moment, wrinkled her brow wondering, then handed it back to the captain. "You think McCreary was *killed* because you found his hat, ID and walkie-talkie here?"

"That's not the only reason. Come over here." The captain reached out his hand to take hers so that she could let go of the railing and walk to where he stood, which was against the railing right beside the number three. He pointed to a stretch of railing nearby.

"The ice has been broken off here. See?"

She could see. The rest of the railing was encased in ice, but on that spot, all the ice was broken off. Then the captain stretched out over the railing and pointed downward, and Rileigh did the same. There was an awning on the deck below, and the ice on the awning in that spot had been broken up. It was no longer a smooth, flat surface as it was on the other awnings.

"And the walkway below. Take a look at that," the captain said. Rileigh had to stretch farther out over the railing, and Rowe took her arm to steady her so that she could see the walkway below the awning. The ice there was pristine, not scratched or scuffed at all.

"It seems to me," Captain Rowe said, "that something large knocked all the ice off the railing up here, then fell and hit that awning before it slid off into the water."

"And you think that something large was Donovan McCreary?" Rileigh asked.

"Nobody's seen him. We searched and he'd definitely missing."

Rileigh's head was reeling, but she ground her teeth and forced herself to be calm and logical.

"You think somebody killed Donovan McCreary, then threw his body over the railing into the lake."

"That's what it looks like to me. What do you think?"

Rileigh wasn't ready to make a pronouncement about what she thought now. Rowe's theory might not be the only explanation for the scuff marks, the blood, and the broken ice, but it certainly was the most convincing explanation.

"So how does Mitch fit into all this? Where was he when the murder was happening?"

"Gus said somebody hit Mitch on the back of the head," the captain said. "Somebody came up behind him and clocked him."

Maybe.

But exactly where on the timeline of events had that happened? Perhaps Mitch had been on the deck with McCreary, and someone hit Mitch in the back of the head and then killed McCreary. Or perhaps McCreary had been out here with the killer, and Mitch had come upon the two of them. But if that was the winning scenario, then who hit Mitch *from behind?*

Well, they had said all along it was ludicrous to believe that one person had managed to do it all: kill two people, destroy the radio, disable the engine, steal the handhelds, and poison the crew all at the same time. Since the passengers didn't know how to disable the engine, obviously some crew member was in on the deal. Maybe McCreary had found the crew member, confronted him, and the guy killed him.

Rileigh wasn't even aware of the cold until she lifted her hand off the metal railing and felt the sting on her skin. The captain reached out and took her elbow.

232

"Come on, we need to get in out of the cold."

"Just a moment."

Rileigh knelt again and looked at the hastily-scrawled number three in blood on the wall beneath the railing. It didn't have the number sign in front of it like "#1" and "#2". But somebody was working with blood and was in a hurry, she supposed.

"Why identify this as number three?"

Number one and number two implied planning ... this is the first and there will be a second. But this killing clearly wasn't one that'd been planned in advance. Why call it number three? Just to confuse things, to muddy the waters? Maybe that's what all the numbers had been intended to do.

The captain shrugged his shoulders. Then he reached down and took Rileigh's elbow.

"You need to get inside."

Chapter Thirty-Nine

THE CAPTAIN OFFERED to accompany Rileigh back down to the infirmary on Deck Two. She thanked him for his generosity, but she needed to go and check on her mother before she went back to stay with Mitch.

"You've got a whole boat full of upset, angry, frightened people to take care of," she said. "I'll manage on my own. Thanks."

She found her mother at yet another slot machine. This was the third one she and Millie had tried. Rileigh considered telling her mother about Mitch, but it would only worry her. Worry seemed to exacerbate the symptoms of her dementia. When she'd been worried about her sister Daisy last fall, she got so dithered she forgot to feed the chickens and put her shoes on the wrong feet. In the relatively smooth emotional waters since then, Mama had seemed to be more centered and lucid, or at least what passed for "Lily lucid" more of the time.

Millie was positively jumping up and down, looked like a little kid trying not to pee. Rileigh couldn't figure out Mildred Hanover. She was a member of the zoning board.

That's why she'd been invited on this cruise, and she'd asked Mama to be her "date." But even though the chairman of the zoning board had been brutally murdered a couple hours ago, Here was Millie playing the slots with Mama. Sometimes Rileigh's mother, even with dementia, seemed to have more common sense than some of her sane friends.

As soon as Mama spotted Rileigh, she poked Millie and the two of them hurried over.

"Thank God you're here," Millie said.

"We've been waiting and waiting," Mama said. "What have you been doing all this time?"

Not a whole lot. Investigating two brutal murders. Fighting for my life in a dark hallway. Nothing special.

"Do you need something?"

The two old ladies exchanged a glance.

"Well, as a matter of fact–" Millie began.

"We need for you to–" Mama said.

"You're the only one who–"

Mama held up her hand to her friend.

"You let me explain it to her," Mama said. Millie made a zipping-her-lip motion and stood silently beside Mama, a cat-that-swallowed-the-canary look on her face.

"Explain what, Mama?"

"Well, we figured out…" She leaned forward then and said the rest in a whisper. "We're certain we're about to hit."

"Hit what?"

"Why the jackpot, of course," Mama said, then gave Rileigh her classic patient-and- forbearing look as she shook her head. "Silly girl."

The two women started talking at once.

"See, we've been calculating …"

"Ran the numbers …"

"The odds and things and…"

"I've got a calculator on my phone!" Millie was quite proud of that.

Then Mama took the conversational ball and started running with it toward the end zone. By the time she hit the fifty-yard line, Rileigh couldn't follow what she was saying. It was some kind of convoluted explanation of how they had figured out the odds of winning the big jackpot on the machines they had been playing. It made absolutely no sense at all. When Mama paused for breath—that was probably a fumble— Millie picked up the ball and kept running.

While they babbled, Rileigh studied the machine — shiny silver, with a red light like on a fire truck on the top and red lettering urging the player to "Play big, win big." There were five reels with symbols on them. This machine was clearly vegan because all the symbols were fruits and vegetables — cherries, tomatoes, cucumbers, pears, carrots — interspersed with numbers and red hearts and WILD CARDs. There was a silver crank on the right side topped with a red ball that set the reels spinning.

Rileigh tuned back in. Mama was still talking.

"That machine over there is a quarter machine, and the big jackpot, if you win it all, is a hundred and twenty-five thousand dollars."

Millie interrupted then. "But you have to feed too many quarters into it to prime the pump. We've done the math on it, and it doesn't work out in the player's favor. So now we're playing the dollar machine."

"The dollar machine?" Rileigh was horrified.

"Over there is a five-dollar machine we haven't gotten to yet."

These old ladies were sitting here feeding dollar chips into a slot machine, getting ready to feed another beast five-dollar chips. They'd go broke in no time. Surely to God the casino wouldn't allow her mother to open a line of credit.

"I know you think we're going to lose all our money," Millie began, "but we won six hundred dollars on the quarter machine, and we've figured out how to take that money—" Millie began.

Mama interrupted. "And use it to play the dollar machine." Mama smiled beatifically as if she had imparted some kernel of great wisdom. "Don't you see? You play this cheap machine, and—"

"—and then you use what you win on the cheap machine to play the more expensive machine," Millie said. She looked over her shoulder as if she was afraid somebody was going to hear her grand plan and steal it. "And the grand prize on the dollar machine, is *two hundred thousand dollars.*"

Rileigh's head was too full of other things to try to understand what her mother and her mother's friend were saying.

"Just tell me, what is it that you want from me?" She kept herself from saying, *And don't tell me you want to borrow money because that's a no. Full stop.*

"We want Gus, dear," Mama said.

"Gus?"

"He's your friend," Millie said. "He'd do you a favor if you asked, wouldn't he?"

"Why do you need Gus?" Before they could answer, she continued, "Gus is busy right now. He's taking care of ..." she swallowed hard, "someone who's injured."

"We thought he might be busy," Mama said. She looked back at Millie.

And Millie said, "Well, could we borrow his head?"

"I am totally not tracking with you," Rileigh said, her own head spinning.

"His head, dear," Mama said. "Are you not listening? He came as the headless horseman. And if we can't get Gus, maybe there's luck in something that belongs to him."

Mama looked at Millie. Millie looked at Mama. And they nodded like two little bobble-head dolls and looked expectantly at Rileigh.

This was insane.

Millie had occasionally been dropping chips into the slot machine as she and Mama talked to Rileigh. She pulled the silver crank then, and suddenly the fire truck light flashed on the top of the machine and clanging bells rang out, signaling that she had won. Millie jumped up and down in place.

"See? *See?*" she cried.

"I *told* you," Mama said triumphantly.

Rileigh looked at the total she had won — a thousand dollars!

"Mama, you and Millie need to quit while you're ahead. Go cash in your chips and keep the money. I don't think you understand how the odds on slot machines work. It's the same as the odds on flipping a coin. The odds are the same every time you do it. It's not like it accumulates, like if you flip a coin five times and it comes up heads, the next time it's bound to come up tails. Every time is an individual event that doesn't affect the outcome of the next event…"

Rileigh stopped, letting her voice trail off. Mama and Millie clearly didn't understand a thing she was saying. And besides, she felt that annoying itch in her mind that she felt every time—

"Mama, excuse me for a minute."

Rileigh got up from the stool beside the machine and

238

walked slowly down the center aisle of the mini casino. It was as Donovan McCreary had described it. There were only twelve slot machines. The game tables were at the other end and no one was playing them. Only a couple of people were playing the slot machines other than Mama and Millie, who had spent the entire night doing nothing else.

Math had never been Rileigh's strong suit. She'd never been able to do it in her head like Mitch could. He could figure out how many miles to the gallon he was getting without even using his calculator.

But this wasn't hard math. It was pretty simple. The slot machines that took quarters paid out a hundred and twenty-five thousand dollars for the grand prize. The slot machines that took dollars paid out two hundred thousand dollars as the grand prize. The big win on the lone five-dollar machine would net you a cool three hundred thousand dollars. Rileigh stood very still, doing the math in her head. Six of the machines had a hundred and twenty-five thousand dollars jackpots — payout for a jackpot win on *all of them* would cost the casino seven hundred and fifty thousand dollars. Five machines paid out two hundred thousand dollars for a jackpot win— it would take a million dollars to cover them all. One machine paid three hundred thousand dollars.

Rileigh was having trouble keeping the first number in her head, but she thought it was seven hundred and fifty thousand dollars. Add that to a million dollars. Then add three hundred thousand dollars to that.

The total was two million fifty thousand dollars.

Rileigh stood very still and let that realization wash over her.

Donovan McCreary had said that the Queen of the Smokies mini casino was not required to carry the kind of cash — one hundred to two hundred million— that the big Las Vegas casinos did because the paddleboat's game tables used chips with no monetary value. And it was at the game tables in Las Vegas that the vast sums of money were won and lost.

But the state gaming commission still required the mini-casino to have enough cash on hand to pay out *every chip in play.* That meant enough cash to pay out a win in any one – *or all* – of the twelve slot machines. In other words, the Queen of the Smokies was carrying more than two million dollars in cash.

True, that was nothing like the hundred and sixty million dollars that had attracted the likes of Danny Ocean and his expert crew of thieves in Ocean's Eleven.

A mere two million dollars would attract smaller fish than Danny Ocean. But they'd still be sharks.

Chapter Forty

RILEIGH HAD no trouble finding the right passageways to take her to Belle's quarters. She hurried through the corridors that were too small and not well lit, rushing because she was uncomfortable here. But more than that, rushing because there was a ticking clock. Mitch needed a trauma center that could assess his injuries and treat them. He needed that *now*, not in five or six hours, or however the hell long it took the boiler to build up enough steam to run the engine again.

She had to find the stolen ship-to-shore handhelds so they could radio for help. Which meant she had to find the murderer. Except maybe she wasn't looking for a murderer at all.

When she got to the cabin with the number three on the door, she knocked twice, loud. There was no response. When she'd come here before, Belle had yelled at her to come on in but to keep her mouth shut because Belle was deep into a video game that Rileigh interrupted, and she consequently lost. But Rileigh could hear no sound at all. No video game. No Belle.

She made her hand into a fist.

Bang, bang, bang.

"Belle, are you in there?"

She heard words from inside, not angry words. Muffled.

"Belle, dammit, open the door."

Stumbling sounds and a thump came from beyond the door and then it opened, revealing Belle, half asleep. She was wearing something that resembled hospital scrubs instead of pajamas, but her short hair was in that state of bedhead you only got to after rolling around trying to go to sleep for hours. Rileigh looked at her watch.

"What the hell do you want in the middle of the night?" Belle asked, leaning against the door frame. "It's three o'clock in the morning and I only get two hours off, then I gotta be back in the wheelhouse. I answered every question you asked. I don't have anything else to tell you."

"Belle, can I come in?"

"What for?"

"Just let me come in, okay?"

Belle stepped back and held the door, and Rileigh crossed in front of her into the small, stuffy, and window-less quarters.

"If you're standing there waiting for me to ask you to sit down and let's have a talk, you came to the wrong room. Now, what do you want?"

Rileigh ignored what Belle said, took a couple of steps and sat down on the edge of Belle's rumpled bed.

"I need a favor."

"Girlfriend, we don't know each other well enough for you to ask me for a favor."

"I have a reason, a really good reason." Rileigh lost it for a moment. She put her head in her hands and shook it, then looked back up at Belle. "It's about the three murders—"

"*Three?*"

"Hunter Dobson, Ruby Cunningham, and Donovan McCreary."

"Donovan?" Belle was stunned. "Are you telling me somebody murdered McCreary?"

"Well, we haven't found his body yet, but somebody attacked Mitch."

"And Mitch is?"

"Oh, I forgot. You don't know anybody's name. All right, Mitch Webster is the Yarmouth County Sheriff. I came as his date tonight." She almost smiled. "We were the Big Bad Wolf and Little Red Riding Hood."

Belle pulled a chair out from the desk, spun it around, and straddled it. "Can I interrupt and ask why in the world a closet person like you wanted to come to a big party with a lot of people in the first place?"

"I came because I *didn't* want to. I came because I knew I had to do shit like that or I'd be stuck in my house forever."

"Copy that," Belle said.

"I'm a former police officer. I've been helping Mitch out with cases in Yarmouth County because he's not local and nobody will tell him anything."

"And the two of you have gotten…" Belle paused, then just said, "*Close.* Am I right?"

Rileigh opened her mouth to deny it and found herself saying, "Yes, we have. And a little while ago, somebody attacked him on the deck outside the lounge. They found him lying there unconscious."

"I thought you were going to tell me what happened to Donovan."

"We think he was somehow involved in whatever

happened to Mitch. He came upon Mitch fighting with someone, or Mitch came upon him fighting with someone. The ice is all scuffed up on the deck. Mitch was found unconscious. There was blood everywhere. McCreary's dwarf hat was lying on the deck beside Mitch, as was his walkie-talkie, which somebody had stomped on. His ID badge was under the ladder and '3' was written in blood on the wall beneath the railing."

Rileigh took a breath and continued, explained what the captain had said about the ice on the railing and the awning.

"All right, you think somebody killed Donovan McCreary and threw his body over the side. But none of this tells me why you're here to ask a favor."

"We have been scratching our heads. Mitch and I and Gus. Gus is a friend, the coroner. The three of us have been trying to figure out who could possibly have committed two murders right under everybody's nose. But more than that, we couldn't figure out why whoever did it also stranded the boat out in the middle of the lake and destroyed all the communications. Why would you kill somebody and then disable the engine so everybody's sitting here for hours?"

"Do you know?"

"No … but I'm wondering if we've been looking at what's happened on this boat from the wrong viewpoint." Rileigh paused. "You do know, don't you, that there's *two million dollars* on this boat."

Belle looked shocked and whistled softly.

"I knew there was a lot, but two million?"

"What if this was never about the murders at all? What if somebody is trying to steal that money and the murders were just a distraction, a red herring?"

Belle's eyes opened wide and she sat back. "Now *that's* an interesting theory."

"If we stop looking for a murderer, and start looking for a thief, that puts a new spin on things." She paused. "I told you when I was here before that somebody on the crew has to be involved. The disabled engine, the missing handhelds, the spiked chili."

Belle nodded. "Two million dollars. That's a lot of money."

"About the crew ... there are just things that don't add up, little things that probably mean nothing at all, but..."

"Like?"

"Like the engineer said somebody sneaked up behind him when he was reading the pressure gauge and hit him on the head. That gauge is right out in the open. You'd have to "sneak" across twenty feet of open deck in every direction to get to him." She paused. "And the wound. It was on top of his head, right above his eyebrow. If somebody sneaked up on you from behind, the wound would be on the back of your head." She thought, but didn't say, *like the wound on Mitch's head.* "A wound right above his eye would do minimum harm and cause maximum bleeding — it had be easy to clock yourself on the head in that spot."

"And what else?"

"Why would McCreary lie? When we were getting on the boat, he was complaining to the captain that it was his birthday and he was missing his own party to come in and cover for the guy, Burkett, who didn't show up. But I saw his ID badge a little while ago. Donavan McCreary was born in May, not January."

"I thought he was dead."

Rileigh just shrugged. "There's no body." She paused, "And there's no Dopey."

"No Dopey?"

"The seven members of the security team are dressed as the seven dwarves. I've been keeping track and I've seen six of them — Sneezy, Happy, Bashful, Sleepy, Grumpy and Doc. Everyone but Dopey. Where's he been hiding out all this time?"

Then she took a deep breath. "And there's one other thing that may mean something, may mean nothing at all. I don't know. My mother is on the boat too."

"You people made this a family occasion, didn't you?"

"She has dementia. It's getting worse."

Rileigh thought about it. Thought about making her sound more sane, more reasonable, more a reliable source of information. But she couldn't do that. This was truth time.

"She's so crazy she thinks she's dating Rhett Butler."

"If you have to come up with a delusion, that's a pretty good one."

"My mother wandered off tonight. And when my best friend found her—"

"Your best friend? You really did bring everybody you know."

"Mama had been wandering around in the hold. And she told Georgia all kinds of bizarre things she'd seen."

Rileigh paused, took a breath. "And we totally wrote off everything she said because it was coming from a woman who thinks she's dating Rhett Butler. But one thing sticks out now. One thing could be the final piece of the puzzle."

"What's that?"

"Mama said she saw some guy down on his knees cutting a hole in the wall."

Belle wasn't tracking.

"The two million dollars on this boat is in a safe in a

246

room it takes three keys to unlock. There's 24/7 video surveillance. Go to the surveillance room right now and I guarantee nobody's tried to open the safe room door. But what if the thieves don't need to open the door, because they've drilled a hole in the wall?" Then Rileigh played her final card. "It explains the biggest mystery. Why would a murderer strand the boat in the middle of the lake for hours? He wouldn't. But a thief would, if he needed longer than a four-hour cruise to drill a hole into the safe."

Belle was tracking then, firing on all cylinders.

"So why did you wake me up? What's the favor?"

Rileigh pointed to the floor plans that hung on Belle's walls. "Those. I need to figure out what's on the other side of the wall from the safe. Where are they digging from?" She took a breath. "I need you to help me find the right spot."

"And when I do?"

"I'll go check it out, see if the woman who shoved Scarlet O'Hara out of Rhett Butler's bed actually saw something that was really there."

Belle went to the wall, took down the drawing of the hold of the Queen of the Smokies and laid it on the desk where she could light it up with the desk lamp.

She showed Rileigh where the safe was located, in an unmarked room off an unmarked hallway. Then the two of them examined the rooms that backed up on it. Finally, Belle tapped on a little box on the floor plan off a different passageway on the other side of the boat.

"There. That's your best shot. It's a storage room, full of supplies, but those could have been moved. There's easy access in and out, and it's a place your mother could conceivably have wandered into."

Rileigh nodded.

"Show me how to get there from here."

Belle traced the route for her with her finger, showing her a couple of different ways to approach that spot. Rileigh asked for landmarks, what she could look for to orient herself. A fire extinguisher on the wall. Markings on cabin doors. Even a bent step on the stairs.

Finally, she felt confident she could find that spot.

Belle looked at her then and surprised her.

"You got a gun?"

"I *wish.*"

"You got to know that whoever's involved in all this is packing."

"Oh, they're armed all right. If they weren't before they attacked Mitch, they are now. His service revolver is missing."

"You want some company?" Before Rileigh could speak, Belle said. "I can handle myself."

Rileigh was genuinely touched by the offer.

"I could gather up all kinds of firepower, if that's what I wanted. I can think of half a dozen reeeally tough guys upstairs … who happen to be dressed as cartoon characters right now but they're still tough. They'd go with me if I asked. But Belle, the whole thing might be… *probably is* a wild goose chase. I *want* to believe I've cracked this. But the whole premise rests on believing that my mother — my befuddled, crazy mother — actually saw what she says she saw. I'm not pulling anybody else into this until I'm sure."

"So if you get caught you're just going to … what? Stick out your index finger, cock your thumb and say bang?"

"That *is* a dangerous weapon alright, but I don't expect to need it. I'm not going down there to kick ass and take names. This is a stakeout and stakeouts are my gig. I'll hide somewhere and wait to see if anybody comes out that door. All I want is to find out the truth. If I find anything, and I mean *anything at all*, I'll haul ass out of there and go back later — with an army!"

"Watch yourself. And I expect you to buy me a beer one of these days for all my help."

"Copy that," Rileigh said.

Chapter Forty-One

RILEIGH MADE her way out of Belle's quarters and down the passageway. The room had been so very, very small and there were no windows. The longer she'd stayed, the more trapped she'd felt. But she had stuck it out and was discovering slowly and painfully that when she did, when she just gritted her teeth and forced herself to do the thing that made her anxious, her anxiety began to ease.

Still, she hurried down the passageway, up the steps, and out onto the freezing deck and gulped huge lungfuls of fresh air.

The freezing rain had slathered the entire boat in a sheen of ice that made taking even a single step on the deck treacherous. Visibility was five feet, maybe. Rileigh hunkered down as much as she could, but the sleet felt like pellets of birdshot from a shotgun blast. She took long, deep breaths, tried to calm herself.

She was going to have to go back down into the bowels of the boat and stay down there for who knows how long. She'd have to find a place to watch the door that Belle had pointed out. Belle had said there was a bit of a recessed doorway, something like an alcove on the opposite wall about forty feet beyond it. The passageway was a dead end beyond the alcove, so no danger of somebody passing by on their way to somewhere else. That was probably as good a cover as she was going to get. Belle said the door in the alcove was small, a janitor's closet. If it wasn't locked, she could step inside.

Goody. The only thing that sounded worse than going back down into the bowels of the boat was going into a very small closet and closing the door.

Dear God in heaven, how she hated this anxiety.

Though she would have preferred to stay on the deck longer, it was just too damn cold out here.

Rileigh pictured the diagram Belle had shared with her. She could picture it perfectly when she closed her eyes. But picturing it perfectly and being able to find the different passageways that it displayed was something else entirely. She sighed. She never had been good at corn mazes as a kid.

Drawing in her last breath of frigid air, Rileigh let it out with a sigh and headed down the steps. She would feel much better if this really was a wild goose chase, if her mother had seen absolutely nothing, if the whole thing was just one more of Mama's crazy delusions.

But she didn't believe it anymore. The tectonic plates in her mind had shifted and now the continents lined up perfectly with the belief that the two million dollars on this boat was at the root of all the evil that had been done. And it didn't matter anymore to Rileigh what her mother had seen.

She walked down the final passageway past the unmarked door beyond which she believed somebody had cut a hole into the back of the safe on the other side of the wall. There was no one in the passageway. So she slowed and put her ear to the door. She could hear nothing inside.

She continued down the passageway to the alcove — shallow, just an indention in the wall — with the little door that led to the janitor's closet. There was a shiny silver fire extinguisher right where Belle had said it would be, on the wall across from the door. Rileigh tried the door handle and discovered that it wasn't locked.

The little janitor's closet was stuffed full of cleaning supplies. There was barely enough room in it for Rileigh to stand. She stepped inside, closed the door almost completely behind her, and peeked through the crack she'd left. Thirty seconds later she had broken out in a cold sweat. Thirty seconds after that, she was afraid she was about to start hyperventilating. She had to get out of this small space. Had to get out of it *now.*

She managed not to throw the door open and bolt out into the passageway gasping, which is what she felt like doing. Instead, she kept her eye to the crack, opened the door slowly, and did a ground-squirrel peek — pop up, pop back.

The door to the room down the hall opened and a hooded man stepped out. Holy shit!

He headed down the hallway beyond Rileigh's line of sight through the small crack, so she couldn't see … the fire extinguisher! She glanced at it and could see a blurry reflection of the man in the shiny surface. From what she could tell, he went to the end of the hallway where it joined another hall, looked up and down that hallway, then returned to the door and went back inside.

And *that,* boys and girls, was the ballgame.

It told her what she'd come here to find out. There should not be anybody in that locked storage bay. The fact that there was a man in there doing *something* was …

Not enough.

It was like being on a stakeout and seeing the unfaithful husband sitting in his car outside a motel room when a car carrying the unfaithful wife pulls up beside him. That wasn't enough. Nobody who hired her as an investigator at the Good Guys would have settled for that. She had to get pictures. She needed them in each other's arms, at the very least. Passionate embrace, lip-lock pictures sealed the deal.

No, she needed more than she could see right now. She stood still and watched the closed door, concentrated on it ferociously to hold at bay the rising anxiety of the close quarters.

She didn't have to wait long. The door opened and the hooded man reappeared, stepped out the door and looked up and down the hall. He turned and spoke to someone inside the room, then held the door open. The man inside the room pushed a cart carrying a large metal box out into the passageway. That man was hooded, too. He was much smaller than the first man. He closed the door and the men began to push the cart down the hallway, one in front, one in back. At the end of the passageway, the men and cart turned left, and they were gone.

Was the box they'd carted away big enough to have contained two million dollars? How the hell would Rileigh know? It would depend on what denominations. If the casino kept its money in packets of a thousand dollars each, yeah, sure, it would fit in that box. But if they kept the money they would have to pay out for a jackpot in denominations of fives or tens or twenties, who knew how much space two million dollars of it would take up?

But there was something in that box.

Rileigh stepped out of the tiny room into the small passageway, shook herself, tried to reorient. Okay, fine, something was in that box. Surely to God it was money, given what she believed was going on. It didn't matter whether it was the whole two million or just a portion of it. Two men had come out of *that* room and hauled that box away. That's all she had to know. Now was the time to bail. She needed to get upstairs and gather up a posse. She'd talk to Pete, get him to grab some other firemen. There was Ian, of course, and...

And what if the two guys were hauling a keg of beer they had stolen from the ship's stores? Or some other item, some *valuable* item. After all, that room was a storage room, and it was always locked to keep whatever was inside safe from somebody who might have sticky fingers.

Nope. Rileigh didn't have quite enough yet to go for the posse. She needed more. Those guys could return from wherever they took that box at any minute. If she was going to get proof, she'd have to do it now.

She stepped resolutely out of the little closet and walked with purpose down the passageway. That's what you did. You didn't sneak. You acted like you had every right to be there. If she met those guys in the hall, she'd smile, say hello. She slowed as she came to the door they had exited. Again she put her ear against it, heard nothing. She tried the handle.

The door was unlocked.

Which likely meant they'd be back soon. She had only seconds. She eased the door open, stepped inside, pulled it closed, and found a pile of boxes directly in front of the door, almost blocking it. She edged around the boxes farther into the room. There was no overhead light shining in the room, but there was a light on the other side of the boxes that cast harsh back shadows toward the door.

She squeezed quickly around the side of the boxes and found more boxes she had to squeeze around. When she bumped into the next stack of boxes, the pile almost fell —

must be empty boxes. She went past them down what was obviously a small lane that had been created between the boxes for the cart that had just left the room. Around a corner, around another corner, and then she stopped cold, staring.

Well, there it was: the unfaithful husband in a lip lock with the unfaithful wife. Eight by ten glossies suitable for framing, film at eleven.

Before her was a mess of broken drywall in front of an irregular hole— maybe four feet across, in the wall of the room. Beyond that was a smaller hole, maybe three by three, that had been cut in something metal with a blowtorch that lay on the floor. She didn't try to see what was on the other side of the holes. She had what she needed. Now it was time to get the hell out of Dodge.

Turning quickly, she bumped some more empty boxes, but grabbed them before they could topple over. She hurried around the first corner, the second corner, the third corner, squeezed past the boxes in front of the door and put her hand on the handle. She began it ease it open, to make sure the coast was clear before she —

The door handle was yanked out of her hand, the door flung open. Blocking the doorway, dressed in a black hoodie, was a dead man.

Donovan McCreary.

Chapter Forty-Two

RILEIGH'S REFLEXES were faster than Donovan McCreary's, but not by much. She grabbed his jacket and aimed her knee toward his groin —if she had been able to land the blow, he would have been incapacitated. But he turned aside, caught her knee on the inside of his thigh, groaned, and grabbed her by the front of the cape that had saved her from the man with the knife she had fought in the dark. This time it was her nemesis. Donovan used the cloak to hold her still long enough to land an upper cut to her jaw that turned the world black.

When Rileigh came to, she tasted blood in her mouth. Not just a little, not like she'd nipped her tongue, like maybe she bit it off.

She kept her eyes closed as she reoriented herself to the world, felt with her tongue inside her mouth to assess the injury. A big gouge had been chunked out of the right side of her tongue by her own teeth. She swallowed blood.

Pretending to still be unconscious, she listened to the voices of the men who stood over her. One of them was McCreary, of course. She didn't want to believe she recognized the other voice, but it was unmistakable. Charlie Hayden.

Charlie appeared to be dead set — no pun intended— on killing her.

"We have to kill her. Let me do it. That bitch broke one of my ribs."

"Just be grateful she didn't see your face. Your little solo vendetta could have screwed the pooch for all of us."

"She *owes* me."

Charlie didn't even sound like Charlie. The voice was the same, but the man speaking the words wasn't the Charlie Hayden she knew, the charming man who'd flirted with her when she went to his office last summer — that Charlie Hayden had left the building.

"Shut up and let me think," McCreary said. "We've come this far and haven't dropped a single ball. Now's not the time to screw something up."

"What's to think about? She's a witness. We have to get rid of her. How hard is that? Come on, Mac. Let me do it." Rileigh heard a yearning, a hunger in those words that was truly chilling.

She'd found the murderer they'd been looking for. The guy who was pleading for permission to murder Rileigh had buried a hammer in the top of Hunter Dobson's head and stabbed a knitting needle into Ruby Cunningham's brain. He was the crazy son of a bitch Gus had referred to, the killer who was not satisfied by the killing alone, had to gut Hunter's corpse, had to stab a knitting needle into Ruby's other eye. Her mind flashed to what Mama had said about how Charlie Hayden had been going downhill ever since he stumbled over the corpse of the woman Brandon Hollister had murdered. That had been a gruesome sight, but instead of horrifying Charlie, it had turned him into a killer just as merciless and brutal.

McCreary kicked her in the side and she managed not to groan. Then he used the toe of his shoe, slid it under her, and flipped her over onto her back.

"Stop pretending to be unconscious. You are not that good."

He reached down and grabbed a handful of her hair, used it to pull her up into a sitting position, leaned her against a stack of boxes. She opened her eyes and glared at him.

"So tell me, how did you do it? How'd you figure it all out?" McCreary asked. He had a pistol, but it wasn't Mitch's service revolver. Did Charlie have that?

Rileigh said nothing.

"Come on, Mac. Quit playing with her. Let's kill her and be done with it."

Charlie kicked at her in impotent rage, landed a glancing blow off her hip.

"Payback for the slap, huh? Now we're even." Rileigh said, though it was hard to talk with a severed hunk of her tongue flopping around in her mouth.

Charlie started to lunge for her, but McCreary held him back.

"Who knows about this? Who helped you figure it out?"

Rileigh realized that McCreary was ticked off that she had managed to unravel the mystery. He thought he was so smart that he was a step ahead of everybody, and it hurt his pride that someone had caught onto his little game. Narcissists loved the spotlight. She could use that.

She turned her gaze on Charlie Hayden and said, "You came up with a helluva plan."

She dribbles … she shoots …

McCreary bristled. "It wasn't his plan, it was mine."

Score!

"Your plan?"

"All Charlie brought to the party was a gambling debt the size of Cleveland. *I* was the one who figured out how to kill two birds with one stone — cover his losses and sink Dobson's huge Gum Tree Hollow project so Blarney Stone could swoop in behind him and snatch it up one little piece at a time."

McCreary was on a roll.

"This little charter cruise was the perfect storm. All the money on the boat, but half the normal security force because of the small crowd. So Charlie kills Dobson in some really outlandish way, showy and gruesome, and everybody's concentrating on that, not paying any mind to all that money sitting in a safe in the hold."

"Oh, so it was *Charlie* who did all the heavy lifting."

"You missed the part where I got rid of Winston Burkett," McCreary snapped.

"Who's Winston Burkett?"

"The son of a bitch head of security who was getting ready to fire my ass. Couldn't locate the references I'd listed on my job application … hell, nobody ever checks those. I timed it just right, so I'd be called in to take his place when he didn't show up for work."

McCreary looked again at Charlie, then back at Rileigh. "I believe I made a killer out of Mr. Hayden here when I killed Burkett and let him watch." He seemed to forget Charlie was even there, was just talking to Rileigh. "I could almost see it happen on his face — the change, you know, the shift. I could see it in his eyes."

"So that's why you killed Ruby Cunningham," she said to Charlie, sounding horrified. "Because you *enjoyed* it."

It worked. Charlie didn't like being portrayed as some sort of mad dog.

"It was all part of the plan!" he snapped.

Was killing Rileigh part of the plan? Probably not. Best not to mention that part.

"We had to keep upping the ante to *keep* everybody distracted while we got into the safe," McCreary jumped in, clearly annoyed at Charlie for stealing his limelight. "Which would take hours, and neither of us had the … proper skill set to do the job. So Team McCreary drafted a couple of new players."

Rileigh knew who one of them was. Hector Quiñones, the chief engineer.

"One provided the time, the other the skill — did it way faster than we expected." Then Dobson shook his head. "But the son of a bitch got greedy, wanted more than the fifty grand we agreed to pay him for the job, decided he wanted a cut of what was in the safe he was cutting a hole in. He was 'Dopey' alright. I silenced him."

So, Dopey's was the body that went over the side.

"Damn it, Mac. Stop preening in front of the pretty girl and let's do what we got to do." Charlie looked at Rileigh with hungry eyes. He pulled a knife — obviously the one he's used to gut Hunter Dobson — then set it on top of a stack of boxes. "You don't get off *this* easy. I'm going to strangle you slowly. Watch the light start to go out in your eyes — then let you breathe, just enough air so you come back around. Again and again."

Charlie was psychotic. McCreary was a mere sociopath, so she engaged him, ruffled his feathers.

"And you don't think somebody's going to go looking for you as soon as they find this hole in the back of the safe? Surely you're not so stupid that you think you won't be a suspect. The prime suspect."

McCreary bristled, then just chuckled.

"Nobody's going to find the hole in the safe. When we're done, there won't be enough of boat left to find the hole in it." He stepped back and looked at her, gloating. "You ever heard of the Lucy Walker?" He didn't wait for her to tell him she hadn't, just continued with a little smirk on his face. "It was 1844, I think. The Lucy Walker left Louisville down the Ohio River, bound for New Orleans. She didn't make it more than ten miles before all three of her boilers exploded. Set the boat on fire and she sank. They say the blast shot one sailor fifty feet into the air — when he came down, he crashed through the deck like a missile. Another fellow was sliced in half by a jagged piece of the boiler. Of course, that's probably just myth. Only a handful of the hundred and ten people on the boat survived, and they were all burned so badly — by the steam and the fire — that they probably weren't very reliable witnesses."

Rileigh couldn't breathe. He couldn't mean …

"The Lucy Walker was only a hundred feet long and the Queen of the Smokies is four hundred feet with five decks and all — so when our boiler blows, it probably won't sink the boat. At least not right away. But the explosion will take out the whole stern."

Rileigh's voice was thready. "You'd do that? You'd kill everybody on this boat just to hide—?"

"Oh, they won't all die. Your boyfriend saved most of them by telling everybody they had to stay together in the lounge and the casino on the bow of the boat. The explosion won't get them, and neither will the fire. It won't kill everybody."

McCreary's smile broadened.

"Of course, they won't ever find all the bodies. Some people will just vanish. And Charlie here gets to be a hero. Just happened to be out on the bow on the deck next to the lifeboats when it blew. Helping people board. They'll remember."

"I don't get it. How can the boiler blow up when it's not even hot enough to run the engine?"

"And who told you it wasn't? Heck rigged that gauge to look like all the pressure had been let off the boiler. He's been working down there by himself with half the crew sick for hours, feeding that firebox, and that boiler's pressure is getting higher every minute."

"Which means we need to kill her and get out of—"

"You planning to swim to shore with two million dollars on your back?" Rileigh asked, desperate to keep them talking about something other than murdering her.

"Oh, we already dumped the money overboard," McCreary grinned.

She could tell he liked confusing her. He went on:

"In a water-tight container. With a transmitter going beep, beep, beep on a special frequency. Sometime next summer when things calm down, we'll come out here some moonless night, haul it up, and divide it up."

McCreary's walkie-talkie crackled to life. As he drew it out of his pocket, Rileigh looked at Charlie and cringed away from him in fear. He took the bait. He advanced on her, leaned over as a voice from the walkie-talkie said, "Fifteen minutes."

Rileigh struck fast. Reaching out, she grabbed Charlie's foot and yanked. Off balance, he toppled backward into McCreary, who was holding the walkie-talkie to his ear rather than pointing the gun at Rileigh.

She leapt backward between the boxes and shoved them as she passed. The pile of empty boxes cascaded down like an avalanche between her and the two men.

"Shoot her!" Charlie cried. Rileigh zigged and zagged as she ran, the words of her firearms instructor ringing in her ear: "Contrary to what you see on television, it is seriously difficult to deliver a fatal shot to a moving target."

McCreary didn't fire, maybe because he feared a gunshot could be heard upstairs, though the sealed doors made that unlikely.

She was out the door in seconds and racing down the passageway, pursuit only a few steps behind her.

Chapter Forty-Three

RILEIGH FLEW DOWN THE PASSAGEWAY, could hear footsteps behind her but didn't take the time to look back. She slammed into the wall on the opposite side of the left turn, bounced off it and raced down that hallway too. The footsteps were coming. She had to hide, had to find somewhere …

She grabbed at the knob on a door as she ran, could feel it was locked, grabbed at the next and the next. All locked.

Then she felt a knob turn. She skidded to a halt, threw the door open, leapt into the room, and shoved the door closed behind her. If they'd made the turn into this passageway, they saw her go in. If they hadn't, she could hide.

She had expected to find herself in a storage room, a place full of boxes and shipping containers she could hide behind. But Rileigh wasn't in a storage room. She gaped at her surroundings as she gasped for breath. No. Oh, no.

Rileigh was in Gerbil Village.

Rileigh could see in the shadows in front of her, the tangle of tunnels snaking around each other like a giant pile of spaghetti. She looked around for somewhere to hide. There were tables bolted to the floor, and chairs where you could sit down and have a soft drink and some candy. There were shelves to hold little kids' shoes, because you weren't supposed to wear shoes inside Gerbil Village. Memories of that day flashed through her mind. Connor ducking under the tape blocking off the closed-for-cleaning Gerbil tunnels and racing toward one of the entrances. Georgia sending his two older brothers to get lost in there with him.

The men were coming, Rileigh had to hide.

Where?

There was absolutely nowhere in this room to hide. Nothing to get behind. Nothing to crouch down beside. Nothing at all. There was almost nothing else in the room but the Gerbil tunnels.

Time did one of the hiccup things it did now and then with Rileigh. It didn't exactly stop. But it seemed to pause and take a breath, which let her take a breath. And in that pause, Rileigh had a heartbeat or two to understand with gut-numbing terror that there was only one place in this room she could go. Into the tunnels. Oh, they were little kid tunnels, but Rileigh was thin ... ok, skinny. She'd fit. It would be tight, but she'd fit.

She had offered at one point during the years ago fiasco with George's children to go in there and drag them out one by one. But the deck hands who had been summoned to rescue the children wouldn't have it. Maybe some liability issue with insurance allowing a grown-up to go into a children's play area. She'd considered the possibility that the upper ranges of the tunnels up by the ceiling were not strong enough to hold the weight of an adult, though she'd weighed less than a hundred twenty pounds then and was waaay skinnier now.

In that pause, that hiccup of time, Rileigh faced the dilemma in front of her and realized there was really no decision to make. If she stayed where she was or went back out into the passageway, Donovan McCreary and Charlie Hayden would catch her and they would kill her. She had only one place to hide —inside the gerbil tunnels. *Take it or leave it, sweetheart, that's your option.*

When time returned to its normal rate, Rileigh didn't hesitate. She raced toward the first of the tunnels where the door stood open and dived into it, scrambling as fast as she could deeper into the tunnel, away from the sections that were transparent where mommy and daddy could see their kid crawling around.

The tunnels were too small for her to get up onto her hands and knees and crawl through them like the kids did. All she could do was commando crawl. And even then, her knees and elbows banged into the sides of the tunnel as she crawled. She barely made it around the first curve of the tunnel, where she would no longer be visible by someone looking into the entrance, when she heard the room door slam open and the lights in the room flashed on. Rileigh tried to move soundlessly, scooting farther up into the tunnel. But about four feet in front of her was one of the clear sections. There was another one a couple of feet behind her. She flattened out on her face where she was, panting, listening.

"You think she came in here?" That was Charlie Hayden's voice.

"If she did, where the hell is she?" She heard footsteps as they came into the room, looking around.

"She could be in there, in them tunnels. She's small

enough to fit," Charlie Hayden said. She heard his footsteps approaching the entrance to the tunnel. And to her horror, he leaned over and called out into it. "You in here, sweetie pie? You in this little hidey hole?"

Charlie was only a few feet from where she lay, trying not to breathe loud, hoping her heartbeat wasn't hammering as hard as it seemed to be. Because if it was, you could have heard it in the next county.

McCreary sounded like he was standing in the doorway.

"We don't have time for this shit. Come on. If she made it up those stairs, she'll bring a posse back here."

"No, she didn't get away. She's in here, hiding in here." It sounded from the nearness of his voice that Charlie had gotten down on one knee and was peering into the tunnel.

"Come on out of your hole, little mousy." He crooned. "The cat's waiting out here to gobble you up."

"Come *on*, damn it," said McCreery. "Either there's a posse after us or that damn boiler's gonna blow. We do not have time to play games."

She heard Charlie Hayden get to his feet.

"If she's in here, I'll see she *stays* here."

There was a sickening bang that she felt through the plastic of the tunnel. It reverberated through her body and through her soul. It was the sound of the door on the end of the tunnel clanging shut. She heard a clicking sound, a latch. Then another sound, just like the first, closing off the second tunnel.

She heard footsteps hurrying to the door. Then Charlie Hayden's voice called out, "Won't get to see the light go out in your eyes, sweetie pie. I hate that. I'll just have to daydream about you being blown to pieces. Have a nice day."

The door of the children's play area banged shut behind him.

Silence.

Rileigh let out a huge sigh of relief that he was gone. The next intake of breath was a sucked-in gasp of terror. He'd closed the doors on the tunnels, latched them *on the outside*. Maybe she could get them open somehow. There was not enough space to turn around. She'd have to back up, commando crawl backwards, kick at the doors maybe. But her recollection of the hours she'd spent in the room was that everything in Gerbil Village was well-made. She figured the doors on them would hold. She could go back and try, of course. Or …

Or *what?*

Realizations slammed into her like freight trains, one after another, each one hitting her dead center in the chest.

She was in this place … too tight.

They'd closed the doors; she couldn't get out.

She was *trapped*.

It was like being inside a coffin and buried alive. It was the same thing. It was the fate that Mitch had saved her from when he had killed Brandon Hollister, before Brandon could bury her alive in the coffin he'd locked her in. This was a coffin too, though. As surely as the one Brandon Hollister had stuffed her in. She'd been trapped in that coffin— *alive*—listening to the sound of the clods clunking onto the wood as Hollister shoveled the dirt in on top of the coffin.

This was the nightmare she had lived through every night for months after she'd got out of that wooden box. But this wasn't a dream. This was reality. She would die here, sealed up in this coffin of plastic.

And she wouldn't die suddenly, painlessly, when the boiler exploded. She wouldn't die with all the other people

— *Mitch!* Mama. Georgia. Ian. Gus. She wouldn't die when they died. She would die before they did. She would be crushed to death by the walls of plastic closing in on her, tighter and tighter. The shrinking plastic would squeeze the life out of her.

Her chest would be constricted so she couldn't breathe, tighter and tighter. Maybe she would die before she had to endure the pain of all her bones breaking, her ribs being crushed into her lungs. She wondered if her eyeballs would bulge out as she was crushed, like that toad she had seen after her father ran over it, its insides squashed out of it, its eyeballs protruding from their sockets.

Would Rileigh look like that?

No, no, no, no, no, no.

She screamed at the top of her lungs, but no sound came out. How could it? The walls were already tightening around her so she couldn't breathe.

Panic went off like a nuclear explosion in her chest.

She beat her fists against the bottom of the tunnel, tried to raise up, tried to crawl forward, banged against the plastic sides, screaming with a sound that could be heard now. But there was no one to hear.

The panic consumed her for a minute, for an hour, a lifetime, a geologic epic.

Every second of her life was the worst second of her life … until the next. She flailed against the sides of the tunnel, commando-crawled as fast as she could, screaming and crying and banging her head against the top of the tunnel.

She had to get out.

She had to get out, out, *out*. And she heard her mind form the same words she'd prayed when she was nailed in the wooden coffin with clods of dirt falling on the lid.

She'd cried out soundlessly to God, "Please, please don't let me die like this."

After that, her mind formed no more words. All that was rational shattered into tiny pieces that tinkled soundlessly through her hollow chest into the darkest pit of her soul.

She continued to scream and scream and scream.

Chapter Forty-Four

You done yet?

The words formed in Rileigh's head. Not like some voice had spoken or anything like that, more like — earth to Rileigh: message from your essential self.

Because if you're not done, I'll wait.

"Done?" Rileigh was trembling violently, more like vibrating. Her throat was raw from screaming. The back of her head ached from banging it against the top of the tunnel, as did her elbows and knees. Her fists were scraped raw from pounding against the plastic. Her tongue was bleeding in her mouth, but she heard herself speak the words out loud anyway.

"Done what?"

Done throwing a tantrum. Actually, it's 'FINISHED' throwing a tantrum. Turkeys are done. People are finished.

Aunt Daisy always said that when she was correcting Rileigh's grammar.

"Throwing a tantrum?"

Yeah, a tantrum. Just checking to see if it's over yet. If you still need to flop around some more in a hysterical pity party, I'll wait.

Pity party? Rileigh didn't say the words out loud, but the voice heard the thought.

What else would you call it? You're still alive, you're not even injured anywhere. You're scared, but there's no real danger. Still, you want OUT and when a little kid doesn't get what he wants ... what does he do? He throws a tantrum.

The image of three-year-old Conner Stump flashed through her mind. A crewman had finally managed to grab the kid and lifted him up out of the opening in the tunnel. But Conner did *not* want out, he wanted to stay and play. So he'd defaulted to his go-to behavior in such circumstances — he went postal, kicking and punching and thrashing around, screaming ... shrieking. He looked like ...

He looked like ... Rileigh. Like she'd looked only moments ago.

The terror that was fueling her hysteria, having its way with her, ripping her guts and her soul apart in wild abandon ...faltered, paused. And in that pause, she remembered the voice's words, *remembered* because the voice had fallen silent.

No. Real. Danger.

Rileigh knew fear, so scared your stomach clenches and you almost vomit. She'd felt that terror in her bowels in every fire fight in Afghanistan. And she felt the same terror *right now.*

But she wasn't in danger of dying right now.

That kind of mindless terror didn't belong to this little-kid playground, as it did the bloody battlefields of war. It was only here because she had brought it here. She'd been hauling it around with her everywhere she went for three months, clinging to it in white-knuckled determination. She had dragged it into the tunnels with her, embraced it, was at this very moment clutching it tight to her chest.

Let it go.

The voice didn't say that, *Rileigh* did. Not out loud, but Rileigh said it.

It was suddenly scary to think about letting go, she'd held on so tight for so long, it felt normal. To let go felt … uncomfortable.

She forced herself, struggled to pry her fingers loose from it, determined to leave the hot stinking pile of terror right here, not to drag it along with her another step.

She closed her eyes and made herself take a deep, shaky breath.

Waited.

The walls squeezing her so tight she couldn't breathe — she could no longer feel them crushing her. In fact, they weren't really touching her at all. Close, but not *touching* her. They were, after all, just plastic walls, not some maniacal being with murderous intent. Just walls.

Shadows of terror flitted around in her belly, frantically taking little bites out of her. She ignored them.

Then the voice spoke one last time.

You got this.

And Rileigh did.

With her return to reality, the world as it really was instead of what her phobia had made of it, she felt the return of fear — but a different kind. Real fear, not remembered terror. McCreary had said the boiler on this boat was going to explode. Quiñones had said, "Fifteen minutes." She looked at her watch, her eyes blurry with tears she hadn't realized she'd been crying.

Quiñones had said that *twenty* minutes ago.

Borrowed time.

She had to get out of this stupid maze, get to the engine room and … do *something*. She began commando crawling forward as fast as she could, came to an intersection where tunnels went off in other directions. She picked the right tunnel, crawled through it. But it went up, higher into the maze. She needed to go down, down to floor level and toward the back of the room. That's where the tunnel went through the wall, the one that opened up outside in the water park. If the door to it was latched, as Charlie Hayden had latched the other two… she'd figure that out when she got there.

She went through the red tunnel until it connected with the green one that went downhill, and then she chose that one. Every time she came to a stretch of tunnel that was clear plastic, she shoved on the ceiling, praying that she'd find one of those "escape hatches" un-hooked. But they all held tight. She also looked out into the room through the clear spaces. She was up high, near the ceiling. She needed to go down and to the left. The back wall of the room was to the left.

Out of the green tunnel into an orange one, she crawled, feeling the pain in her bruised and battered knees and hands as a distant distraction, a pain belonging to somebody else. She ignored it, as she ignored the pain in her mouth, just kept swallowing blood and crawling forward.

Through the orange tunnel and into a blue one. Through the blue one and into another red one. Going down now, but the tunnel curved out right farther into the room rather than toward the back wall. She passed another intersection, but the intersecting tunnel went back right, and she needed to go left. Still going down, but in the wrong direction, she finally came to a purple tunnel that angled back toward the left and she crawled frantically down it. The purple tunnel led to another red one — that went back up, but she could see that was just a little bump, that up ahead the tunnel dipped back down again.

Red led back to blue. At the next intersecting tunnel, she could feel it. The tunnel on the left was colder than the one on the right. She followed the cold, going up for twenty feet or so, and then back down. The air got colder the farther she went.

Blue into red again. Red into orange. Orange back to purple, slanting downward. It was cold here, seriously cold. She finally rounded a bend in the tunnel and saw something blocking it about thirty feet away. It was darker there than where she was. A door.

She crawled toward it, and suddenly it was frigid. She'd passed through the wall of the boat; this section of the tunnel was outside on the deck. The ceiling and sides of the tunnel were too cold to touch, and the only light was the little bit that filtered through the clear section of tunnel behind her. When she got to the door, she shoved hard. It didn't move. She pushed again and she thought she felt it give a little. Maybe it was unlatched, just frozen shut. But she couldn't push hard enough to find out because the effort merely shoved her back down the tunnel rather than shoving the door outward.

Her heart was pounding, her breath coming in gasps.

Think! How could she get leverage to—

She started crawling backward. It was awkward, wasn't a natural motion and she got tangled in her cloak. Back into the warmer tunnel that was inside the room. Backing through it, she came to the portion that'd been slanting downward when she came to it before. Now it was slanting upward, which made going backward even more awkward.

She struggled up the slant. It wasn't far now. Another few feet. Her left foot kicked out and didn't hit the side of the tunnel. Yes!

She had reached the last intersection she'd passed, and she continued crawling backward until she was beyond it.

Then, like turning into a driveway to change directions, she crawled forward into the cross tunnel, then backed into the tunnel where she'd been before. Now, her feet were pointed toward the door instead of her head. Then she began to crawl backward toward the door.

She passed through the wall of the boat, felt the cold, and then her feet connected with the door.

Now, she had to turn over. She had to get off her belly onto her back, so she'd be facing the ceiling of the tunnel instead of the floor.

Grunting and straining, her long skirt and cape had bunched up around her waist when she started crawling backward, and she could barely budge the mass of fabric to turn over.

Finally, she lay on her back, panting, catching her breath. Then she bent her knees — there wasn't much space, couldn't bend them far — and slammed both feet as hard as she could against the door.

It moved! It did, it gave a little. She did the same thing again and again. Each blow inched the door of the tunnel farther open, allowing the freezing wind to blow in on her bare legs and thighs.

Bam! Bam! Bam! She didn't have to get it all the way open, just enough for her to squeeze out.

Bam! *Bam!*

The last blow seemed to break something loose — maybe she'd crushed through thick ice on the deck — and the door was halfway open. She stuck her feet out the opening and used them to drag her body out onto the ice. Farther. Inches at a time. When her butt was on the ice, she could reach up and catch hold of the edge of the tunnel above her to drag herself the rest of the way.

She scrambled to her feet outside on the deck to get

her bare legs off the ice, wiggled to allow her long skirt to drop down in place, pulled her tangled cape around her.

Then she stood gasping in the frigid air, figuring out what she had to do next. The boiler was about to explode. It had already held longer than the engineer had said it would.

She had to find a way to release the pressure somehow. She'd figure it out when she got there.

Chapter Forty-Five

RILEIGH HURRIED as fast as it was possible across the slick-as-glass icy deck toward the door that led into the hold. She almost went down a couple of times, had to grab the railing. She didn't have time to fall down. She had to get in there and let the pressure off the boiler.

Right, and exactly how did she plan to accomplish that task? She was just about at the "put up or shut up" part of "I'll figure it out when I get there." She was almost *there*.

She had been there when the engineer talked about how the engine had been disabled, how someone had let off the pressure, how someone had doused the fire in the firebox. All of it a crock of shit. She'd seen him gesture, he had gestured toward some pipes and some gauges when he was talking about the pressure, and toward this big metal thing when he talked about the firebox. She thought about the plaque she'd read on the wall in the engine room, tried to remember what it had said.

Suddenly, Rileigh's feet went out from under her and she landed painfully on her butt on the icy deck. Which is what would happen to all those people forced out onto the decks if she didn't make it in time, if that boiler blew. Falling on their butts and a whole lot worse. There'd be a huge fire, eating up the wooden structures on the boat. The people who'd been ordered to stay together in the bow of the boat would survive the explosion and then they'd have to get off the boat before the fire consumed it and it sank.

All that might work in good weather, but tonight? The lifeboats were surely frozen in place, encrusted with an inch-thick layer of ice. How would they even get them free to launch them? And the freezing temperature — the people on the boat were dressed in storybook character costumes, not swaddled in parkas, heavy boots, and thick gloves. How many of them would even make it into the lifeboats? The ones who didn't, the ones who fell over the side or jumped — she didn't know what the temperature of the lake was, but she did know hypothermia would kill anybody left in it for long before they were rescued. And who would come to their rescue? They couldn't radio for help, and with visibility down to ten feet, the people on shore would hear the explosion, but would they even see the fire? Even if they knew about the disaster on the lake— how would anybody be able to muster the necessary resources for a rescue — emergency vehicles on icy roads and all.

The truth in long johns with the buttflap down was stark — it would take a miracle for any of the hundred and fifty guests, not counting the crew, to survive what would happen if the boiler exploded. It was staggering to comprehend. In a town the size of Black Bear Forge? Just about every one of the "movers and shakers" in the whole county were here tonight. And they'd all be dead if she couldn't get this right. Mitch. Mama. Georgia. Ian. Gus. They'd all die.

She scrambled to her feet and held onto the railing, the ice numbing her fingers, and hurried on, trying to call to mind everything she knew about steam engines. It wasn't much. She had understood precious little of the explanation of how steam engines worked that'd been framed in the engine room.

A steam engine had four steam cylinders, a high- and low-pressure cylinder on each side of the paddlewheel — which on the Queen of the Smokies was made of oak and steel and weighed twenty-six tons.

None of that gave even a hint about how you let off the pressure of an over- pressurized boiler, how to do what the engineer had claimed someone had already done. The assistant engineers knew, the guy who'd come into the engine room after Captain Rowe took Chief Engineer Heck to get his head sewn up… from his self-inflicted wound. But there was no time to go find that guy, no time to go for help. It was up to Rileigh.

She shifted gears then, felt it like she hadn't since she was in the military. She went to the place soldiers go when they're about to step into overwhelming enemy fire and probably won't survive the next ten minutes. It was a calm and resolute place, a fatalistic pace. If it's your time, it's your time. It was a place of heightened awareness, logical thinking. She'd never even get the chance to let off the pressure on the boiler if she ran into the men who were willing to kill hundreds of innocent people just to get what they wanted.

Assess the enemy, soldier.

What are your resources?

The enemy was three men, one of them armed with a knife — the one Charlie Hayden had slit open Hunter Dobson's belly with, the one he had tried to stab her with in the dark. It was a nasty-looking blade. The other two were armed. She had seen the gun that McCreary had pulled on her. But when she'd bailed, he could have shot her, and he didn't, so maybe the gunshot could be heard upstairs on the main deck. They had Mitch's gun, too — somebody did. They had taken it from him when they attacked him and left him for dead on the icy deck of the boat.

She shook herself, shook it off. Couldn't think about that now.

Three men, a knife, and two guns. One woman, no weapon at all. That didn't look good.

If they caught her, she had to be able to defend herself somehow. But with what?

A particularly strong gust of icy wind blew across the side of her face and down into the back of her cloak, and she pulled it closer around her, stuffed the hand not holding onto the railing down into her pocket for warmth. And her fingers came upon... what was this? It was a pair of socks. The socks that Mitch had shoved at her when he put on the matched socks Gus had given him. She'd stuck the other socks in her pocket. She pulled them both out now. One was a white gym sock, classic green stripes at the top. She looked at it and thought.

When she finally stepped into the warmth of the boat from the frigid deck, she had a weapon on her. What they used to call a BTN weapon, because that's all it was— better than nothing.

Chapter Forty-Six

RILEIGH CREPT down the small passageway that led to the engine room quietly, listening, though the engine room was the last place she'd find the three thieves. They'd be putting as much distance as they could between them and the about-to-blow boiler.

But as she drew closer to the main hallway, she heard a voice. It was Heck, Hector Quiñones, obviously talking on a walkie-talkie.

"... told you this ain't an exact science," he said. "It'll blow when it blows. I've added more fuel to the firebox, and with everything clamped down tight, it's a ticking bomb."

"Get your ass down here," came a voice through the crackling of the walkie-talkie. McCreary. "The Sea-Doos are ready to launch, just gotta shove them into the water. I'm not waiting for you. I'm pushing mine in, cranking it, and I'm outta here."

"On my way," Quiñones said.

Rileigh stepped back down the passageway the way she'd come, away from where it intersected the main hall, flattened herself against the wall. She heard his running footsteps as he raced out of the engine room and down the main hallway in front of it. She stood ready, tensed.

Quinones flew past the hall where she stood, running dead out, never even glanced her way. Rileigh leapt out into the passageway behind him, twirled the sock filled with chunks of ice around as hard as she could once, and then slammed it into the back of his head. He went down hard, landed on his face. Blood squirted out onto the floor.

Grabbing his feet, she dragged Quiñones across the slick deck back toward the engine room, leaving a bloody trail on the metal floor. He wasn't a whole lot bigger than she was. She dragged him out into the middle of the shiny clean red floor she had noticed earlier and dropped him there. Grabbing the gun that he had stuck down in his pants — Mitch's service revolver — she rolled him over onto his back stood over him with the gun pointed at him. She poked him with her foot. "Wake up," she said.

She poked him again, harder. "Come on, wake up."

He moaned, but didn't open his eyes. She had better sense than to stand close enough to poke him with her foot again, so she stepped back two or three steps and called out, "You've got to the count of three to open your eyes before I put a bullet in your skull right between them."

He didn't move.

"One. Two. Thr—" Before she could say the rest of the word, his eyes popped open.

"That's better. Now, get on your feet and let off the pressure on that boiler."

His eyes never left her face as he sat up slowly, but instead of getting to his feet, he got as far as a crouch and remained there.

"Planning on launching yourself at me, are you? Think

you can get to me before I can shoot you? Me being 'just a woman' and all."

"I'm the only one who knows how to let off the pressure on this boiler." Heck glanced over his shoulder nervously, then slowly got to his feet and stood fifteen feet away, poised and ready. "You won't kill me."

"Who said anything about *killing?*" His expression changed slightly. "Let off the pressure on that boiler or I'm going to shoot you in the kneecap."

"No," he said defiantly, but there was a quaver in his voice. "You won't shoot me."

"Oh, that's right, the whole me being a woman thing." There was no time for playing games. It was put up or shut up. She lifted the pistol, pointed it at his left knee, and pulled the trigger.

Blood exploded out of his knee. He shrieked in agony and collapsed on the floor, holding onto his leg and wailing.

"Believe me now?"

He kept screaming.

"Let off the steam on that boiler, or I will shoot you again."

"I can't," he moaned. "I can't stand up."

"Well, then I guess you're going to lose another kneecap." She moved so she had a better line at it, pointed the gun, and...

"No, no. Please don't. Don't shoot me again. I'll do it. I'll do it. Just don't shoot me again."

"Get after it. From what you told McCreary a few minutes ago, this baby's more than ready to blow."

The engineer began to drag himself across the floor slowly toward a part of the tangle of inexplicable pipes and dials that he'd nodded to when he told the captain someone had disabled the engine.

"You're going to have to move faster than that, pal."

"I can't go any faster."

Rileigh took aim again. She didn't shoot him in the knee, though. She shot him in the left foot. The gunshot sounded like an explosion. And the man's shrieks were deafening. They had to be audible on the decks above. "Get your ass moving unless you want another bullet to go with the first two."

He couldn't crawl, could only drag himself across the floor, and he did, pulling himself across the shiny red deck that was now redder with his blood. But there was no time, he had to move *faster*.

"I'm going to let you pick this time. Do you want the bullet in your foot or in your knee?"

He picked up the pace, moaning and crying, but moving faster, got all the way to the railing around a big piece of machinery. Tears flooding down his cheeks, snot pouring from his nose, he held up a bloody hand and begged for mercy, "Don't shoot me again, don't shoot me again. I can't stand up. I *can't*."

She lifted the pistol and pointed it as his other knee, then his foot. "If you don't pick, I'll pick. I'm kind of partial to knees myself." And she pointed the gun at his knee.

He screamed, "No!"

"No, no, please. I'll do it. I'll do it." He dragged himself a little farther to a piece of machinery she didn't recognize and grabbed hold of it, used a pipe on it to pull himself to a crouch, with the injured knee and leg sticking out in front. He leaned against the pipe, panting, almost lost his grip and fell. Then pointed with a blood-smeared finger. "There, right there. That's the valve. You have to turn the wheel counterclockwise. I can't do it. I can't reach it."

It could be a trap. She'd have to get fairly close to him to turn the dial. She'd have her attention focused on the crank and not him. And for all she knew, if she turned that crank, she'd be blasted with steam that would melt the skin off her face. If she had to fight him in his condition, she'd win … but there was no *time*.

"Not buying it, pal. You do it or you get shot again." She lifted the pistol higher. "Maybe an ankle this time."

The man was sobbing now, could barely talk. "Please don't shoot me again. Don't … I'll do it. I'll do it." He dragged himself toward the big metal wheel he had told her to turn, pulling himself along the railing toward it, then leaned against the railing, and with bloody fingers began to turn the crank.

"How am I supposed to know if you're turning the right crank?"

"There," he said, and gestured with his chin toward the dial that had previously said there was no pressure at all on the boiler. The needle had been lying on its side in the blue area on the left.

"I unhooked it. But it's hooked up now."

The needle on the dial was no longer in the blue area. It had passed the midpoint where the colors changed from blue to orange and had gone down the other side in the red zone. If it had been the hour hand on a clock, it would be five o'clock in the red zone. The dial didn't go past six o'clock.

He cranked the wheel around and around. She heard the sound of escaping steam somewhere in the bowels of all the equipment. The room heated, clouded up like a bathroom after a shower. As Rileigh watched, the hour hand on the clock slowly began to move back up from five o'clock to four, and then to three. He continued to turn the dial. When it was noon, no longer in the red zone at all, she told him, "Stop right there. That's enough."

She didn't want him to let off all the pressure on the boiler. There had to be enough left to run the engine. She didn't know how much was enough, but she wouldn't let it go all the way back down into the blue area, so they had to start all over again. Mitch didn't have that kind of time.

Quiñones collapsed on the floor then, blood pouring from his knee and his foot.

"You got to help me. I'm going to bleed out."

"We should be so lucky," said Rileigh. "Now where are the others?"

"Down there," he coughed out the words and gestured toward the door. "In cargo bay four, starboard side."

She had no idea where that was.

"How do you get there?" But he was too far gone now. All he could do was roll around on the floor, crying in agony, holding his knee and his foot and blubbering. She didn't have time to drag it out of him. She'd just have to find it herself.

Crossing quickly to the other side of the room, she picked up a coil of soft rope and tossed it to him.

"Might want to make a tourniquet," she said.

Quiñones had been going down the center hallway when she'd clobbered him, so she raced down that one, hoping it would lead to bay four. She very much wanted to get to McCreary and Charlie Hayden before the bastards got away.

Chapter Forty-Seven

THE MAIN PASSAGEWAY where Rileigh was running full out intersected with another one, a smaller one. Which way? She continued straight ahead because it was a main passageway, and because she had to pick, and that's the direction she picked.

At the next intersection of passageways, the other passageway went left, only left. Left was starboard, so she turned that way and kept running. It wasn't fear driving her now, not terror that she and everyone she loved was about to die, be blown apart or freeze to death. Not fear for Mitch, either. She had already shoved that down into the back of her consciousness so she didn't have to deal with it.

Fear didn't propel her forward. *Rage* did.

The passageway curved first one way, then another and she was afraid that around any of those bends she would see a dead end, that the passageway had run into the hull on the side of the boat.

Then she heard a sound ahead of her that sent a thrill running up her spine — an engine cranking. She rounded a bend and saw the dreaded dead end of the hull in front of her, but the sound was coming from behind a closed door near the end.

She ran to the door, tried the knob, it wasn't locked. Now she could hear voices as well as the engine sound. She pushed the door inward slowly and a blast of freezing air struck her face. Peeking around the door, she saw a large room with a high ceiling, and bay doors that opened out over the water. The doors were open and a Seadoo was resting at the end of skids that led into the water. It would take only a single shove to launch it. The engine was idling and Donavon McCreary was astraddle it. He was no longer dressed in baggy dwarf clothing. He wore a black neoprene wetsuit.

A second Seadoo rested on skids near the first. It wasn't all the way down to the waterline yet. It would need to be shoved another five feet or so before you could crank the engine.

Charlie Hayden stood inside a door on the other side of the bay. He'd obviously just come in and was headed toward the second jet ski.

"What the hell …?" McCreary cried when he saw Charlie making for the second Seadoo. "What do you think you're doing?"

"I'm not staying on the boat."

"You have to stay on the boat, asshole. That's the plan."

"I'm changing the plan."

Charlie had begun pushing the Seadoo down the skids toward the water.

"Exactly how you gonna pull it off, showing up tomorrow high and dry? The explosion blew you all the way to shore, didn't leave a mark on you?"

"I just know I'm not going to be on this boat when the

boiler explodes. You don't know what's going to happen. You don't know that all the people bunched together in the bow of the boat will be fine — you don't *know* that."

"How will you explain it?"

"I'll think of something. But I'm not gonna get blown up because you miscalculated something, burn to death or drown when the damn boat sinks. I'm getting off right now."

"On Heck's Seadoo." It wasn't a question.

"With or without him. It'll carry two people. Where the hell is he?"

"On his way."

Charlie had shoved the jet ski to the end of the skids, and he leapt onto the seat, looked down and turned to McCreary with a stricken look on his face.

"Where's the key?" He began searching around the machine frantically looking for it. "Don't tell me Heck has it!"

McCreary indicated a rubber bracelet around his wrist with the key and the plastic cork that'd keep it from sinking if you dropped it in the water. He pulled the bracelet over his hand and tossed it to Charlie.

"Crank it up, make sure it runs."

Charlie put the key in the ignition, turned it, and the machine purred to life.

Rileigh opened the door and stepped into the bay, was raising her gun as McCreary continued to speak, conversational and non-threatening.

"You're a liability, Charlie, a crazy son-of-a-bitch who could go off and do God only knows what. That look on your face when I ran over Winston ... I knew then. You've lost it. You're insane." He paused, shook his head. "And the only thing you can do with a mad dog is put it down."

Rileigh didn't see the pistol in McCreary's hand until

he fired it, point blank at Charlie. The bullet caught Charlie square in the forehead and blew out the back of his head. He flew off the side of the jet ski into the water.

Rileigh was shocked into inaction for only a second. Then she planted her feet, held Mitch's service revolver out in front of her in a two-hand grip and called out.

"Drop the gun, McCreary."

He whirled toward her.

"You! Where did you come from?"

The shock, surprise and rage she heard in his voice warmed her heart.

"I already shot your buddy Quiñones — twice. I will shoot you too, if you don't drop that gun right now."

"Okay, okay," he said turning around on the seat, holding the gun loosely as if he meant to drop it into the water. "Just don't get trigger happy and shoot me."

She knew what was about to happen, could read Donovan McCreary like a first-grade primer. He wasn't going to drop the gun. He wouldn't surrender. She just had to decide what she'd do when he pulled it on her. At this range, she couldn't miss, got to decide where to put the bullet. Kill shot? The man had just executed his partner and had a gun on her, so she was justified in using deadly force.

She watched his eyes. The instant he twitched, before he had a chance to lift the pistol more than an inch, Rileigh pulled the trigger, watched the gun fly out of his hand in something like slow motion as his body was propelled backward by the slug she had put in his chest. The *right* side of his chest.

Killing was too good for Donavon McCreary. He needed to face the consequences of what he had done.

Chapter Forty-Eight

As SHE CHOPPED the last of the carrots for the salad, Rileigh looked out the kitchen window at the bare limbs on the sycamore tree. The tree was home to a family of cardinals, and she longed to see one, a splash of bright red on the dull brown winter landscape. Maybe that's why Valentine's Day was in the wintertime, so that red hearts would brighten the world.

Except she didn't particularly like red hearts, and she definitely didn't like Valentine's Day. She had hated it ever since she was a little kid. In elementary school, all the children had to bring a box of some kind to school, a shoebox, bigger if you thought you'd need it, to collect your valentines. You could decorate it any way you wanted it, put wrapping paper on it, bows, ribbons, hearts, whatever suited your fancy. Then you'd put a slit in the top of it where your classmates could slide in valentines. The teachers made certain that no kid went without, of course. Every child in the class was required to bring enough valentines for every child in the class. So it quickly became rote. It wasn't about wanting to give somebody a valentine.

It was about walking around and sliding the required valentines into the required boxes. Like delivering mail.

Even as a little kid, she had never liked the emphasis on showing your love for somebody by buying them something. You *bought* a valentine or you *bought* candy or you *bought* flowers or something else to demonstrate that you love someone. She didn't like that, just on the face of it. She always thought about the kids in her class, and there were a lot of them, who didn't have the money to buy anybody anything. Kids for whom it was a stretch to buy the packet of 36 generic valentines for them to give out to their classmates. It just seemed like a raw deal all the way around.

As an adult, she didn't like Valentine's Day because it could screw with normal relationships. You have a *friend*, a male friend. You're getting along swimmingly and then comes Valentine's Day and — *awkward!* Do you expect a valentine? Do you give a valentine? It was such a waste of energy to figure it all out.

She had Valentine's Day on the brain because she'd seen the first holiday display in the store when she went to get lemon juice so Mama could make a lemon meringue pie for Mitch, who was coming to supper tonight. Valentine's Day, and it wasn't even the middle of January.

She dumped the chopped carrots into a bowl and looked around. She needed seasoning salt, the kind Mama kept on the top shelf in the pantry. And she needed to make sure there was a full jar of vinaigrette dressing. Mitch drowned his salad in dressing. She went into the pantry, found the salt, then had to unfold the step stool to check out the top shelf for dressing.

The pantry. For months, she made up excuses not to go into the small, windowless room. Now ... when you've crawled through ten miles of gerbil tunnels, the pantry loses its sting. As does the shower stall, and she definitely needed to pay it a visit before Mitch got here.

She was cleaned up and dinner was almost ready when he arrived, a minute before he'd said he would.

He was out of uniform tonight, looked thin, but she was sure that was her imagination. He'd only been in the hospital three days. She'd been at his bedside when he woke up. He had looked at her, smiled a crooked smile and wanted to know if she liked raspberries.

Yeah, the concussion had scrambled his brain a little, but in 24 hours, he was making perfect sense and wanting to go home, but Gus wouldn't sign off on it. It made her smile to remember Gus hovering over Mitch, making light of his own concern, of course, but hovering all the same, watchful, determined to catch any sign of … but there was no closed head injury.

Mitch would be fine. And back to work on Monday.

"I don't know if you want this or not, but John Joe told me you left it in the ambulance." He held up her tattered Red Riding Hood cape.

"I'd been freezing all night, and that ambulance was like a sauna." Rileigh took the cape and tossed it over a chair. Mama had worked so hard on it.

"Dinner is just about ready," she said and sat on the couch. Mitch folded his tall frame into the big comfortable chair across from it.

"I can smell the pie."

"I watched," Rileigh whispered. "I made sure she put sugar in it this time."

She didn't want to ask, but he saved her the trouble.

"I thought I'd see you at the courthouse today," he said. "At the arraignment."

"I didn't want to … go *there*." Rileigh's part in the

whole thing was over, let the justice system deal with it from here on out. "Tell me about it."

"No surprises. McCreary was standing there with some big-time lawyer in a three-piece suit. Took the bailiff half an hour just to read the charges. Murder, four counts."

Quinones had told them where to dig up Winston Burkett's body.

"Attempted murder, two-hundred-sixty-five counts. Grand theft. Using a firearm in the commission of a felony. On and on. The only way he'll ever see the outside of a prison cell is if they execute him."

Tennessee was a death penalty state. "That'd be my vote."

Quiñones had survived with all his body parts still attached, but it would take months for him to regain full use of his left knee. When Mitch heard that, he pointed out that prison gyms were great rehab facilities, which was good to know since he'd be spending the rest of his life there. Unless he joined McCreary on death row.

Quiñones had made noises about Rileigh, demanding she be charged with assault. But that wasn't going to happen, not in Yarmouth County. The county prosecutor tore up the paperwork and tossed it in the trash.

Mama came into the room, gave Mitch a big hug and said that dinner was ready. Then she saw Rileigh's Red Riding Hood cape draped over a chair.

"I thought you lost that."

"Misplaced it." Rileigh scooped it up off the chair and held it out in front of her.

"Why it's got a big ole tear in the back. Did you hang it on a nail or something?"

Rileigh paused. "Yeah ... or something."

"I'll sew that up and we can put it in the clothes bank at church."

"Is there a stray sock in the pocket perhaps?" Mitch teased. Rileigh had told him what she'd done with the gym sock.

"Maybe the other one's in here, if you want it." She stuck her hand down in the left pocket and found nothing. When she put her hand into the right pocket, she found no sock, but there was something there, a small card of some kind.

Rileigh pulled the card out of the pocket and looked at it.

She couldn't breathe then, stood frozen.

"What's wrong?" Mitch leapt to his feet and took her arm. "You're as white as a sheet."

She didn't say anything. Couldn't. She just shoved the card at him wordlessly.

It was a postcard with a picture of the Tennessee State Capital Building's gold dome … in *Nashville*. There was no postmark.

Mama snatched the card out of Mitch's hand.

"There's no postmark because it was never mailed!" Mama cried, absolutely jubilant. She looked at Mitch. "Don't you get it? It was never mailed because Jillian slipped it into Rileigh's cape pocket when we were at that costume party."

Rileigh took the card back from Mama and turned it over, then sat down suddenly on the arm of the chair because her knees had collapsed out from under her.

On the back, there was a smiley face … but this one was winking.

THE END

What To Read Next

A lavish riverboat casino should be the perfect place to unwind after nearly being buried alive, but ex-police officer Rileigh Bishop knows better.

The killer wants to turn the casino into a floating graveyard.

And Rileigh is his big prize.

Pick up your copy of Calling My Children Home today.

About The Author

Lauren Street has always loved a mystery. As a kid growing up in bible belt country she devoured every whodunit book she could get her sticky little hands on and secretly investigated all of her (seemingly) normal boring neighbors. Sometimes their pets and farm animals too. All grown up now and living in the UK with her thoroughly unsuspicious (and often unsuspecting) husband, she writes domestic psychological thrillers about families torn apart by secrets and lies. And she sometimes still peers over garden walls to check up on the neighbors.

Also By Lauren Street

The Bishop Smoky Mountain Thrillers

Hide Me Away

Fuel To The Flame

Closer By The Hour

A Gamble Either Way

Calling My Children Home

Replaced with Nolon King

Replaced

Irreplaceable

In Her Place

Printed in the USA
CPSIA information can be obtained
at www.ICGtesting.com
CBHW020936250524
9098CB00042B/792

9 781629 553610